THE PENTAGRAM MURDERS

EMMA K BLACKER

2QT Limited (Publishing)

First Edition published 2023 by

2QT Limited (Publishing)
Stockport UK

Cover design:Robbie Associates Ltd.
Cover images: shutterstock.com

Printed in the UK by IngramSparks

A CIP catalogue record for this book is available from the British Library

ISBN 978-1-914083-98-3

Other books by Emma K Blacker

Lismarian Series

HANNOKI'S WILL
LOVOA'S CHALLENGE
MESRRA'S POWER

To my first fan

Pauline Rosner

Prologue

SOMEONE WAS FOLLOWING her; Amy was convinced of it.

She was sure she could hear footsteps behind her. It wasn't unusual for her to leave work late; staff shortages and emergencies at the hospital were a regular occurrence but, for some reason, she felt ill at ease this time. She paused, turned around and saw nothing but shadows.

Amy was not reassured and started walking faster towards home. She pulled her phone out of her pocket and dialled her flatmate, disregarding the advice to not put your valuables on display. She just wanted to hear a reassuring voice, and she reasoned that if anything happened then someone would know where she was.

The phone rang for some time before Susan answered. 'Amy, what's wrong?' she mumbled.

Amy knew she had woken her up and felt guilty. Convinced that she was overreacting, she was just about to apologise, to tell Susan that everything was okay and end the call, when someone grabbed her around the waist and placed something over her mouth.

It happened so quickly. Amy froze for a second before she started to fight. She clawed the hand covering her mouth, but her limbs became weak very quickly and her brain clouded over. The last thing she remembered as the phone fell to the ground was that she had not told Susan where she was.

Susan woke to her phone buzzing. Annoyed because she had an early start the next day, she looked at the caller's name – and her annoyance turned to worry. Amy wouldn't ring at this time unless there were a problem.

'Amy, what's wrong?' she asked. There was no reply, just a muffled scream and the sound of a struggle, followed by silence.

'Amy, Amy?' Susan shouted down the phone.

Nothing but silence. Scared to hang up on her friend in case she heard anything that might help, Susan placed her mobile onto loudspeaker, jumped out of bed and ran into the kitchen. She grabbed the flat's landline and called the sector police. She listened to the standard message.

'We are sorry for the delay; we are currently experiencing a high volume of calls. Please consider reporting through our website, as this might receive a faster response. Otherwise, please hold the line.'

Putting the landline on speaker, Susan placed both phones on the kitchen table then grabbed her laptop. As she listened to the message repeat again and again, she logged on and searched for the sector police's website.

She clicked on 'Report a Crime' and nearly screamed with frustration when she saw the mandatory fields to complete for which she did not have the information, including crime type and location.

With the automated message still advising her to report online, Susan tried adding information like 'unknown' and 'other'. Finally, she was able to submit it, though it worried her that they'd not asked for a contact phone number, only an email address.

A message appeared, thanking her and informing her that the status of the investigation was being reviewed and any questions would be posted under the following reference number. Knowing it could be days before anyone came back to her, she stayed on the phone and waited for it to be answered.

She called out to Amy on her mobile again and again as she waited for the sector police to get back to her but got no response – then suddenly the call was disconnected. Susan tried calling Amy back with no success.

Finally, the automated message from the sector police on the landline stopped and someone spoke. 'Thank you for waiting. How can we assist you?'

Susan quickly picked up the phone. 'My flatmate Amy called me. I think she's in trouble.'

'Why do you think she is in trouble?'

'She rang me and woke me up – she's never done that before. All I could hear was some sort of muffled noise as if she was struggling with someone. I kept the line open but she didn't speak, and then the call was disconnected.'

'Do you know where she is?'

'No, I assume she was coming home from work at Sector 2 Hospital – she was working the late shift there.'

'Could she have called you accidentally?'

'No. She's not allowed to carry her mobile when she's working. They have a paging system. Surely you know that?'

'Each hospital is different. Do you know where she might be?'

'No, I've no idea where she is! All I know is that I answered the phone to a muffled noise. Is there no way you can track her mobile? The call was still live until a short time ago.'

'I'm sorry but you have not given sufficient evidence of a serious offence having been committed. If you gain further information, or she has not returned after seventy-two hours, you can report her as missing. Please call us back.'

'Amy wouldn't have called me unless she had to,' Susan protested. Looking at the time and realising how late it was, she added, 'She should have been home by now and she isn't.'

'I appreciate that, but we can do nothing without further information. Please call us back or submit information online if you have any more details.'

The line went dead. Susan sat there, looking at the phone for a moment before putting it down. She picked up her mobile; the line was still dead no matter how often she dialled it, but it didn't stop her from trying.

'Amy,' she whispered. 'Amy, where are you?'

∞

Amy woke up slowly. She was lying awkwardly and her wrists and ankles hurt; she wanted to move to ease the pressure and realised she couldn't. She tried to remember what had happened. She remembered finishing her shift and walking out of the hospital car park, then nothing more.

She opened her eyes, hoping her surroundings would jog her memory, but saw nothing but blackness. She had been blindfolded. Panicking, she again tried to move her arms and felt the bindings dig into her wrists. She could feel grass beneath her hands as she struggled against the bonds.

'Though I love to see you struggle, there isn't any point.'

Amy stilled at the male voice that whispered into her ear. The man was so close that she could feel his warm breath as he spoke. 'What do you want from me?' she whispered.

'To be a sacrifice to my master.'

'If you don't let me go, I'll scream.' She heard him laugh. Something cold ran down her arm, then up towards her neck; she guessed it was a knife and went silent, not knowing what he was going to do to her.

'I'd love to hear you scream. That's why I didn't kill you when I knew you couldn't feel the pain; it takes the fun out of it.' The knife didn't cut into her as Amy feared; instead, he trailed it back down her body, past her chest to her stomach.

Then he stopped.

Amy held her breath, not knowing what would come next. Suddenly he grabbed her blouse and ripped it apart.

She knew she should scream, but she guessed he had moved her to a location where no one would hear or care if she did. Maybe he was about to rape her. She started crying at the thought. But if she stayed quiet, maybe he'd let her go afterwards.

Without warning, the knife cut into the left side of her stomach and was slowly dragged in an upward arch. Then Amy knew she had it wrong and she started to scream.

∞

He stood and watched as she lay bleeding. Her screams had pleased him, but he'd been disappointed how quickly she had passed out. It had taken the fun out of it.

He waited as long as possible to see if she would regain consciousness and used the time to clean her nails where she had scratched him. He'd wanted to see her face as he cut her throat. Disappointingly, he had to complete the ritual with her still unconscious.

He hoped his master would instruct him to kill another.

Chapter 1

Johnson walked out of the interview with her suspect. The prosecutor had already agreed on the charges if she could get a confession, and she was determined to get it. It had been a long time coming; he had been burgling houses across all the sectors, and it would be a relief to have him locked away.

Johnson retrieved her firearm from the locker outside the interview room before stopping to talk to the detention officer to ensure the burglar was returned to the cells.

'Well, is he going to court?' a sector officer asked her as she watched the suspect being led away.

'Oh yes. I've got the charging authority here.' She showed him the paperwork from the prosecutor.

'Let's hope the courts actually remand him and give a decent sentence for once.'

'That would be nice.' Space was limited in prisons, so they were normally reserved for those that committed very violent or repeated crimes. Johnson was not hopeful for a long custodial sentence. As the burglar's crimes were non-violent, a short custodial followed by a home curfew and electronic tag were a strong possibility.

She went up to the desk of the sergeant who reviewed the prosecutor's charge authority. 'I'll make sure he's charged when the investigation file has been submitted,' he promised.

'It will be with you soon.' Johnson had twenty-four

hours to complete it; if it wasn't done by then, the sector police would have to release him and a summons would be issued for his attendance at court – if they could find him.

Johnson was leaving the sector police building and heading to her car to return to headquarters when her phone rang. She looked at the caller ID and saw it was her supervisor. 'Johnson,' she answered.

'Michelle has identified a possible linked series of murders.' Inspector Kerten got straight to the point as usual. 'There was a murder last night with the same MO as two other killings last month. I want you to get down to the crime scene and assess it before I take the case to the director.'

'Yes, sir. Can I ask why the doubt?'

'The way they span across the sector jurisdiction. The most recent is in Theron Park, Sector 2. The other two bodies were in Sectors 9 and 16.'

'Is there anything linking them, other than the MO?' Johnson asked. 'Such a wide area is unusual.' Though the Central Law Enforcement Agency – CLEA's – remit was where crimes went over sector boundaries, they were usually clustered within a sector before moving out into neighbouring areas. Sectors 9 and 16 shared a border, and the murders could have just been a road away from each other, but Sectors 16 and 2 were a distance apart.

The sectors were divided into two circles. The inner circle ran clockwise 1–8, the outer circle, Sector 9, was north of Sector 1 and again ran clockwise up to Sector 16. So though 9 and 16 didn't sound like they were close to each other, they were neighbours while Sector 2 wasn't, though it wasn't far away.

'Michelle is working on it,' Inspector Kerten told her. 'She'll send you the details of the other two murders. I want you to go down to the scene at Theron Park. See what you can find out and get back to me. Don't say CLEA is taking over the investigation just yet,' he warned.

'What about the case I'm on currently?'

'I understand you have the charges and it will be handed over to the sector prosecutor ready for court – good result, by the way – so you have twenty-four hours to submit the file. Do it when you get back from the crime scene. Let me know if you can't complete it in time.'

Kerten ended the call and Johnson sighed with frustration; he was a good supervisor, but he had brought a lot of his military police background with him when he joined CLEA, including his rank, so he was an inspector and not an agent.

Johnson had seen case files before with sector police trying to pass a 'linked series' to CLEA because they were all stab victims. Still, they had never asked an agent to attend before. Had the senior bosses got involved?

Curious about the case, Johnson got into her car and put Theron Park in the GPS. Michelle was one of CLEA's best criminal analysts; if she thought there was a link then there was one. Johnson knew Kerten had the same opinion of Michelle's skills but he probably needed more information to make a case to the director.

⚭

Johnson drove to Sector 2; the number of cars at the scene made finding a parking space difficult. That was unusual because those who could afford cars should have been at work. She started to worry about what exactly she would see in the park.

Having found a space, Johnson checked her phone to see if the files had come through. She had an email from Michelle with a brief summary of the previous offences and crime-scene photographs. As she read through them, Johnson could understand why Kerten was concerned.

The previous killings were similar in style, and that there had been three of them raised serious questions.

Unlike many parks within the sector jurisdiction Theron Park was large and you couldn't see across it, but Johnson didn't have to ask where the crime scene was; she just followed a group of people talking about the 'gruesome death'. It always amazed her that so many people were drawn to the macabre.

She had to push through the crowd when she arrived. At least the crime scene was well-staffed. From the way the officers were gathered, she imagined the body was just out of sight. She ducked under the cordon tape.

'Stop! You can't come into this area,' an officer challenged her. Johnson smiled, pleased he was paying attention. She had learnt long ago that trying to ask permission to cross the line took too long; if you just did it, you either got the attention you needed immediately or walked in – which raised serious security concerns.

'CLEA,' she said and showed her ID.

'Sorry, Agent.'

She was allowed to continue. She heard the crowd whispering, curious about her presence, and hung her identity badge around her neck.

The body was just behind a tree. Johnson had seen many bodies over the years, but she was shocked by this one. Although it wasn't the most gruesome she had seen, it was the most unsettling.

The victim had been blindfolded, tied down, spread-eagled and bared to the waist. A symbol had been carved into her stomach and something about it was ritualistic. Johnson had read a description in the files Michelle had sent, but seeing it was something different. The carving was not the cause of death; that was the large cut across the victim's neck. She hoped the woman had been dead when the mutilation happened but, looking at the blood loss from the abdomen, she doubted it.

'What do you know?' Johnson asked as she squatted next to the local detective and the crime-scene officer. He turned to look at her, and she saw a flicker of annoyance flash over his face as his eyes went to her badge.

'Not much at the moment. We suspect her name was Amy Hood.' The detective handed over an evidence bag; inside was the victim's photo-identity card from the local hospital. 'It was in her pocket. Nothing else was found on her.'

'What do we know about her?'

'Nothing beyond the ID. We're still waiting for the checks to come back.'

Johnson handed back the bag. 'Anything else?' she asked.

'Only what you see. We won't know if there are any forensics for a few weeks, and the autopsy could take a while – though the cause of death is obvious.'

'Who reported it?'

'One of the local park wardens early this morning. Couldn't give any information other than that he'd found a body.' The detective looked at her. 'You looking at taking this case off our hands?'

'That hasn't been decided yet.'

He grunted. 'Don't know why you bother to come if you aren't going to take the job.'

Johnson ignored him and leaned in to take a closer look at the marks carved into the dead girl. The other reports had only mentioned abdominal mutilation and there had been no detailed description. These marks were not very clear due to the blood but they were better than anything in the files. She took some pictures of the injuries to send to Michelle.

Finally she stood up and walked a short distance away before taking out her phone and calling Kerten. 'From the information Michelle sent, I'd say all three murders have a similar MO,' she told him.

'Do the local officers have any ideas about suspects?'

'Nothing. They have the victim's name from a hospital ID on the body. She was Amy Hood, a nurse at Sector 2 Hospital. They don't expect anything from the crime scene or autopsy for a few weeks.'

'That's to be expected. What are your thoughts?'

'I think we need to take the case. The perpetrator was cruel in the killing – evil. I think there will be more murders and we need to get ahead of this.'

'Damn! Send Michelle what details you have for her to run checks. She'll get results quicker than any sector analyst. I don't like that the victim was a nurse – that hits home. I'll talk to the director and make an argument for CLEA to take over the murders. For now, shadow the local officers, see what you can find out from the crime scene and try to make sure they don't muck it up.'

Hanging up, Johnson went back to where they were loading Amy's body onto a van for the journey to the morgue. She was divided on where she needed to be.

She went back to talk to the detective. 'Will the crime scene be in place for some time?' she asked.

'For too long,' was his irritated response.

Johnson clenched her fists. There were some good officers in the sector police but others didn't understand the benefits of taking a bit more time to do the job properly. Satisfied that the scene would remain for a while, and unable to direct anything here until CLEA had officially taken over, she couldn't even call in their own forensic team.

'Mind if I go back to the morgue with you?' she asked one of the mortuary staff.

'Suit yourself. Are you taking the case?' he asked.

'Not yet. Call it curiosity,' Johnson replied.

There was no room in the van, so Johnson collected her car and drove to the morgue. When she arrived, Amy's body had already been removed and taken inside.

Johnson cursed; she wished she'd arrived at the same time so she could have followed the body inside and had a chance to talk to the admitting staff, maybe persuaded them to accept the body as the next in line for autopsy. Now she would have to go through reception.

She was met by a frosty welcome. 'Whose autopsy are you here for?' Johnson was asked once she'd identified herself.

'Amy Hood.'

'I don't have that name on record.'

'She was just brought in.'

The receptionist stared at her for a moment. 'Is she a CLEA case?'

'Not yet.'

'Then if you want to leave your details, I'll make sure you're informed when the autopsy takes place.'

'Do you know when that will be?' Johnson asked.

'We have a backlog. The team will get to her as soon as possible, but it won't be today.'

Frustrated, Johnson forced a smile. If CLEA had the case, Amy's autopsy would be completed next; as it was, she would have to wait. 'Make sure you call me when you're ready to start,' she said and handed over her contact number.

Leaving the morgue, Johnson walked across the street to a coffee shop. It was small and bare but surprisingly clean. She ordered a coffee, found an empty seat, pulled out her phone and made a call.

'Good morning,' a bright, very formal voice answered.

'Michelle, it's Johnson. I've a name I need you to run a check on – Amy Hood, I don't have a date of birth but I'd place her in her early twenties, and she was a nurse at Sector 2 Hospital.'

'I will see what I can find for you.'

'I was also wondering if you have access to the sector police reports on the case and if you've found out anything else?'

'Yes, I do. The reports should be in your email. And it is not good news. I was about to call Inspector Kerten with an update.'

'Anything you can tell me first?'

'I have looked at the information and pictures you sent me and compared them to the reports and crime-scene photographs from the two previous murders. The way the bodies were tied down is the same. The carvings were not clear on the other bodies but, based on limited descriptions, they are likely to be the same. I still do not know what they mean, but I will continue to investigate.'

'Thanks, Michelle.'

'There is one other thing. All the females were killed at the time of the new moon.'

'That's a very specific MO. Is there any connection between the three victims?'

'Not that I have been able to find, but I will keep looking.'

'Cheers, Michelle.'

'I will let you know what the inspector says,' Michelle hung up.

Johnson knew better than to try and call her back; she would receive an update when Michelle had one to give. Sighing, she opened the email reports on the previous two murders.

She read through the first file. The similarities in how the victims were killed were shocking enough, but the dates and locations – all in parks – were incredibly disturbing. There was no evidence that the sector police investigating officers were aware of similar MOs, so they had not been flagged as linked crimes. Michelle had identified the connection, which Johnson found worrying. Why had the sector police not flagged them as a potential CLEA case?

As she continued reading, she started to understand why. To her disgust, the investigating officers had made assumptions about the victims' lifestyles; in one of the cases, they claimed the victim had been tied down for 'other reasons'.

Crime rates were so high that only serious crime was investigated adequately, and there was pressure to write off 'less serious' ones. Johnson understood that pressure; it was one of the reasons she had left the sector police and joined CLEA. But it left her wondering how many more bodies might be out there.

Her phone rang. 'The director has authorised CLEA to take over the case based on the information Michelle has found,' Inspector Kerten told her. 'Ensure the autopsy on this most recent victim is done next. I'll let the sector police know.'

'Yes, sir,' she managed to say before he hung up. She finished the last of her coffee before walking back into the morgue.

'Have you decided if CLEA is taking the case?' the receptionist asked. 'Otherwise, I don't know why you're here.'

'We're taking the case, and Amy Hood's autopsy is to be conducted next.'

'I'll let the pathologists know.'

'Tell them I'll be witnessing it.' Johnson paused at the security barrier until the receptionist opened it, then went towards the examination room. She was glad that government buildings all followed the same plan so she knew precisely where she was going without having to ask.

Johnson looked around the examination room. The wall to her left consisted of floor to ceiling body storage units, well over a hundred in total. All of the bodies here would be connected to a serious offence, murder or suspected murder. Autopsies weren't carried out if there was no reason to suspect foul play. Most of these bodies would be the result of domestic arguments, drunken disputes or gang-related violence. Coroners used to decide when an autopsy occurred. When the volume became too much, the decision was taken away from them, the coroners office was dissolved, and the pathologists did the autopsy and law enforcement took over everything else.

The tags on the drawers indicated that the morgue was nearly at capacity. Johnson was not under any illusion about the murder rate but seeing this made it more real than numbers on a page.

At the end of the room was a refrigeration unit where the 'fresh' bodies were brought in and swabbed for evidence before a freezer drawer was allocated. In the centre of the room was a row of tables where the autopsies were performed. The pathologists dictated as they worked and made audio recordings, so reports were released quickly. A thin plastic screen separated each table. Johnson winced; it wasn't great for forensics but better than some places she had been to. At least there was a divide between the areas.

One space was free and Johnson approached it as a body was brought to the table. 'Is this the autopsy of Amy Hood?'

'So we have been ordered,' the pathologist said.

'You have a problem with that?'

'Do you know the average waiting time for an autopsy?' he demanded. 'How many people are waiting for answers about their loved ones? What's so special about her that she takes priority?'

'Her cause of death may be the same as two previous ones. I'll be interested to hear your views.'

He muttered as he turned away from Johnson, but she thought she heard the words 'bloody CLEA' and 'entitled idiots'.

'Amy was a nurse at a hospital here in Sector 2,' she continued. 'She was attacked on her way home from work.' The pathologist's hand paused as he went to unzip the body bag. 'Her death was not pleasant and we want to get the person who did it.'

The pathologist opened the body bag and saw the deep cut across Amy's throat. He paused for a moment before unzipping the bag all the way down. When he saw the symbol cut into the body, his face drained of colour.

'Are you alright?' Johnson couldn't resist asking.

Chapter 2

Johnson left after the autopsy. The pathologist had promised to email his findings to her a short time later.

She debated whether to go to the station next door or back to the coffee shop. The coffee shop won; she needed to get the smell of the morgue out of her nostrils and check her messages. Would a quick stop matter that much? Once she went to the station there would be a limited chance of her reviewing her messages and emails until she left.

She breathed in the glorious scent of hot coffee as she checked her phone. There was nothing new from either Michelle or Inspector Kerten. She was about to leave for the station when the preliminary autopsy report came through. She stopped and sat down again to review it.

It did not make pleasant reading. Hearing the details during the autopsy had been bad enough, but the report made them more real. Johnson did not see a victim as a person as she watched a cold and clinical procedure, but reading about it afterwards made it harder.

There was bruising to Amy's wrists and ankles and friction burns where she had struggled against the restraints, but otherwise there was little sign of her having fought. There were traces of chloroform on her mouth, so Johnson assumed that the attacker had taken Amy by surprise and she'd had no chance to fight back. More personal details were also recorded that made the woman more real. Amy had spent a lot of time on her feet; she was used to making dexterous movements with her hands and was not a drinker or smoker.

Johnson remembered the volume of blood around the body and wasn't surprised to read that Amy had been killed where she had been found. The pathologist surmised that the killer had abducted Amy, rendered her unconscious with chloroform, transported her to the location, tied her down and waited for her to regain consciousness before making the cuts to the abdomen. There was a jaggedness to the start of the cut, as if the body had jerked in response to the pain. The cuts then became smooth and precise, which suggested that Amy had lost consciousness. The incisions were so precise that they were unlikely to have been done quickly, and they were not deep enough to be fatal. The cause of death was a deep cut across her throat.

There was no forensic evidence. Though the pathologist had taken swabs from Amy, it would be a few days until the results came through.

After closing the email, Johnson headed back across the street to the sector police station.. She was pleased that the two buildings were so close together, though it was a poor reflection on society that this was now necessary.

People were clustered in the front office waiting to be seen by one of the five reception officers. Even though there were many ways to report offences or seek help, the poverty levels in some areas were so high that many residents didn't have computers or mobile phones and could only get help in person.

As soon as a cubicle became free, Johnson walked in. The people queueing started to shout in protest but when she turned and showed her badge, they stopped.

Turning to the station officer, she said, 'I am Agent Johnson from CLEA. Please tell the officer on the Theron

Park murder to come and meet me. I'm taking the case.' She didn't wait for a response but walked out to wait, ignoring the curious looks.

Experience had taught her that asking one of the CLEA support officers to make calls on her behalf wasted time. Walking into the station and saying she was taking over a case would get a much quicker response. Sure enough, five minutes later the detective she had spoken to at the crime scene walked into the front office. 'Made up your mind then?' he asked.

'Invite me in, if you want me to take the case.'

The detective stood aside and allowed her to walk past him. He led her down a corridor; light bulbs had failed and not been replaced, the walls were dirty and damaged and it was clear no maintenance had gone into the building for a long time. The lift at the end of the corridor had an 'out of order' sign on the door. Johnson guessed that when finances were tight, cosmetics were low on the list.

'Hope you don't mind stairs,' he said and opened the fire-exit door to the stairwell. It was a not-so-subtle dig that those who worked in CLEA had an easy life with better funding and resources. In reality, the CLEA offices didn't look much better, but the unit did have better resources.

CLEA received a huge number of requests to take over cases so they had to be selective to target the biggest offenders and be most effective. Johnson knew it caused resentment among front-line sector police officers, but CLEA would be ineffective if they didn't. However, the sector police just saw it as their cases being rejected. They forgot that there were sixteen sectors and only one CLEA.

'Stairs are fine,' Johnson said. When they arrived on the fifth floor, the detective seemed almost annoyed that she was not out of breath.

He led her to his desk in a crowded and noisy open-plan space. She had to step over wires; people had found inventive ways to plug in computers, monitors and anything else they needed to get the job done. He rolled over a chair from a neighbouring desk. 'I'm going to need evidence of the authority before I hand over the case. The boss will demand it,' he said as she sat down.

Johnson pulled out her phone, navigated to her email and showed him the formal order from the director. 'If you want a copy, let me know where to send it.'

'No, it's fine,' he said when he saw his superintendent's name as one of the recipients. He turned and pulled up the murder file on his computer. 'Where do you want me to send this?'

Johnson gave him both her email and the central one that the file would have to go through to be formally accepted and recorded. Once it arrived in her inbox, she scanned the contents. The only point that stood out was that someone called Susan had filed a report online and called the police. She was concerned that her flatmate had been attacked. The system had linked the two reports.

Johnson made a note to talk to 'Susan' as soon as possible. 'I'll need the forensic report once it's complete, and the scene must remain in place until our team can examine it.'

'I'll send you the report when I have it, but the scene was reopened over an hour ago.'

Johnson cursed to herself; she hadn't expected the scene to be released so quickly. When CLEA took a case, a notification to preserve the scene and allocate a forensic team was despatched but experience had taught her these were not always actioned quickly. She had been so focused on getting the autopsy completed that she had failed to check the notice had been received. The murder had happened in a public park; how many people had walked through it in the last hour? How much evidence would be left?

'You didn't see the notification?' She knew the answer but had to ask to cover the CLEA.

'What notification?'

'When we take over a case, we send a notification to the sector police to let them know and freeze activity.'

'I guess no one's seen it. Maybe your forensic team should have done the same as you and just shown up,' the detective replied sarcastically.

Johnson bit her lip to stop herself saying something that would damage relations further; no forensic team would just 'show up' and the detective knew it. 'Any chance of your officers maintaining the scene until I can get my own people there?' she asked.

'Not a chance. It's your problem now.'

She was frustrated but knew that anything she said would only cause more friction between their organisations. 'Please make sure I get that forensic report as soon as possible. If you could send it to me direct, I'd appreciate it.' She stood up and left without waiting for a reply, then pulled out her phone and made sure a CLEA forensic unit was on its way to the scene.

ⵙ

When Johnson arrived back at Theron Park, the sector police had left but not cleaned up. Amy's blood was still on the ground.

People were still standing around, curious about what had happened, but no one was keen to walk over the scene; it was as if they sensed something evil had happened there. Maybe, as a result, there would be a chance to find something.

She didn't have to wait long for the CLEA forensic team.

'Agent Johnson.' She turned to see Matt, one of the team leaders. He looked happy to see her.

'Thank you for getting here so quickly.'

'No problem. I wish a decision could have been made sooner then the scene wouldn't have been so compromised. We might have been able to stop the samples that the sector police collected from being submitted and redirected them to our labs. It is as it is, though. Is there anything we need to focus on now?'

'The details aren't in from the sector forensic unit, so I don't know what they did. From the previous murders, one did not have a scene examination and the other reported that nothing of note was found.'

'I'll get one of my team to contact them to see what samples they retrieved, and we'll see what we can find out about a link to another crime scene. Just be aware – anything we find at this point might not be related to the case because of contamination.'

'I'll take anything you can find for me, Matt.'

∞

It was late when Johnson finally left Sector 2. Matt and his team had been thorough and collected an array of samples to take back to the lab for testing. He expected the results in the next day or two, faster than the sector team could turn them around, but he reminded her again that there was unlikely to be anything useful.

It was with relief that Johnson turned off the car engine outside her apartment block. She was used to murder but this series disturbed her in a way no other had.

Inside her apartment, she took a hot shower before heating up a pre-prepared meal and settling on the couch with her laptop. She had to complete the file for the burglar she had interviewed that morning, otherwise he would be released. With over a hundred offences to his name, no way was that happening.

She sent the completed file to the sector detention centre and prosecution ready for court the next day, then turned her attention to the last few hours. She typed up everything that had happened to send to Kerten. She finally logged off in the early hours of the morning to get a few hours of sleep.

Her dreams were haunted by the symbol carved into Amy's body: two sides of a triangle with the corner breaking through a half circle, and a full small circle with the skin gouged out, making a bloody hole.

Johnson woke up feeling disturbed and uneasy. Something cold and dark was lurking just out of view. Something evil was waiting...

∞

Back at headquarters, Johnson sat at her desk and logged onto her computer and phone network. Before calling Michelle, she checked to see if anything new had come through.

She couldn't remember if she had ever met Michelle because she'd never bothered going to the analysts' floor before. She didn't even know how old she was. The way that Michelle spoke was very formal and precise, indicating an older generation, but she was good with modern technology, which made Johnson think she was in her early twenties. Stereotypes were a bitch.

'Good morning,' Michelle answered when Johnson phoned her.

'Were you able to find anything else for me?' Johnson got straight to the point.

'Nothing helpful, I am afraid. The three victims were all law-abiding and had no connection to each other that I could find. I cannot identify where they were taken from, which would indicate the suspect knew the location of CCTV cameras. Amy called her friend Susan when she was attacked, and Susan called the sector police and logged her concern online. I listened to the call – they would not deploy anyone without an exact location; Susan knew that Amy was between her place of work and home. There was a good chance she knew her friend's route home.'

'Well, Susan seems like the best place to start. Thanks, Michelle.'

'I am running searches to collect intelligence on any other people who have been killed or registered missing on, or near, the time of a new moon.'

'You think there could be others?' Johnson asked.

'Amy is the third that we know of. Why do you think there would not be more?'

∞

Johnson's next stop was her supervisor's office. Inspector Kerten looked up as she knocked on the open door. 'I read your report from last night. Not much to go on. What are your next steps?' he asked.

Johnson updated him on her conversation with Michelle, 'I plan to talk to Susan first and then Amy's colleagues at the hospital before trying to retrace her steps home.'

'Good. I'm posting Eric Badu to work with you. Don't start!' he said as she opened her mouth to protest. 'You have three murders in three different sectors, two of them now cold cases. That's a lot of ground to cover. And to be honest, Eric has much better people skills than you do. When it comes to talking to Katy Jones's family, he'll probably get more from them than you will.'

'Who is Katy Jones?'

'My point exactly. She was the first victim.'

Johnson took a deep breath. She had not looked at the names of the other two murder victims. And, if she were honest, she had to admit that she was terrible at dealing with families – and people in general – which was why she often worked alone. There had been complaints that she was too cold, unsympathetic and abrupt. She knew Eric's reputation; he was good at empathising with people and talking to them, but Johnson didn't like admitting that she would need him. She didn't like admitting that she needed anyone.

'I'm going to Amy's flat to talk to her flatmate. When Eric gets in, tell him to check in with me.' Her comment implied that he was late.

'He's already over at the Sector 9 police station getting the reports. I'll let him know *you've* made it in.' Kerten's words grated as she turned and walked out.

Chapter 3

Eric Badu was standing outside the address of Katy Jones's ex-partner, Simon. Michelle had emailed the file to him yesterday evening. Once the director had accepted that this and the other two murders were linked and CLEA had taken on the investigation, Inspector Kerten had briefed him on the case and the actions he was to take.

'You'll be working with Johnson,' Kerten had informed him. Eric had tried to argue that he didn't need help but was quickly silenced. 'She's already on it and you will assist her. She is currently in Sector 2, supervising the autopsy and the scene of the most recent murder. There is a lot of ground to cover – Michelle seems convinced she will find more bodies now that she knows what she is looking for, so we need to get a grip quickly. Once you've spoken to Katy's family, link in with Johnson and Michelle and send me a full report.'

Kerten had hung up and Eric had cursed. Johnson wasn't known as a people person; previous attempts to partner her with other agents had never been successful.

After the call with Kerten, Eric had opened the file. It hadn't made pleasant reading; he could understand the inspector's concerns and also why he'd been assigned to work with Johnson.

He rang the intercom at the communal entrance to the apartment block. The conversation with Katy's ex-partner was not going to be pleasant. Simon had been hesitant about agreeing to a meeting, but Eric had reassured him that all he wanted were the facts.

When the door buzzed, Eric pulled it open and walked up to the third floor. As he turned into the corridor, a door opened and a man came out of one of the apartments. 'Agent Badu?'

'Yes.'

'Come in. My folks have taken Sammy early, so we can talk without interruption, but I need to be at work in a few hours.'

The flat was a small studio, clean but cluttered with children's toys. Clearly Simon had never expected his son to move in with him, and he was struggling for space.

'Thank you for talking to me at such short notice,' Eric said. 'Looking after a young child and working must be difficult.'

'My mum is great – I couldn't do this without her,' Simon admitted. 'But it's been hard. I've been demanding answers from the sector police since me and Sammy got back from holiday and discovered what had happened to our Katy, but they decided she wasn't worth investigating.' He paused and took a breath. 'What's changed now? Why is CLEA interested in Katy when the sector police ain't?'

'There have been two other murders, both female victims found in the same way as Katy,' Eric admitted.

'Did the sector police think that they were prostitutes, too? That's what they said about Katy – why they didn't care. They thought that because Sammy was visiting my sister with me, she'd decided to earn some money on the side.'

'No, they didn't think they were prostitutes.'

'Then why did they think that about Katy? I didn't report her missing until we got back because I hadn't expect to hear from her when we were on holiday. I took Sammy with me so he could see his auntie. Katy was glad that she could do extra hours because her phone had been cut off and she was behind with the rent. I always gave her what I could, but I've got to pay my rent as well. The police took the "extra hours" as sexual favours. She was never like that. Never,' Simon said vehemently.

'I'm sorry that assumption was made,' Eric apologised. 'It delayed you getting the answers you need. To try and understand what happened to Katy, I need more information. Do you know where she worked? Any friends and family that I can talk to?'

'She worked for cash, doing odd jobs for a lady called BB. That's all I know. It wasn't great work but it was flexible. Besides Sammy and me, Katy had no family and no time for friends. If she wasn't working, she devoted her time to Sammy.' It was clear that Simon was very defensive about Katy, and that she had loved her son very much.

'Do you know anything about what she was doing on the day she died? Is there anyone I can talk to who saw her that day?'

'No, Sammy and me had already left and I don't know who she saw. You may get something if you can work out who BB is. I told the police everything, but it ain't much, I'm afraid.'

'If Katy didn't have a phone, how did she get work from this BB?'

'I don't know. I'm sorry, Katy and me – we ain't been together since before Sammy was born. She lets me see him and take him to see my family, which I was thankful for, but I ain't been in her life. I can't help you. Sorry, I wish I could.'

'I hate to ask, but how do you know she *wasn't* making money as a prostitute? Not that it will change how we handle the investigation.' Eric reassured him.

'She hated sex. We only did it a couple of times, but it

was the main reason we broke up. As far as I know, I'm the only person she liked enough to even try it with. The police assumed she was on the game because she was broke and had no job they could identify, and that it was a trick that had gone wrong. But I tell you, she wasn't like that. Now you say there were two others that died like her?'

'The circumstances around the deaths are similar.'

'If the police had listened to me when they found Katy, would it have made a difference? Would the others still be alive?' Simon asked.

'It's unlikely, though we think the murders could be linked. The connection was only made because of the most recent victim who was found last night. Could I look at Katy's flat? Check to see if anything links her to the other victims.'

'The landlady let me keep some of Sammy's things, but she got rid of everything else and let the bedsit out to someone else. I'm sorry I can't help you.'

'Can you give me the landlady's details?'

'Yeah, give me a minute.' Simon looked through some paperwork before handing over a card.

'Thank you.' Eric noted down the details.

'I don't need that anymore, you can keep it.'

Eric put the card in the file. 'I appreciate your time. Please call me if you remember anything that might help.'

'I will. Can you do me a favour? Can you correct the police record, so Katy isn't shown as a prostitute? She wasn't, and I don't want Sammy ever to think that of his mum.'

'I'll do what I can,' Eric promised as he left.

He found it interesting that BB had given Katy work because it suggested that Katy had a phone no one knew about. There hadn't been one on her body and a detailed search of her home had never been conducted. He messaged Michelle to ask if she could find any evidence that a phone had existed.

∞

'So when I called saying Amy was being attacked, you didn't care. Now she is dead. now you care?' Susan said acidly.

Johnson had gone to visit Amy's flatmate and best friend. She understood Susan's anger and grief, but she wished Eric was with her as she struggled to come up with the right words. 'I'm sorry,' was all she could think to say.

'Sorry Amy is dead, or sorry no one cared while she was still alive?' Susan demanded.

'Even if the sector police had sent someone, Amy would still be dead,' Johnson said.

'Oh my God, is that how you justify them doing nothing?'

'No, of course not, I'm just stating a fact. But if you have a complaint against the sector police that's a separate matter. I can advise you who to speak to.'

'I don't believe you. Please leave.' Susan stood up.

'You didn't know where Amy was, her route from the hospital or when she'd left. The sector police wouldn't have found her, even if they'd looked,' Johnson argued. 'With a search area from here to the hospital, it would have taken time – time that Amy didn't have.' Despite her words, Johnson wished a sector unit had done an area search of the likely route; it wouldn't have saved Amy but they might have seen something of note like a dropped mobile phone.

'That doesn't mean they shouldn't have tried.' Susan refused to be placated.

'I'm not here to argue about what should or should not

have been done. I need to learn more about Amy, her habits and her friends, and to see if there is anything among her things that could indicate who did this to her.'

Susan sighed. 'Fine. You're welcome to anything that could help you find the culprit.' She led Johnson to a room off the hallway. 'That's her bedroom.'

The walls were covered with cheap prints of animals and flowers. There was a handful of popular novels on a side table, and photos of Amy with either Susan or an elderly couple that Johnson assumed were her parents. Michelle would identify them to let them know what had happened.

Johnson found nothing unusual. Amy seemed to have been a private person with a lifestyle that revolved around her family, Susan, and work. An old laptop was open on a small desk; Johnson picked it up to take with her in the hope that something might be stored on it. There was very little else in the room besides a bed and some clothes, so little left of someone's life.

Susan was waiting for her in the corridor. 'I'll need to take this.' Johnson said, showing Susan the laptop.

'If you think it'll help,' Susan replied. 'Is there anything else you need?'

'What can you tell me about Amy's life? What did she like to do? Did she have any other friends or family?'

'Amy worked long hours – we both did to afford this place. Her free time was mainly spent here at home.' As Susan showed Johnson out of the flat, she said, 'You'll let me know if you find out anything?'

Johnson reassured her that she would. She didn't want to say that any updates would be limited because Susan wasn't a relative.

Next she drove to the hospital where Amy had worked and circled the grounds in frustration, looking for somewhere to park. Law enforcement had a designated set of bays but there were never enough of them. She wondered how patients and their visitors managed. Suddenly she saw someone leaving and took the space. Getting out of the car, she entered the hospital and went to the nurses' station.

'I'm from CLEA and I need information about Amy Hood. Is there a supervisor I can talk to?' Johnson didn't know what information the staff had been given, but it turned out they knew a lot. The receptionist started crying at Amy's name and struggled to put through a call. A supervisor arrived a short time later, together with several nurses who all said they wanted to help.

Johnson wondered cynically how many of them had come out of curiosity, but she didn't really care; the gossip would circulate quickly enough. 'Did you know Amy well?' she asked the supervisor.

'No, she wasn't part of my line management team, but I've requested the HR files for you – though they can take a few hours to come through. The nurses have come because they knew Amy. I've arranged a private room for you to talk to them.' She led Johnson to a small interview room off a quiet corridor.

It would take too long to question all the nurses, and it would take them away from their own duties, so Johnson decided to speed things up. 'Who knew her best?' she asked.

At first, there was just noise as everyone started to speak at once, so Johnson interrupted. 'Let me be clear. I'm not interested in talking to anyone who is curious or wants to get away from their work for a bit. Amy was brutally murdered and I want to find the person who did it, so please don't waste my time. Who here knew Amy?'

One of the nurses spoke up. 'No one really. She never came out with us for a drink after early shifts. But she was always polite and a good worker. You could rely on her to help you out if you needed a shift to be covered, but she never got involved, you know?' The others nodded agreement. 'That doesn't mean that we don't want to help. We do.'

'Do any of you know anything about her private life?' There was silence. 'What about anyone she was seeing?'

'No one,' another nurse called out. 'She wanted to, but the hours here stopped her going out on dates.' Several people nodded. 'We all work extra hours to pay bills and there isn't time for anything but work. And Amy did more than most of us.'

'Is there any way to find out what hours she worked, especially what time she left the hospital last night?' Johnson asked.

'You'll need to ask human resources for a full schedule of her work hours, but her time card for this week should still be in place so I can check what time she left,' one of the nurses said before disappearing to get the information.

'How accurate would that be?' Johnson asked.

'It's how our hours are calculated for pay,' the supervisor said. 'It's the last thing we do as we walk out. No one wants to get caught up with another patient and not get paid for it.'

The nurse returned and handed over a copy of the time card. 'Thank you,' Johnson said. She looked at the slip of paper and saw that Amy had called her flatmate only twenty minutes after leaving the hospital. 'If you remember anything that happened that night that seems relevant, please let me know.' She handed out her contact details, though she wasn't hopeful about getting a call. 'Do you know what exit she would have left by and if there is any CCTV?'

'Of course. The hospital managers like to check we actually leave when we say we do. I'll take you down to security. They should be able to help you with that.'

One of the nurses took Johnson to a room away from the wards and knocked on the door. To Johnson's surprise, she walked away before it was answered.

'What?' a man's voice shouted as the door was yanked open. Maybe not so surprising, Johnson thought.

'Agent Johnson from CLEA.' She showed her badge. 'I'm investigating the murder of Amy Hood, a nurse at this hospital, and I need access to your CCTV. I was told you could help me with that.'

'Yeah, of course,' the man said. 'Anything for a law enforcement colleague.' He stood aside and let her in. Something about him made Johnson's skin crawl.

∞

Johnson left the office with relief; the security guard had been in her space the whole time, sitting too close, wanting to know what she would do with the CCTV, information she refused to give him. She knew the sort of guys who wanted to get into either sector police or the CLEA but couldn't.

His colleague sat quietly in the room until finally he told his mate to 'leave off'. Johnson didn't need his help, but she smiled at him politely as she got up to go.

Once out of the hospital, she called Michelle. 'I have the time Amy left the hospital and I've taken copies of the CCTV that shows her leaving the hospital, as well as for the previous hour in case anyone was waiting for her. I'll send it over.'

'Thank you. That is a good starting point for me.'

'Can you check the cameras between the hospital and the park? See if she was followed or where she dropped off the CCTV?'

'Of course,' Michelle replied.

Chapter 4

MICHELLE READ AMY Hood's autopsy report. At first, she wasn't fazed by the details – it wasn't the worst she'd read – but as it got to the details of the symbol carved into the abdomen, she paused. The other autopsies had not given a full description of the symbol, either through laziness or because of the decay of the bodies. The photos Johnson had emailed from the scene had been unclear; blood obscured the symbol, making it hard to see.

When Inspector Kerten had questioned her before CLEA had taken the case, Michelle had bent the truth about what she could prove. Luckily the date, the park, the victim being tied down and something carved on her abdomen were enough. She had known that the murders were linked, though not in any way she could hope to explain.

She swore. She searched her desk for a piece of paper and cursed the digital age when she couldn't find one. She rifled through her handbag for the notebook she always carried. Pulling it out with a sigh of victory, she drew the symbol as it had been described. She hoped that she was wrong.

'Damn.' She had hoped to identify the carving once she had a clear description. Although she knew many of the symbols used by demons, her information was out of date since her father had cut her off. To be sure, she re-read the autopsy report on the first body to see if the vague details would match what she knew. They did.

This was not good.

When Michelle had come across the first body while running searches of linked crimes, she'd hoped it was a coincidence. She'd refined the search criteria and discovered the second victim. She had known then that there would be others, though if she tried to explain how she knew nobody would believe her.

She had created a new search parameter that would run in the background, which was how she'd found out about Amy Hood's murder a few days later. She knew that wouldn't be the end of it. Demons loved a sacrificial ritual when the moon was either new or full; the symbol was the essential element that identified which demon was trying to come out of hell's dimensions. She would have to determine which one it was, based on her memories or what the internet could tell her.

Most of the time, she was thankful that her father had withdrawn from the mortal world, especially after the destruction that her brothers had unleashed when they had decided they wanted power for themselves. They had turned their backs on their father and been killed as a result. Michelle was now the last of her kind. Only rarely did she miss the information her father could have given her, but being mortal – or mostly mortal – was the price she'd paid for her life.

Pulling up a map of all the sectors on her computer, Michelle plotted the locations of the three deaths. Demonic rituals normally required five sacrifices; once completed, the locations would place each victim at a point of a pentagram. She hoped to see three of the points; however, while two fitted the pattern, one was definitely too far away to be part of the same pentagram.

Maybe she was wrong, maybe it was a coincidence and a demon occultist had just happened to take a fancy to

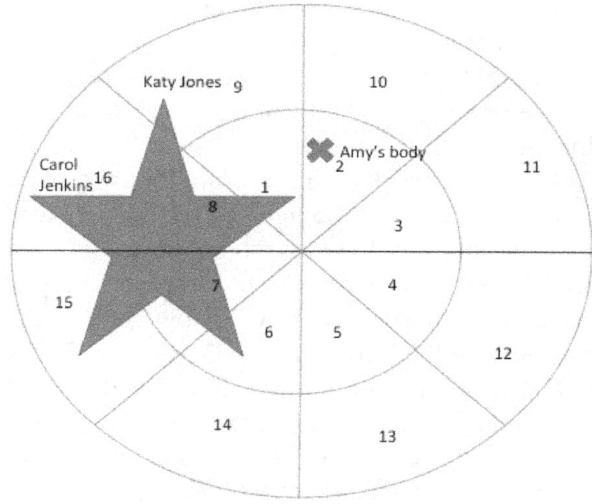

this symbol, but it was so similar to ones she had seen before. If all three had fitted into the same pentagram, Michelle would have been sure. However, the location of Amy Hood's murder was not even close.

She scanned the image onto her computer and searched the internet to see if it was known, but only a few results were returned. None was associated with anything demonic. Looking at the results, she was confident the symbol was not in the human world, but she was aware that was not the whole picture. Sites that she could access on the dark net might give her some answers, but that would have to wait until she got home. If she asked for permission to use the dark net whilst at work, she would have to explain why she needed to access it. She couldn't do that without revealing the demonic connection and how she knew that the sites existed. Also, she would have to be careful how she targeted her searches; she couldn't afford for them to be questioned in a court of law.

For now, Michelle tried to piece together what she could to give Johnson something she could understand and use to progress the investigation. She worked on two theories.

1. The symbols were a coincidence being used by fanatics, and the CLEA only had to find a psychopathic murderer.
2. A genuine ritual was being performed – and there would be more sacrifices.

Michelle pondered the location of Amy's murder. Could two teams be working in two different sectors on two different pentagrams? If that were the case someone else had died last night and not been found yet, but she had no idea where to suggest a search, let alone what reason she could give for one.

If people already thought the world had gone to hell, it would be nothing compared to what could happen if the demon behind this got its way.

Michelle was wondering how best to approach the problem when the phone rang and she heard Johnson's voice. 'Michelle, I have the time Amy left the hospital. Can you start checking cameras for me?'

'Of course.'

Johnson passed over the details and ended the call; at least Michelle now had some definite parameters to work with.

∞

Michelle reviewed the hospital CCTV footage. She watched as Amy went into the ladies' changing rooms, came out a short while later, went to the exit and swiped her time card to book out. Michelle saw no one near her in the hospital, so she switched to the external cameras.

Amy walked across the car park out of range of the cameras. Now she knew when Amy had left the hospital grounds, Michelle accessed the sector's cameras and found the one covering the hospital exit Amy would have used.

She followed Amy to the transit station and watched as she boarded a train. Still no one was following her or paying her any attention. When Amy got off the train, the camera coverage was limited and Michelle had to check video footage from the surrounding cameras between where she was last seen and her home address. Amy entered an area not covered by CCTV and Michelle couldn't see where she had emerged; this had to be where she had been abducted.

She pulled up a map and marked where Amy was last seen, the route she'd have taken, alternatives, and where the cameras were. She sent the data to Johnson and flagged up the areas of highest probability to search, based on vehicle access and routes to the park.

It was a five-block area and several routes were not covered by CCTV. Michelle sighed. Plotting the shortest path between the train station and Amy's home on the map, she looked at the routes to Theron Park. The only way to get Amy to the park where she was found would have been by using a vehicle.

Michelle created an algorithm to look for vehicles large enough to transport a body arriving at Theron Park. There were many possibilities, so she set the computer to run the owners and licenced drivers against the criminal database. It was a long list. Once there was more information about the movements of the other two victims, perhaps she'd be able to cross-reference the data. Hopefully the sector police had seized any relevant footage, otherwise it was probably too late; most areas only kept recordings for a month.

She called Johnson with the bad news. 'I am sending you a list of all vehicles that left the area when Amy went missing. I have highlighted the ones linked to people with criminal records, and those that have been reported stolen.'

'Thanks, I'll take a look. Are you doing any further checks?'

'I cannot with the limited information I have. When you talk to the families of Katy Jones and Carol Jenkins, try and get anything about their movements so I can look for similarities between them and with Amy.'

'Eric spoke to Katy's ex-partner today. I'll make sure that he gives you anything he learned.'

'Do you know yet when you will be talking with Carol's family in Sector 16?'

'Not yet. I'll talk to Eric and let you know.'

Chapter 5

JOHNSON LOOKED AT the list of vehicle registrations Michelle had sent her and her heart sank; it was too long to be helpful. She needed to find something to help Michelle narrow it down. Picking up her phone she rang Eric, hoping he had some leads from his meeting with Katy's ex. 'It's Johnson,' she said when he answered her call.

'So I assumed by the caller ID. I'm guessing you are calling to ask how I did talking to Simon.'

'Of course,' Johnson replied after a pause. She was trying to remember where she had heard that name before. She had gone over the facts of the case but barely glanced at the personal details. She hated personal information, learning about what life was like for those who had been killed.

'I'm just about to enter headquarters to catch up with Michelle,' Eric said. 'Can you join us? Inspector Kerten wants a report on how the investigation is going.'

'He always wants a report,' Johnson stated. She wasn't surprised Kerten had asked Eric; she completed her reports but she wasn't good at getting them in on time. 'I can be there in thirty minutes.'

∞

Johnson dropped Amy's laptop onto her desk. She couldn't see Eric so she rang him to see where he was. 'I'm with Michelle,' he said.

'See you in a minute.' She realised that although she had worked many cases with Michelle, she'd never met her and didn't know what she looked like. Neither could she remember if she'd met Eric; she'd never worked with him and didn't spend much time at headquarters, preferring to be in the field.

Walking onto the analysts' floor, she saw two people sitting together and realised that she did know Eric. He was in conversation with a, thin, very pale, blonde female. When had that woman last seen sunlight, Johnson wondered.

'Johnson, it is good to see you on the analysts' floor for once,' Michelle said, 'Eric and I were just going through his findings. Find a chair and join us.'

Michelle's tone grated. Johnson rolled over a chair. 'What have I missed?' she asked as she sat down.

'Michelle was taking me through the list of vehicles that went to the park and seeing if there's any way to narrow it down,' Eric said.

'Was Katy's family able to tell you anything?' Johnson asked hopefully.

'Other than an unknown woman called BB who employed Katy, he couldn't add anything to the investigation.'

'Do we know anything about BB?'

'Nothing, not even a number.'

'But if she was giving Katy work, they must have been communicating somehow. Michelle, is that something you can help with?' Johnson had no idea what Michelle could do with such limited details, but it never hurt to ask the question.

'Eric has already given me what he knows. If I find anything, I will update you both.'

'Thanks, Michelle.' Johnson felt that both Eric and the analyst were ahead of her and being polite about it.

'What did you find out from Amy's flatmate Susan?' Eric asked.

'Not much, just that she had a dropped call from Amy and was convinced something was wrong. The hospital gave the time that Amy left, which is where the long list of vehicles came from. Oh, and Amy had a laptop in her room and I brought it in. I was going to see if there was a way past the password.'

'Bring it to me and I will see what I can do,' Michelle said. 'I can turn it around quicker than anyone at the lab can.'

'Thanks.' Johnson stood up to go and fetch the laptop then turned to Eric. 'The other victim, Carol Jenkins, have you made arrangements to see her family yet?'

'I was about to contact her sister Gemma to arrange a time to meet.'

'Great. Let me know when it's set up. We can go together.' It wasn't a question and they both knew it. As Johnson walked off, she had to admit that she was relieved that Eric was taking the lead in reaching out to the family; she didn't relate well to families, but she got results. That's what mattered to her.

'Of course.' There was an edge to Eric's tone as if he resented her intrusion. But she didn't know Eric, didn't trust his work yet, and if she wasn't there she could miss facts. That wasn't acceptable. Once she was confident about him, it would be different.

∞

Johnson returned to Michelle's desk with Amy's laptop. Eric was still there, eating a pastry and chatting with Michelle. They were clearly at ease together, and she wondered if Eric always made a point of seeing the analysts in person.

Johnson placed the laptop on the desk. 'Any luck?' she asked him.

'Gemma is happy to meet now if you're ready to go.'

'Good. After you.'

Michelle reached for the laptop and muttered something under her breath as they walked out. When they reached the garage, they both headed in different directions to their cars. 'I don't think we need two cars,' Johnson said.

'Neither do I, but I have the address,' Eric pointed out. Taking a deep breath, Johnson got into his car. 'You don't like giving up control, do you,' he said as he turned on the ignition.

'Is there anything I should know about Carol's family?' Johnson asked, changing the subject. Eric started to brief her on what he knew.

∞

Eric rang the doorbell of the flat Gemma had shared with her sister Carol. The woman who answered the door was pale with dark circles beneath her eyes; she looked like she had not slept well since her sister had died.

'I'm Agent Badu and this is Agent Johnson. Are you Gemma Jenkins?'

'I am. Thank you for coming so quickly. Please come in.' Gemma led them through to the living room. There were still signs of Carol's occupancy; looking around, Johnson suspected that Gemma couldn't bear to move her sister's belongings.

'I'm more than happy to talk to anyone who might give me answers about what happened to my sister – though I was surprised to hear from *you*. I thought the sector police had the case.'

'We have taken it off them.' As Johnson explained why, Eric remembered his conversation with Simon and wondered how many more times this would happen.

'We would appreciate you telling us more about your

sister,' Eric cut in, getting back to why they were there. 'Who she was in contact with, her routine and, most importantly, anything about her activities the night she died.'

'Of course, though I don't know how much help I can be. We were close as sisters but our friends were different, and I'm afraid I don't have their details. The sector police took her laptop and I don't know what happened to her phone. It was with her when she died.'

'We're having your sister's property transferred to CLEA, so we'll make sure we get those items,' Eric said. 'What can you tell us about the day she died?'

'Not much. She was out with her friends.' Gemma wrung her hands together. 'We talked all the time. She complained to me about them, her day, everything – or so I thought – but I only had first names. I knew about their lives and weird facts about them, but I didn't know who they were. Now it matters and I can't help you. What else didn't I know?'

'I know this is hard for you, but not knowing Carol's friends doesn't mean you did not know *her*. They were *her* friends, not yours. We can find out who they were and talk to them. But there are other things you can tell me. What about Carol's routine? Did she prefer to walk or take a bus? Did she choose main roads or shortcuts,' Eric asked.

Gemma paused before answering. 'She kept to the main roads. She didn't like the dark, so she always took the best-lit routes, even if they were longer. When she went out, she liked to stay local – she didn't want to risk public transport stopping early and taxis were too expensive.'

Eric reassured her. 'You are helping us already.'

'The sector police said they'd talk to the other teachers at the school where Carol worked. Most of her friends were from there, so maybe they can tell you more. The police never told me what was said.'

'We'll review all the interviews and redo them if needed,' Johnson told her. 'Would you mind if we searched her room? We want to make sure the sector police missed nothing.'

'Of course, anything that would help.'

⦿

Nothing in the room helped, and Gemma couldn't add any information that the sector police had not recorded. 'It's far too late to go to the school now,' Johnson said as she climbed back into the car with Eric.

'I'll try to set something up tomorrow. See what you can get back from the sector police,' he responded.

As he drove them back to headquarters, Johnson sent requests to the sector police for the interview transcripts and evidence seized from her laptop. 'Coffee?' She suddenly broke the silence as they neared headquarters, the first word she had spoken during the journey.

'God, yes.'

'Drop me off at the corner and I'll meet you at Michelle's desk.' Neither of them even considered that Michelle would have gone home, though it was gone 10pm. It was a joke in the office that Michelle's only life was work; although some researchers and analysts covered the night shifts, Michelle never trusted her assignments to them so she was always in early and left late. When someone had questioned her about that, she had retorted, 'We are here to support the agents. If they are still working, then so am I.' As a result, she was permanently assigned to the more complex cases.

Eric stopped outside a 24/7 café so Johnson could jump out before parking at headquarters. Walking into the intelligence support area, he saw the night-duty team sitting at their desks. Michelle was at her desk on the other side of the room; the box of pastries that usually accompanied her had been replaced by chocolate.

'Have you already scared Johnson off?' she asked without looking up from her computer.

'She'll be here in a minute. She's just getting the coffees.' Eric pushed two chairs to Michelle's desk and collapsed into one of them.

'I hope she does not think I want one,' Michelle said.

'I hope I know you better than that,' Johnson said, walking up behind her with three drinks in a cup holder. She handed one to Michelle who took it and smelt it.

'Hot chocolate. Thank you. How did you know?'

'We might have only just met, but it doesn't mean I'm not aware of your addiction to sweet things,' Johnson responded.

'So, are you going to keep me waiting?' Michelle berated them. 'What did you find out that I can use? You are both bad at keeping me updated, you know that?'

'Sorry, Michelle. We found nothing that we needed you to research immediately. If we had, we'd have been in touch,' Johnson replied.

'How do you know what I can use?' Michelle challenged.

Johnson was about to retort when Eric interceded. 'Apologies. Let's summarise what we know, then hopefully we can see our next steps. Tell us what you can use of the information we've gathered, and what else we need to find out. Honest communication will help Johnson and me in the future in what we share and how quickly we share it.'

Johnson watched as Michelle relaxed and smiled at Eric. She had to admit he had a way with people that she had never achieved.

'Johnson, do you want to summarise, or shall I?' Eric was asking because he knew how she liked to control the situation; she hated herself for not being able to delegate.

'The murders of Carol and Amy happened a month apart in different sectors,' she summarised. 'We have the exact dates for them thanks to friends and family, but we don't know when Katy died. The decomposition of her body only gives us an approximate date.'

'What was the estimate from the pathologist?' Michelle asked.

'That she was the first victim, about four weeks before Carol.'

'Carol and Amy were murdered on a new moon. Could Katy have been killed at the same time of the lunar cycle?'

'Possibly,' Johnson admitted. 'Do you think that's a coincidence?'

'I do not know yet. I am still trying to ascertain the facts.' Michelle couldn't explain what she suspected about the murders; they wouldn't believe her. If she were honest, she wasn't sure what she had yet. Amy's murder didn't fit the pattern, which could only mean one of two things: either this was a mortal murderer obsessed with the occult, or a second pentagram was being created and not all the bodies had been found yet. Either way, next month would see two more females murdered – and a month searching for suspects could pass very quickly when they had so little to go on.

'Carol had nothing in her property that stood out. She liked to exercise and belonged to a local running club and gym,' Johnson said. 'We'll arrange meetings with them and her work colleagues tomorrow. However, nothing indicated that Amy was a runner or went to a gym. She worked long hours at the hospital and had little time for hobbies. What did you learn about Katy?' she asked Eric.

'When she wasn't looking after her son Sammy she was working, so I doubt she had the time or money for either pastime. All her personal possessions had been disposed of and her ex didn't know her well enough to give much insight into her life.'

They went through everything they had learned. 'Unfortunately, it does not seem we can add much to the original reports,' Michelle admitted. 'What about phones and computers?'

'Carol's laptop was seized by sector police and should be delivered shortly. She had her phone with her when she was killed but it hasn't been found,' Johnson said. 'We don't know what happened to Amy's phone.'

'Do you have the phone numbers?'

'Of course.' Johnson read them out.

'If Katy had a phone, it was never recovered,' Eric said. 'There was no indication that she had a computer.'

'I want Carol's laptop once the sector police release it,' Michelle told him. 'When you talk to the teachers she worked with, get as much detail as you can about when she left and the route she took. I will run a similar search to the one I did with Amy for any vehicles in the area, cross-reference the vehicle details and hopefully develop a more concise list.'

'We'll do our best,' Eric promised.

'Also, though the others have no gym membership, explore the running. There are a lot of informal running groups in all the sectors that are free and do not require membership. People with busy lives and limited budgets are attracted to these to meet people socially. I will see what groups exist in the areas that Amy and Katy frequented.'

'Thank you. Did you have any luck identifying any similar MOs? Did you find out what the symbol carved into the victims could mean?' Johnson asked. When Michelle did not respond, she continued, 'if you don't have anything, just say so.'

'It is not that I do not have anything.' Michelle paused, weighing up what she should say. Although she doubted that they would believe her, if her suspicions were correct the sooner they started accepting them the better. 'You are not going to like it. The way the victims were tied down and mutilated is symbolic of a demonic ritual. Unfortunately, the symbol does not come back on the intelligence database or on the internet, but that does not mean it is not trending on the dark net.'

'You think it is some sort of satanic sect?' Eric asked.

'Something like that, yes,' Michelle replied, relieved that her suggestion had not been discounted immediately.

Both Eric and Johnson were silent for a moment. 'I'll ask Inspector Kerten to apply for authority to access the dark net,' Johnson promised. 'Can you identify any demonic groups we can talk to in the meantime?'

'I will see what I can find and send it over to you.'

∞

When Johnson and Eric left to get some sleep, Michelle requested the data from Amy and Carol's phones; she might not have the handsets, but some data could still be retrieved from the network provider. Then, knowing the networks had no overnight cover and nothing would be returned that night, she went home.

Getting special access to the dark net would take time, time the next victims did not have. However, the beauty of the dark net was that it was nearly impossible to track anyone unless they started posting and revealing details about themselves that led back to their real identities.

Letting herself into her apartment, Michelle pulled back a section of carpet in her living room and removed a floorboard. Reaching down, she pulled out her laptop and charger. Her hand brushed against the clothing that they had rested on. She kept her laptop, as well as other items, separate from her main computer. Though she rarely had visitors, she didn't want anyone looking where she didn't want them to.

CLEA couldn't track people who logged onto the dark net, where they were and what they looked at; that was a bonus for her. But what if CLEA found her laptop and ran a forensic check on it? They would be able to tell if the dark net had been accessed and, depending on how careful she'd been, they could ascertain details of the searches.

Keeping the laptop in the flat was risky but keeping another clean computer in full view limited that risk. And if anyone found her laptop and tried to log on without the correct details, the first fail would release a virus and corrupt it. That would protect her data, but if CLEA ever found it she would have a lot of uncomfortable questions to answer.

Logging on, she navigated to the dark net. From there, what she looked at was not traceable because her IP address bounced around various sectors, cities and other countries. Co-operation between countries was limited; even if they agreed to supply information, they would not support any law enforcement activity, which meant no trial.

Michelle started with basic searches for demonic rituals and symbols; she wanted to see if there was anything obvious. She was already a member of numerous forums discussing rituals because she liked to monitor what was happening, but nobody was discussing the murders. The silence surprised and worried her. Whoever was responsible was not advertising it anywhere obvious. With these sorts of murders, she would have expected attention; the perpetrator would need people willing to follow them as much as they needed fear.

The connection between the murders hadn't made the

news yet, so Michelle was careful not to enter anything that was not common knowledge. She didn't want to risk someone noticing that she knew more than she should. Once the news broke, she could expand on what she looked at.

She was tempted to search under other parameters to try and find the demonic influence, but there were so many demons and it was hard to know who was trying to escape from hell. It had been several centuries since the last attempt.

She still knew a lot about demons; though her information was old, it was probably still correct because demons were eternal and not known for change. Her worry was that her education from her father had been incomplete.

Michelle decided against searching the dark net outside the basic parameters; she didn't want to risk her account being flagged for any reason. While they wouldn't know who or where she was, she could trip a marker if one had been set and give away more than she wanted to be known.

She looked at the hidden compartment from which she had retrieved her laptop; there were other ways to get information. There were underground clubs for those who worshipped, or were fascinated by, the demonic. She had been invited and attended a few of them more than a decade ago but, other than disgusting her nothing occurred that sparked alarm and she had stopped going. Maybe it was time to go again. She still had her outfits hidden away.

Looking at the time, Michelle saw that she could get an hour or so's sleep. She logged off the laptop and put it back beneath the floorboard before heading to her bedroom and lying down. She would shower and change when she woke up.

It was at times like this she was glad she needed very little sleep.

∞

Michelle had felt there was something wrong when she arrived in the town. It wasn't just that everyone was staring at her as she walked through the quiet dusty street; as a female on her own, that was to be expected. No, it was something else. Coming here had not been her intention, but she had felt a pull, a need to come. She had not felt that since her brothers had died and her father had left.

Michelle knew that there was trouble here.

'Evening, miss.' A man in uniform came up to her. 'I can't remember seeing you here before.'

'No, I am just travelling through.'

'This isn't a place for lone females to wander around.'

'I am travelling to stay with family,' she lied. 'Is there somewhere I can spend the night? It is too late for me to continue further on my journey tonight.'

'Miss Jones keeps a boarding house just down the road on the right. But if I were you, I would make sure I leave as soon as the sun comes up tomorrow.'

'Is there a problem here?' Michelle asked. She knew that travelling on her own was not the done thing, but she suspected there was something more.

'Nothing you need to worry about if you keep off the streets tonight and leave tomorrow,' the man replied.

Thanking him, Michelle continued on her way. She found the boarding house easily, was given a room and warned not to go out again until morning. 'Why? Is the town not safe?' she questioned.

'It used to be, but there have been several murders lately. All young girls, some taken from their beds at night.' Miss Jones locked the door. 'I've locks on all my windows so we're alright here.'

Michelle wasn't convinced; she could feel the lady's terror. Taking her key, she went up to her room and locked the door before lying down.

She was still awake when the sun started to rise. She heard a scream. Jumping up, she raced out of her room; others were reacting to the noise as well. Michelle opened the front door and ran towards the noise. She did not have to look hard; there was a small green by the church and a crowd of people was forming around it.

As she approached and eased her way through, she saw the body of a young woman tied down, a symbol carved into her chest. Michelle was moving forward to get a better look at the symbol when the smell of sulphur filled the air and the ground shook. She had arrived too late. She saw the demon rise and knew real fear. What hope was there now?

Looking around, she saw the locals staring at him in horror. 'Run!' she shouted, though she had no idea where they could run to.

Fire spread from the demon as he laughed, and the townspeople screamed in pain as the flames engulfed them. Michelle felt the heat surround her and thought her end had finally come. But then her wings appeared and wrapped around her, wings that she thought had been lost to her, protecting her from the hell fire.

Her father had said she would be Nephilim again when there were demons, but that was hundreds of years ago and she had started to doubt. Now, as the fire receded, a smile spread across her face. She knew she could do this: she could send the demon back to hell.

∞

Michelle woke up with a start. That was the first time she had had to fight a demon on her own. With the body that was found that morning, the ritual had been complete.

She remembered standing in terror for a moment as she saw the demon rise before her. Then, for the first time since her brothers had been killed, she became Nephilim again, felt her bladed wings on her back and knew what to do.

The demon had looked down on her, considering her irrelevant, a runt compared to her brothers. She had proved him wrong and sent him back to hell, but not before the town had burnt to the ground. Most of the townspeople had died during the battle. The ground was now nothing more than a rubbish heap, tainted by evil so that nothing grew and no one wanted to live there.

She hoped she could stop another demon rising before history repeated itself. With a heavy heart, she got up. Not enough sacrifices had happened yet.

Chapter 6

Sector 15 – two days after the
new moon

'COME ON, IT'LL be fun,' Jon called to his friend as he ran towards a closed-off conservation area.

'My mum will be mad,' Jose called after him, even though he followed as fast as he could. 'We're supposed to be going to the park and we aren't allowed in there.'

'Mummy's boy.'

'Am not.'

'Are too! I only want a quick look to see what's here. I heard there's a pond with tadpoles.'

That was enough for Jose; he wanted to see the tadpoles. Together they climbed over the fence. They knew they would get into trouble if council officers found them out because no unauthorised personnel were allowed in the conservation area in the hope of preserving what remained of nature within the city.

'Why don't they cut the grass and trees?' Jon asked.

'You're an idiot,' Jose retorted. 'That's the point – so the bugs and things are okay.'

'I'm not an idiot,' Jon shouted and pushed Jose, who stumbled. His foot went into the foliage to steady him, but he still slipped and fell.

Jon laughed as he saw his friend collapse, but then Jose screamed and Jon stopped laughing. Thinking Jose had hurt himself, Jon pushed aside the greenery and saw his friend half-lying on a dead body. He was covered in blood – her blood. Jon turned and ran away, screaming, leaving his friend behind.

∞

Michelle was in early as usual. She stopped by her favourite baker around the corner from headquarters. It wasn't open yet but she had an agreement with the owner, who opened the side door and smiled as she handed over a box with Michelle's usual order still warm from the oven. Michelle paid well for that box; it was all about life's small luxuries.

She walked into the office and sat at her desk, picked up a pastry and started to eat it as she logged on. She checked to see if any new bodies had been discovered overnight. It was a negative result and she didn't know if she should be worried or relieved. She set the search to run every hour.

She looked at the map she had plotted. It just didn't add up; the deaths should be three points of a pentagram but Amy's did not fit. Michelle placed a ring around the abnormality; was it an error, or a second pentagram? There wasn't enough data to know where the next victim would be, which frustrated her.

Part of her wished she still had the connection to her father; he would know who she should be looking for. But his interference, and that of her brothers, had been catastrophic so she put the thought away.

Michelle turned her attention back to the crime scene and pathology reports to see if she could identify any discrepancies between the murders. She sighed in exasperation. There was not enough information in the reports for Katy and Carol to compare against Amy to determine if two murder teams were working or not.

She closed the files and checked the search; a result had come in this time. A body had been found in a conservation area by two boys. The sector police were on their way and the details were limited. The mother of one of the boys, Jon, had called the police but her son was hysterical and couldn't give much information. The main detail was that her son's friend had fallen on a dead body and was still there.

The computer search had identified the death by location, sex of the victim and approximate day of death. Michelle looked at the map unlike Amy's, this death created the third point of a pentagram with Carol and Katy. This was the body she had been looking for, but being right felt awful.

Hoping that Johnson trusted her and wouldn't ask too many questions, Michelle called to let her know there had been another murder and gave her the location.

∞

Johnson was about to walk out of her apartment to meet Eric when Michelle called her with the news of a body in Sector 15. 'Damn it,' she cursed. 'Are you sending through the details?'

'As we speak.'

Johnson's phone buzzed as the email came through. There wasn't much – a location and the name of the boy who had found the body.

'Are you going to talk to Kerten now about taking this case, or do you need me to assess the scene first?' Johnson asked. Usually a review from an agent at the scene was needed, but Michelle was so accurate that the supervisors listened to her even when they didn't trust any other analysts.

'If you are happy, I will talk to him as soon as I can,' Michelle replied.

'Please. The sooner I can get forensics to the scene, the better. I want to avoid the situation with Amy.' Hanging up, Johnson called Eric to let him know.

'Do you want me to join you there?' Eric asked.

'No. Michelle needs the information from Carol's friends to narrow her search parameters. Get what you can from them first, then we'll see where we're at.'

∞

Johnson had to push through a crowd when she arrived; it had taken her longer than she liked to get to Sector 15, and the delay annoyed her. Trusting Michelle's judgement and that Kerten would take the case, she contacted Matt to see what his thoughts were about coming out. It wasn't protocol to come out before the case was formally accepted, but she was willing to bet it would be a CLEA investigation before his team could arrive.

This wasn't a large public park like the one where Amy had been killed but a small area that no one should have been in. She guessed that the news must have spread in the community quickly to bring in so many people.

Johnson ducked under the cordon and showed her identity badge when she was challenged. 'Where's the body?' she asked.

'Just past the first bush – you won't miss it.' At first, she was reassured at what looked like a large crime scene and hoped that, with her arrival, the sector police wouldn't just pack up and leave before Matt and his team arrived. But when she walked around the bush, she realised the scene was not that big. The body was in front of her; someone had cut back the greenery that had hidden it from view revealing a secluded space. The killer would have had as much privacy as he needed.

She had to admit that having Eric with her would have been beneficial; he could talk to the sector police better than she could. As it was, she had to rein in her anger over the contamination of the scene. Still, Johnson had to balance priorities; some sectors did not keep their CCTV for long and cancelling Carol's grieving friends could restrict the information they would give, so Eric's interviews were essential.

The new victim hadn't been moved yet, which was something. The scene appeared to be the same as that of Amy Hood; the victim had been tied down, her top cut open and the same symbol carved into her abdomen.

'Can I help you, agent?' one of the local officers asked her.

'I've come to see if this murder is connected to a series we are looking into. What can you tell me about the victim?'

'Not much. We have no idea who she is – she has no personal items on her.' Johnson wasn't surprised; only Amy had been found with any personal belongings so far. Dental records had identified Carol and Katy. 'We'll check for any missing females when we get back to the station,' the officer went on. 'It was lucky the boys found her. People aren't supposed to come in here.'

'Do you know the time of death?' Johnson asked. She almost hoped it kept to the new moon rule and gave all the deaths an order that could be worked on.

'Not yet, but it's definitely been a few days. Rigor mortis has passed.'

Rigor mortis usually dissipated after two days. Johnson cursed; the time scale was not clear enough for her to tell if the latest victim had been killed the same night as Amy or not. Based on what she could see, she was sure the murders were linked but the bosses would need more convincing without the exact time of death.

She messaged Inspector Kerten with the details that she had. He responded that he was with the director and would let her know if CLEA had the new case. Michelle had already briefed him. 'How soon will you be able to get an exact time of death?' she asked.

'That's for the pathologist to say once we get the body back to the morgue.' Johnson watched as the team cut the bindings, ensuring they were correctly bagged and exhibited as evidence, but she turned around as they started to move the body. It was never pleasant to watch.

To distract herself, she moved towards the cordon and the crowd of people. 'Does anyone know what happened here today?' she asked.

One of the crowd shouted, 'Only what Jon said when he ran home to his mum saying he'd found a body. Left his poor mate behind. Came here to see what I could find out.' Some of the others seconded the comment.

'Who and where is the "mate"?'

'Little Jose Davies. The police took him away. I heard he was still here crying when the officers arrived.'

'What about Jon? Is he here now?'

'No,' the woman in the crowd said. 'He's normally a cocky lad – I've never seen him so upset. He's with his mum.'

'Can you tell me where they live?' Johnson asked and the crowd happily gave her the details.

⚭

Her phone buzzed as a message came through from Kerten: *It's ours*. She was relieved because it would give her more authority over the case and she hadn't called Matt out unnecessarily.

One of the sector forensic team approached her. 'Agent, we're ready to take the body to the morgue now. Do you want to travel back with us?'

'Not yet. A CLEA forensic team is en route and I want to ensure the scene stays in place. Once they're here, I'll head to the morgue.' She knew it was a risk, but after the last time she had to trust in the management of the deceased over that of the crime scene. The sector police would see supervising the scene as a waste of resources once the body was removed, especially if the CLEA took over the case.

'Please make sure the pathologist knows that this will be a CLEA case,' Johnson went on. 'I'll be there as soon as our forensic unit arrives.'

As the sector forensic team drove off, the police tried to leave too; this was no longer their problem. 'You will stay where you are,' Johnson ordered them.

'Our sergeant says otherwise,' one of them retorted.

'Then remind your sergeant of Section 5 Cooperative Policing Law, which states that the case is not handed over until the receiving law enforcement body has relevant personnel in place. One person is not relevant personnel.'

After a lot of grumbling, the police officers remained. The law was always good for a quote but rarely enforced in court, but she wouldn't tell them that.

∞

Matt arrived with his team quicker than she expected. Johnson briefed him with what little she knew and, when she was happy he had the scene under control, left for the morgue. En route, she called Michelle. 'You were right about the case – what was done to the body was very like what I saw at Amy's crime scene. I don't know how you found it so quickly.'

'It came up on my search parameters, that is all.'

'I hoped the CLEA would take the case, but I'm surprised at how quickly we got approval.'

'How many murderers are we looking for that tie down their female victims and carve symbols into them on a new moon?' Michelle replied sarcastically.

Johnson didn't know what was in the analyst's original report and found that she didn't want to know. 'Fair enough. The victim had no ID on her. While we wait for DNA and dental, can you check for any white females aged between twenty-five and forty who have been reported missing in the last few days? Once I have a time of death from the pathologist, I'll let you know.'

'Of course, but I doubt there will be anything. The sector police will not take a missing person report until someone has been gone for seventy-two hours,' Michelle reminded her. 'But I can check social media to see if anyone is posting about a missing loved one.'

Johnson suspected she was already on it.

∞

When Johnson walked into the morgue, the victim's body was already on the table. It had been cleaned, making the marks on her wrists and ankles, as well as the cuts on her abdomen, even more pronounced.

The pathologist looked up and nodded but otherwise ignored her as she started working on the body. Johnson listened as she recorded her findings. Samples were taken and sent for further analysis; that could take weeks.

As the pathologist made her assessment, Johnson recognised many similarities to Amy's autopsy. The rope used to tie down the victim appeared to be the same, though it would have to be tested to confirm that. The symbol carved into her abdomen was identical. Johnson thought it had to be the same killer – until the pathologist said, 'The killer was right-handed.'

'Are you sure?' Amy's killer had been left-handed.

'Yes, I'm sure,' the pathologist said and continued her work.

If the pathologists were both correct, there were at least two killers. Had they worked together?

Damn.

Chapter 7

As Johnson left the morgue, she dialled Eric and Michelle into a conference call. She was in Sector 15 and she couldn't get back to headquarters to meet them for a face-to-face debrief. 'Have you found out anything more?' she asked Eric.

'I talked to Carol's colleagues and they gave me the time she left the school. Apparently, there was a team drink after work but she declined at the last minute saying she had to go home and do some marking. They didn't believe her – they thought she'd had a better offer.'

Michelle said, 'Not knowing where she was going, I checked cameras around the school when she left. I followed her for a while until she entered an area with limited coverage. I cannot tell you where she went. I am in the process of checking cameras where she could have exited, but there are some sectors without CCTV and her home is one of them. I compared vehicles in the areas Carol passed through to vehicles near Theron Park where Amy was murdered, but I have had little luck. A few overlapped – delivery vans and taxis – but nothing that raises any concern. I will send you over the details to check out.'

'Thanks, we'll have a look at them.' Johnson knew it was unlikely to lead anywhere but they had to ask the question. Delivery and taxi vehicles were often pooled to operate 24/7 on tight schedules, so the chances were that the companies employing them could account for every second of where they were and who was driving them.

'What did you find out about the latest death?' Eric asked.

'So far her identity is unknown. Two young boys found her and one was still at the scene when the police arrived – he'd fallen on the body. The police seized his clothes and took swabs, but he was very distressed and couldn't tell them anything. His friend ran away and told his mum, and she was the one who reported it. He was questioned by the sector police and said they'd gone in looking for tadpoles. When his friend fell on the body, he was scared and ran off. I don't think either of the boys know anything.'

'Do you think the murder is linked?' Eric questioned.

'From looking at the scene? Definitely. The autopsy also raised many similarities to Amy's. The problem is that the estimated time of death between this victim and Amy is very close; I can't see how the same suspect could have killed both, not with the time they spent with the victims and the travelling time between Sectors 2 and 15.'

'Were there any differences between the murders?' Michelle asked, thinking about her two-pentagram theory.

'A few. Amy still had her ID on her, but the current victim is unidentified. The pathologist also thought the person who did the cutting was right-handed, and the evidence indicated the left hand was used with Amy. Everything else appears to be similar from the autopsies, but we'll have to wait for forensic testing.'

'So we have two murderers copying each other, and we have to wait weeks for forensic confirmation.' Eric stated the bad news that they all knew, but there was nothing they could do about it.

'It certainly looks that way,' Johnson said. 'With the limited information we have at the moment, it's going to be hard enough to find one suspect let alone two.'

Eric cursed at the news, but Michelle was relieved that the evidence pointed towards two murder teams. It would be easier to show Eric and Johnson the pentagram patterns if she had to; she wanted them to be a bit more accepting before delivering the theory so they didn't discount it out of hand.

'Did you find any missing persons' reports that could match the latest victim?' Johnson asked after a moment.

'It is too early. Someone cannot be reported missing until they have been gone seventy-two hours, so there will not be a report until tomorrow at the earliest.'

Johnson swore under her breath; that policy might have reduced the number of people reported missing and eased the stretched resources of the sector police, but it also meant valuable time was lost when someone was genuinely in trouble.

'Is there going to be a press release about the murders?' Michelle asked.

'I wasn't planning to ask for one. Why?' Johnson demanded.

'With the number of people at both this and Amy's murder scenes, I would expect comments to start appearing on social media. It could be beneficial to say we know they are linked and we are investigating. It could help identify new leads by creating awareness so the sector police and the public let us know about missing persons.'

'If an officer is investigating a case that could be linked, an all-sector bulletin will resolve that issue,' Eric pointed out.

'That is definitely a good idea,' Johnson said, 'but I agree with Michelle. With the seventy-two hours' rule, we could lose a lot of vital information. We already have several cold cases.'

'It could also cause panic,' Eric countered. 'The volume of calls that come in will be almost impossible to filter. I don't think it would speed anything up.'

'I understand that, but if we go public it gives women knowledge and the chance to be more aware of danger,' Johnson argued.

Eric still protested. 'Women are more likely to be attacked than males – that's always been the case – and the CLEA runs self-defence programs and awareness sessions. Other than the unusual MO, what makes this different to all the other cases? I'm not against the idea, but we need to be clear about the risk. Why are these murders more important than others?'

'The uptake in those classes is low because most people don't have the time or money to attend them. And if you'd seen the bodies, you'd know why this case is different,' Johnson shot back.

'Stop!' Michelle said. 'CLEA may run classes but they are not widely publicised and can only train a tiny fraction of the female population. They will not suffice.'

She knew that the murders would stop once the ritual was complete, but when they did a demon would come through; when that happened, life would be so much worse. The fact that Johnson seemed to sense something unusual about the cases was a surprise and a benefit.

Michelle continued. 'I know there are many murders against females, but can either of you tell me when you saw anything like these? Most are domestic or opportunistic. These were planned. We could target the message to those missing on the new moon to raise awareness. I know there will be a lot of calls, but they could help drive the investigation. At the moment, no one knows about them. Once there is understanding, people may post on social media. Some groups will take credit, others will look for attention – but others could be genuine. It could open up other search opportunities.'

⊠

'No.' Inspector Kerten said as soon as he heard Johnson's request for a press release.

'Michelle believes it could lead to valuable source of intelligence,' she pointed out.

'I doubt it – I think it will bring out the nut jobs. I don't want it known that we have a killer out there abducting, tying down and cutting weird symbols into women before killing them, not until we have a better grasp of the investigation.'

'Maybe that's why we should be telling people. I don't believe this is related to the normal criminality associated with linked murders. Michelle can't find any connection to the victims, other than that they are female, law-abiding and the dates of their deaths. She thinks that once people are aware of them there will be talk, especially on the dark net. She'll have a chance to see who is boasting and knows more than they should.'

'Michelle doesn't have access to the dark net,' Kerten pointed out.

'Not at the moment, but she could have if you authorised it,' Johnson said.

'No, not a chance. There is enough work to do on this case for the moment without following leads from fanatics. Have I made myself clear?'

'Crystal, sir.' Johnson turned to leave.

'I know you think Michelle is very good, and I trust her more than any other analyst, but she is not omniscient. We can't just give her what she wants without considering the wider consequences,' Kerten said. 'If the details of these murders are released now, they will be seen as exceptional. People will demand to know what we're doing about them and we don't know enough yet. We don't have many victims compared to other linked murders, we have no suspects and we're having to wait for any possible forensic leads. So far, these murders have been a month apart, so we have time before more happen. I don't want to create panic if I don't have to.'

'I understand.'

'If we have no leads in two or three weeks time, I'll release a statement so Michelle can get the information she thinks will be so important,' he promised.

∞

Johnson entered her apartment with relief, tired and desperate for a bath. She had just started running the hot water when her phone rang. Her heart sank as she guessed what was coming.

'I think I have a match for the murder in Sector 15,' Michelle said.

'That's sooner than I expected; the seventy-two hours to report a missing person haven't lapsed.'

'It is not an official report – a local community is posting on social media. A priest has not been seen since she held morning prayers two days ago. Her congregation are angry that the sector police are not doing anything, and they have heard of a body found nearby that has not been identified. They think it is her and are demanding answers.'

'What's her name?

'Jenny Adamson. I cannot see that she has any next of kin. Her curate seems to be the person she is closest to. I will send you his details.'

'Pass them to Eric, too. It's too late to travel there now, so tell him I'll meet him at headquarters at 6am.'

Her boss might not have wanted to do a press release,

but if the most recent victim was Jenny Adamson he might not have a choice.

Johnson pulled the plug on her bath and logged onto her laptop. She read Michelle's information, which included several social media posts about the Revered Jenny Adamson's work in the community.

Johnson looked at pictures of Jenny. With a heavy heart, she had a quick shower and went to grab a few hours of sleep before facing the day ahead,

◑

It was very early when they met at headquarters. Johnson suspected that Michelle had not been home; she was wearing the same clothes as the previous day and her normal box of breakfast pastries was absent. Even so, there was nothing about her that indicated any level of fatigue. Johnson was unreasonably annoyed by that.

'I am sorry I contacted you so late,' Michelle said. 'Do you think the new victim could be Jenny Adamson from the photos I sent you?'

Johnson nodded as she pulled up a chair to Michelle's desk.

'How much were you able to find out for us about Jenny?' Eric asked.

'Not much. She seems to have been a very private woman. Her social media profile is limited to her work in the community, where she is greatly liked and admired. As with the other victims, she is of good character.'

'So we have a type: all female, all upstanding citizens in valued professions – mother, nurse, teacher, priest,' Eric pointed out.

'And none of them with obvious enemies,' Michelle added. 'I cannot link any of the victims. So far, the only variation is that Amy Hood's ID was left on her body,'

'The person who killed Amy couldn't have killed Jenny

Adamson,' Johnson stated. 'If the body I saw yesterday was Jenny, there was no way the killer could have travelled between Sectors 15 and 2 and spent time tying the victims down and carving the symbol before killing them.'

'How close in MO were the killings of Amy Hood and Jenny Adamson?' Eric asked.

'Having seen both bodies, very close. Other than the issue with the ID and that whoever carved the symbol on each body used a different hand, there was nothing to tell them apart.'

'So we have a copycat? Amy's murderer knows about the others and decided to copy them? Why?' Michelle threw out the question. She hoped that they would start to consider the possibility of two teams of killers because she didn't have enough factual information to justify the theory to them.

'To gain notoriety?' Eric asked.

'I could understand that if the murders were in the news, but they're not,' Johnson replied.

'We can't deny the evidence. Maybe when the forensic reports are complete, they'll give us answers,' Eric said optimistically. None of them believed that would be the case, but they could hope. 'For now, we must approach this as a separate killing to Amy Hood.'

Chapter 8

AFTER LEAVING HEADQUARTERS, Eric and Johnson had planned to go straight to the church to find the curate who was demanding answers from the sector police. Michelle had said his social media profile had the name of @DannyJones, and her research showed that a Daniel Jones worked for the church. He was not a big fan of law enforcement, not since his wife and son had been killed a few years ago in a home invasion. No one had been arrested for their murders.

Johnson could understand his view; he had been let down the last time he had trusted the authorities. Michelle had brought up the investigation log for them to read as they travelled to Sector 15, and Johnson knew that there had been significant errors in the handling of the case. Perhaps Danny wanted to drive awareness of Jenny Adamson's disappearance to make sure it got the attention it deserved.

'He'll post about the interview and the questions we ask him to increase interest on social media,' Johnson said as she looked at the existing posts.

'As well as any questions he asks us and we refuse to answer. There's nothing we can do to stop him,' Eric agreed. 'If the relatives of the other victims realise the connection, it won't be long until the news gets out.'

'And Kerten has made it clear that's the last thing he wants. If we reassure Daniel that we'll keep him informed, maybe it will reduce how much he posts.'

'I doubt it, unless we convince him his posts could undermine the investigation. However, he's not family so he has no rights to the details of the murder,' Eric reminded her.

'The conservation area is near here,' Johnson said. 'How much further to the church?'

'It's only a few blocks further down.' Eric took the next right and stopped the car. A crowd of people were walking towards the conservation area.

'It looks like some kind of vigil is about to start,' Johnson said.

'Shall we join them? Show our presence and support?' Eric suggested. Johnson sighed with frustration. 'It'll be fine,' he reassured her as he got out of the car. Johnson followed him reluctantly.

They waited at the back of the crowd. Johnson sent a quick message to Michelle to see if she had seen anything on social media about the gathering.

It is a vigil; it is seventy-two hours since Jenny Adamson was last seen, Michelle texted back. Johnson showed the response to Eric. That meant she could have been missing several hours before she was killed.

A man came onto a stand and the crowd went quiet. Johnson suspected that this was Danny Jones, though she was too far away to know for sure.

'Thank you all for joining us. As you know, our beloved Reverend Adamson – Jenny – has not been seen since morning prayers. It is seventy-two hours since she went missing, and during that time a body has been found nearby. Though we can't confirm it was her, I feel it here.' He put his hand over his heart. 'I know many of you think I should have faith that Jenny is alive and will come back to us, but it's not in her character to leave us. She is gone because she couldn't return to us.'

There was a lot of mumbling among the crowd. Jones

continued, 'I'm not here today to criticise the sector police. The protocols around missing people have been in place for years and it is not in their power to change them. I am here now so we can support each other, continue the work that Jenny started and share what she means to us.' He stumbled over the word 'means' as if he couldn't quite bring himself to say 'meant'.

He called out for people to share memories of Jenny that were important to them and many hands were raised by those who wanted to speak.

Jenny had been much loved and her death would impact a lot of people. For a killer that had previously chosen low-profile victims, Johnson wondered why he'd now selected someone so high profile. Maybe he'd thought the body would not be found for some weeks, or he had not factored in Daniel Jones's determination to take action.

The vigil did not last long but even so people noticed Johnson and Eric, the only people in suits who were not taking part. There were glances their way and whispered conversations.

Daniel Jones thanked everyone for attending and the crowd slowly dispersed. Some people paused to talk to friends, but no one approached the agents.

'Did you want to speak to Curate Jones here, or wait and go to the church?' Johnson asked Eric.

'Here,' he replied. 'It won't take long for the community to point us out to him, and we need to be seen as open. If we go to the church, people might think we are hiding something.'

As they walked through the crowd, a man who didn't seem to fit in caught Johnson's eye. Most of the people there were supporting each other, and many of them were distressed, but this man seemed to be taking pleasure in the atmosphere. She pointed him out to Eric and started to move towards him, but someone walked between them and then he was gone. She cursed; she had not got a good enough look at him to recognise him again.

Johnson turned her attention back to the curate. A woman pointed her and Eric out to Curate Jones and he raised a hand briefly, indicating that he had seen them. Then he turned back to the woman and said something that made her smile before she walked off.

Daniel came over to them. 'How can I help you?' he asked. The question was loaded; he was worried they were there because of complaints about the gathering.

'I'm Agent Badu, and this is Agent Johnson – we're with CLEA,' Eric said. 'We were coming to talk to you when we saw the vigil. We don't mean to intrude but we were hoping to get more information about Reverend Jenny Adamson.'

'Of course. If you can give me ten or fifteen minutes here, I can meet you at the church where we can talk privately.'

⊙

The church was open. Johnson felt uncomfortable as she looked around, but Eric just sat on one of the pews to wait.

'Did you get a look at that man?' Johnson asked, hoping that Eric had noted his appearance.

'No – what about him?'

'I just felt he was out of place.'

'He could have been a local,' Eric pointed out.

She knew that was true, but for some reason she didn't think it was that simple. She was prevented from saying anything further by Daniel's arrival.

'Thank you for waiting,' he said. 'There's an office in the back where we won't be interrupted.' Eric and

Johnson followed him through to the rear of the church. 'I'm sorry for the mess.' He started to move paperwork off the chairs. 'Do you have any information about Jenny? Was it her body in the conservation area? That's why you're here, isn't it?'

'The body hasn't been identified yet, and it will take a few days for DNA tests and dental comparisons to come through. Until then, there will be no formal confirmation. But, having compared a picture of Reverend Adamson and the deceased, I'm sorry to say there's a strong possibility that she is the murder victim.' Eric said.

'Did you see the body?'

'I did,' Johnson told him. Her eyes drifted to the picture of Jenny on the desk, a photo she had seen previously on social media. 'I'm sorry, but there is a similarity between the two...'

'But you need forensic confirmation,' Daniel said. 'I understand. The sector police aren't interested in a missing person's report until the seventy-two hours are up. Trust me, I tried to change their minds. I'd like to know why CLEA is involved.'

'Normally, this would be a sector police investigation,' Eric explained. 'However, there are similarities to another murder. We are investigating to see if the two are linked.'

'I'm glad someone is looking into it. I want to help in any way I can.'

'Can you tell us everything you can about the day Jenny went missing, any friends that could assist, anything that could help us track her movements that day and several days beforehand?' Eric asked.

∞

'You didn't ask him not to post our interview on social media,' Eric pointed out as they got back into the car.

'Neither did you,' Johnson retorted. 'I didn't think it would help. If we'd asked him not to, he would put more weight on the meeting than we want. Legally we can't stop him, and I'd prefer not to make him hostile toward us. All he knows is that there have been two deaths, none of the details.'

'For someone who doesn't talk to people well, you can read their characters,' Eric pointed out. 'If he does post, there's a good chance of the link being made to Amy Hood. Because of our recent interviews, that could connect with the other murders.'

'I know, but it was always a matter of time before reporters made the connection.'

'They may not. Plenty of serial killers never make the news.'

'Normally they are gangs on killing sprees, not law-abiding women who are tied down and mutilated,' Johnson pointed out. 'This will make the news.'

'You're right. I can't remember the last time teachers, reverends, nurses and mothers were targeted. It isn't good.'

'That's an understatement. I'll make Inspector Kerten aware so that social media can be monitored, and a formal statement given if need be,' Johnson said. 'I don't want to sound callous, but if the media does make the connection Michelle can broaden her searches on social media and maybe find new leads.'

'It's not the way I would have wanted it, but you're right,' Eric conceded. 'Since we're here, shall we see if Jon can talk to us. The file said he lived nearby.'

∞

Jon's parents were nervous about the meeting but they agreed to it. They lived so close that there was no point driving, so Johnson and Eric walked the one block. There were still many people in the area because of the vigil, and Johnson couldn't help looking around her.

'Do you mind talking to the family on your own?' she asked. 'Since we're here, I want to take the opportunity to look around the area.'

'Michelle can identify any cameras,' Eric started to say.

'I know but I want to get a feel for it. I can meet you back at the car.'

Eric agreed. As Johnson walked away, he pressed the intercom for Jon's flat. He had to walk up several flights of stairs to the seventh floor because the lifts were out of order.

The boy's father let him in. Jon was curled up on the sofa next to his mother; he looked as if he hadn't slept since he had found the dead body.

'I don't know how my son can help you, Agent,' Jon's father said.

'He might not be able to, but I need to ask him a few questions just in case.' Eric crouched in front of Jon. 'Hi, I'm Eric. Are you Jon?' The child nodded. 'You're not in any trouble but I'm hoping you can help me? Can you tell me what you did when you entered the conservation area?'

'We just wanted to see the tadpoles and frogs,' Jon replied. 'I know we weren't supposed to be there.'

'I understand why you wanted to see them – tadpoles are cool. You're not in trouble for being in the conservation area, but I need to know what happened when you got there.'

'We were on our own. Jose slipped on something and started to scream. When I saw why, I got scared and ran away, I left my mate behind,' Jon sobbed.

'I'd have been scared too. Now, I need you to be really brave. Can you tell me what you saw?' Jon was silent, 'It's okay,' Eric comforted him.

'A body, tied down – and loads of blood. I just freaked.
Jose won't talk to me any more.' Jon started crying again.

'I'm sorry Jose won't talk to you. You said no one was
there – not even any homeless people?'

'Not that I saw.'

'Do you know if there are usually people camping
there?'

'I don't know. I just wanted to see the tadpoles,' Jon
said miserably.

'You've been very brave,' Eric said gently. He stood up
and turned to Jon's parents. 'I'm sorry to have upset your
son, but hopefully I won't need to talk to him again. Please
call me if he remembers anything else.' He handed over
a contact card and they promised that they would.

∞

As Johnson walked around the conservation area and
the busy roads encircling it, she drew a lot of attention.
She didn't know if that was normal or if there was a
heightened awareness in the community after the vigil.
She wondered what it was like at night; it would have
been difficult to unload a body, either unconscious or
awake and struggling, during the day.

She was turning back to the car when she spotted the
man from earlier watching her. When she started to walk
towards him, he ran off. Johnson ran after him shouting,
'CLEA, stop!' but, although people turned to look at her,
no one stepped in to help.

The man quickly increased the distance between them.
She saw him go down a side road but he'd disappeared
by the time she reached it. Walking a short way down
it, she saw numerous blocks of flats that he could have
gone into and other side roads to turn down. Cursing,
she turned back to the car.

Eric was waiting for her. He raised an eyebrow when

he saw her. 'You okay?'

'Yeah, I saw that man from the vigil, but he ran off when I approached him.'

'You think there's anything in it?'

'I don't know. Maybe he just doesn't like police and CLEA. I'll see if Michelle can find him on CCTV when we get back.'

Chapter 9

Back at headquarters, Johnson went to brief Inspector Kerten about Danny Jones and his social media campaign.

'I know we can't stop him legally, but do you think we can convince him in any other way?' he asked.

'No. He has no confidence in law enforcement and thinks that if he remains silent there will be no justice for Reverend Adamson. The sector police did nothing to find the person who killed his family. He trusted them and his trust was misplaced. He doesn't know us yet and has no reason to trust us. Any attempt to persuade him not to post might make him think we're trying to hide information, which would be much more harmful.'

'Understood. However, he isn't family so he isn't allowed to know the progress of the investigation.'

'He knows he's not entitled to details – he is well-versed in what he can and can't be told. But he will take any opportunity to keep up the pressure, including looking for other crimes that fit the pattern.'

'Talk to the communications department and make sure they are aware of the situation. If Danny or anybody else posts on social media, they will release an appropriate response.'

'I think Danny could help us. He has a considerable following in the community...' Johnson started.

'No, I want CLEA to own the narrative on this. Everything goes through the communications department.'

'Understood, sir.' Johnson turned to leave.

'I also want daily updates. I don't want to have to ask. Do you understand?'

'Yes, sir.'

'You should let Michelle know. She wanted the media to be aware and soon they will be, though in a limited way. Let's see if she was right.'

'Her access to the dark net, sir?'

'She will have it by this afternoon,' Kerten promised.

∞

Michelle smiled as she received the authority to log onto the dark net. She downloaded the Tor server onto an unnetworked computer and was logging on when Johnson and Eric came into the office.

'Inspector Kerten said to make sure you only search on the details already in the public domain,' Johnson told her.

Michelle pulled a face. As if she needed to be told – why did they think she wanted a media statement to be released? 'Of course,' was all she said. 'Did you find out anything from Daniel Jones?'

'Not much more than you've read. Jenny was last seen after taking a morning service and she stayed on at the church to work on her sermon. Daniel left once he had tidied up and set up for the next day's service. Jenny was still there when he left. He returned the next day to find the church locked – usually it would have been open and Jenny there already. He tried to contact her and couldn't, and no one has seen or heard from her since. A body that fits her description was found a few blocks away in a conservation area two days later,' Johnson summarised the facts.

'But too far away from the church to be taken there without a vehicle?' Michelle asked.

'I would say so. It's a few blocks,' Eric confirmed. 'I didn't see many cameras in the area.'

'I have already checked – there are only a few traffic and council cameras, and I have already downloaded their footage. What about security cameras at the church?'

'None. It was thought that they would discourage those who needed help the most, and nothing of value is kept there.'

'Not the cameras belonging to the church but to CLEA.' Johnson and Eric looked at her, confused, and Michelle continued, 'The ones that were installed during the religious riots twenty years ago.'

'I don't remember those,' Eric said.

'I do,' Johnson said. She had been in a convent orphanage at the time, having been abandoned by her drug-addicted single mother when she was a baby. She remembered an atmosphere of fear, of whispered conversations. She and the other children knew something was wrong but didn't understand what was happening.

Then she was awoken in the middle of the night by the smell of burning. Johnson remembered the smoke that had started filling the room and the nuns quickly ushering them out. The convent was on fire. The other children began to scream and panic, hindering the nuns from getting them to safety.

She remembered that she was running down a corridor when an explosion outside caused the windows nearby to shatter and spray glass over them. One of the nuns, Sister Mary, protected Johnson with her body.

Johnson remembered lying there for what seemed like ages calling out to Sister Mary, who didn't respond. Sometime later, another nun grabbed Johnson's wrist to check if she still had a pulse before pulling her out from under Sister Mary.

'Don't look,' she said, but Johnson couldn't help herself. She saw the bloodied body lying on the floor, the shattered glass cutting deep. There was so much blood...

'The sector police and the CLEA were both heavily criticised for not doing enough to stop the violence,' Michelle continued, bringing Johnson back to the here and now.

'Even though the churches refused to assist in any investigation because they thought the offenders could still be saved,' Johnson finished with a certain amount of bitterness.

'Exactly. As a result, CLEA placed covert cameras outside religious buildings to catch offenders. The church Jenny is missing from has been there nearly fifty years, so a CLEA camera could have been fitted.'

'They wouldn't still be there, would they?' Eric asked.

'I do not know,' Michelle replied. 'The cameras had a long life and the area has been through limited development. There is a chance that they are still recording, but I do not have access to the relevant database.'

'Why can't you access them like you can the other cameras?' Johnson asked.

'When the CCTV infrastructure was upgraded a few years ago, many of these cameras were not included as they were no longer deemed necessary. However, they were not removed because that was an additional expense. If they are still operational, the footage should be available through the archive database, which I do not have access to.'

Michelle had not worked for CLEA during the religious riots. Johnson wasn't sure whether she had been there when the CCTV changes were made, which was more than the 'few years ago' the analyst had referred to.

'How did you know they were there?' Johnson asked.

'I have learnt a lot in the years I have been here. Footage

from cameras like these has been used in previous investigations and I have seen the reports.'

For some reason, Johnson wasn't convinced by the explanation.

Under Michelle's guidance, Johnson found the CCTV footage that had gone directly into the archive. For someone who didn't have access to the database, Michelle certainly knew exactly how to search it. Johnson decided that she did not want to know how she'd gained that knowledge.

'So how do I find the right folder?' Johnson asked.

'It will depend on how they have archived it. We can search first under sector. Failing that, we can look at date and time.'

'Do you want to type? It will be much quicker that way.'

'It is your account,' Michelle protested.

'I'm not going anywhere,' Johnson reassured her. She moved away and let Michelle take her place. As soon as she had access to the keyboard, Michelle's hands moved quickly. Johnson was amazed anyone could type that fast.

'Found it,' Michelle said.

They held their breath as the footage loaded; there was a good chance that the camera at the church would no longer be recording after years without maintenance. They all released their breath as an image appeared of the front of the church. The quality was poor but hopefully clear enough.

Not knowing what time Jenny had left, voluntarily or otherwise, they viewed the footage from when she was last seen alive.

Eric sat down next to Johnson and she looked at him in surprise. 'You don't think I'd let you have all the fun watching several hours of CCTV footage?' he asked.

Johnson smiled gratefully. A second pair of eyes was always useful.

'Give me a shout if there is any information that I can run checks on,' Michelle said as she returned to her own computer.

Johnson and Eric watched as the congregation left, then Curate Daniel Jones walked away alone. For hours, there was nothing; the odd person walked past, but no one entered or exited the church.

Johnson was about to suggest a break when the screen showed a van draw up and park, blocking the view of the entrance of the church. A man got out of the passenger side and walked towards the door before disappearing from view. After about fifteen minutes, he emerged, got back into the van and it drove off. Johnson couldn't tell if he loaded anything into the back as that was out of camera range.

As the vehicle drove off, Johnson and Eric leaned forward eager to see the licence plate. Eric paused the CCTV suddenly. The image was too small to make out so he slowly started to enlarge it but it blurred further. They couldn't get the vehicle registration.

'I'll give Michelle a call – maybe she can clean it up enough to make out the number. Knowing the time the van was at the church, she might have some luck with the traffic cameras,' Eric said hopefully.

'Are you forgetting you are sitting next to me in my office?' Michelle said, without pausing what she was doing. 'Give me the time and vehicle description.'

Eric apologised and started to write out the details.

'I'll keep watching, just to make sure the van wasn't a coincidence,' Johnson said.

∞

Eric went home after updating Michelle. He had tried to convince Johnson to do the same but she had refused. She wanted to make sure there was nothing else on the footage, but she promised she would leave soon. It had been a busy few days with little sleep, and Eric suspected the next few weeks would be the same.

A few hours later he returned and found Johnson asleep in the same chair. As he shook her awake, she jumped and shouted, 'Sister Mary!' She looked up at him then, remembering where she was, she rubbed her face. 'Sorry, Eric. Is anything wrong?'

'Other than you didn't go home as you promised you would?'

'I meant to. What time is it? Why are you back so early?'

'Michelle messaged to say she's cleaned up the image and has a registration number.' They both looked at Michelle's desk; her chair was empty. 'She knew I was coming in.'

'Why didn't she wake me?' Johnson asked.

'She probably thought you needed to sleep.'

Johnson stood up, stretched and tried to smooth down her suit.

'Who is Sister Mary?' Eric asked.

'I grew up in a Christian orphanage and she saved me during the religious riots. I guess the conversation yesterday brought back some old memories.'

'Want to talk about it?'

'No.'

Michelle walked up to her desk looking as bright and fresh as if she had just had the weekend off and dropped a box on the table. 'I did not expect you to come straight in, Eric. I assumed you would have picked up the message when you woke up. Help yourself to a pastry.'

It was clear she had been out and got double her regular order, though goodness knows where from at that time of the morning. Johnson's stomach rumbled, and she ate one of the pastries gratefully. 'This is so good,' she said. 'Thank you.'

'You are welcome,' Michelle said.

Eric and Johnson pulled up chairs as she brought up the image of the van and the enhanced registration. 'The van belongs to a Henry Ward; he is well known for violent crime. However, most of his victims do not make allegations because of witness intimidation, either by him or other family members. That brings us to the passenger.' Up came the image of the man getting out of the vehicle. 'This is Charlie Ward, Henry's cousin, who is also well known to us for serious assault. They run a business together, for which the van is shown as an asset.'

'Anything they could be delivering to a church?' Johnson asked.

'I do not think so.' Michelle brought up the cousins' website.

'Definitely not the sort of thing you would associate with a church,' Johnson said as she saw the lingerie and sex toys that were on sale.

'Do we know where the van went?' Eric asked.

'There are no cameras between the church and the park, but it was identified entering the Utopia Estate a short time later and leaving almost immediately.'

'Other than the vehicle's locality, is there anything else to tie it to the abduction and murder of Jenny Adamson?'

'None, I am afraid,' Michelle told them.

'Was the van near any of the other murder sites?' Johnson asked hopefully.

'Not that I have been able to ascertain but that does not mean it was not. It just means it did not pass any cameras.'

'It's all circumstantial evidence, but we could try for an

arrest warrant,' Eric said.

'Depends on how sympathetic the judge is,' Johnson responded. 'I'm wondering if we can chance our luck and write up two types of warrant application. If the arrest warrant fails, we ask for a search warrant for the cousins' home and business premises.'

'Sounds like a plan,' Eric agreed.

'It's early, so no judge will be available now. I'm going home to grab a shower and change my clothes.' Johnson checked the time. 'Back in for 9am?'

Chapter 10

MICHELLE WATCHED ERIC and Johnson leave; she knew they expected her to do the same but she had already showered before going out for food, and she always kept clean clothes in the office.

She could see the signs of exhaustion on their faces and knew that they might soon question how she could work the hours that she did. She couldn't claim to have slept at her desk; too many other people worked in the office to know that wasn't true. Looking at the time, she could go home and 'sleep', but then she would have to hand the case over to someone else for a few hours. It wasn't that she did not trust her colleagues, she just didn't like the idea.

Deciding not to pretend to sleep and to plead exhaustion later, Michelle searched more deeply for the Ward cousins. She checked to see what other vehicles they owned; she expected there to be a large pool and was surprised when there were only a few. Either the cousins were smart and registered the vehicles elsewhere, or they were honest and it was a small business. A warrant would be needed to determine which was true.

Michelle added the registrations to search against traffic cameras to see if any of the vehicles had been filmed near the other murder scenes.

She pulled up everything she could find on the Ward cousins, but nothing tied them to demonic cults. Knowing she wouldn't immediately get anything back from the traffic cameras, she turned her attention to the dark net. With the information that Daniel Jones had placed on the internet, she could now run more searches. Knowing the Wards' involvement, she would look first at any results that involved them.

She still had some time before Johnson and Eric returned, so she checked her phone to see if she had gained access to any of the demonic clubs. She had reached out to the ones she had attended previously, saying she'd been in another city but was keen to reconnect. Smiling, she saw that she had been sent instructions that would get her in.

∞

Johnson went to Michelle's desk a few hours later. She had slept for an hour, showered and changed before coming back in. She half-expected to see that Michelle had gone home to sleep or used her desk as a bed, but the analyst was there as always, staring at her computer and scrolling through a list of results. 'Did you get any sleep?' she asked.

'I got what I needed,' Michelle replied.

'Do you sleep at all?' Johnson's tone was sarcastic.

'Of course. Doesn't everyone?'

Johnson was tired and the response irritated her. She was about to point out that no one else looked as unfazed by the long hours and demand Michelle's secret when Eric walked in looking as tired as she felt. 'Do you have anything for us?' he asked Michelle.

'Nothing very helpful, I am afraid. Vehicles owned by the Ward family are active in all sectors. I can eliminate them from the murder of Amy Hood.'

'What about the other two murders?' Johnson asked.

'For Carol, I cannot say with any certainty because the camera coverage in the area where she went missing is inadequate. For Katy, I do not have enough detail.'

'Not much for us to go on,' Eric murmured. 'What about the Ward family? Any association to the reverend, the church or our other victims?'

'There is intelligence that they burgled the church, but they did not take much. There was nothing worth stealing.'

'Were they arrested? It would be good evidence for another arrest warrant,' Johnson asked hopefully.

'No. The theft was reported to the sector police but the reverend withdrew the allegation shortly after the Wards were identified as suspects. As a result, the investigation can be held as information only.'

'Damn,' Johnson cursed.

'We could still use it as a basis for the warrant,' Eric pointed out.

'Send us through everything you have,' Johnson told Michelle. 'Let's see if we can get one.'

∞

Johnson felt like screaming with frustration. She'd had to call each judge's private secretary to ask if they had any availability to issue an emergency warrant. She had been told more than once that submitting a standard application would be better – but the average time for a standard application was four weeks. Four weeks would take them beyond the next new moon. She reported her lack of progress with the courts to Inspector Kerten, who promised to help as best he could.

While Johnson grappled with bureaucracy, Eric tried to gain as much information as possible from the victims' associates but nothing he reported back helped. He persisted, though, hoping that at some point the questions would lead to answers.

Worried about how many other lines of enquiry could

be missed as she waited for an appointment, Johnson was starting to fill out a standard application for a warrant when she received a phone call.

'I am Judge Gilbert's secretary,' the caller said. 'He's impressed by your perseverance. He will hear your application when he breaks for lunch in an hour.' For a moment Johnson wondered if the call was a hoax, then realised she didn't care.

She grabbed her belongings and headed to the court. When she arrived, she was told to wait outside Court 23. A short time later the court emptied, and she was called in.

Judge Gilbert was on a screen in front of her. The judge and jury used to be present in courtrooms, together with the defendant, but after a series of attacks by organised crime gangs they now operated remotely, as did the victim and witnesses. The defendant gave evidence from prison. Only the prosecution and defence lawyers and any observers actually went to the law courts. Johnson wondered why they bothered to keep them.

'I hear from my secretary that you called every hour looking for time with a judge. Your behaviour reeked of desperation, so this had better be good, Agent,' Judge Gilbert said.

'Thank you for seeing me, Your Honour.' Johnson presented her case and told him about the women who had been murdered, how they had been found and the link between them. She explained why she believed that waiting for a standard application could lead to two more deaths.

'I understand your concerns and why you pushed for this hearing,' Judge Gilbert said. 'But I don't think you have enough for an arrest warrant. However, I'll authorise search warrants.'

It wasn't everything she wanted, but it was more than

she'd expected. The warrants covered the home and business addresses of both Ward cousins as well as any vehicles associated with them.

Œ

Michelle had been helping Eric find new leads while Johnson tried to secure a warrant. Suddenly she said, 'I believe I have a name and number for BB. I am sending you the details now.'

'How? We didn't have any contact information for her.'

'I know, but her job is putting people who want a service in touch with those who can supply it. I found a social media site, BB Domestic Connections, and Katy is mentioned in the reviews.'

'Good work. Thanks, Michelle. Can you do intel on her?' Eric asked.

'Who do you think you are talking to?' Michelle asked sarcastically. 'BB stands for Barbara Brice. She has tried to hide who she is, but it is not a very sophisticated cover. I have identified where she lives.' Michelle hesitated before passing over the information. 'She is known to be a repeat victim of domestic violence, which stopped when she killed her partner. She served five years for the offence and since then has been connecting people who need odd jobs done with people who want the work. She takes a small cut.'

'Any connection to the other victims?'

'None at all. BB's conviction aside, she is clean. Her customers pay a small monthly fee and she ensures they pay fairly for the work before matching them to someone to do the job. The money is paid directly to the worker, not into a business account.'

Thinking through what Michelle had told him, Eric said, 'Her business supports those that are vulnerable and gives them an independent income. Is there anything to indicate that Katy's relationship with her ex was more hostile than it seemed?'

'Nothing, I am afraid.'

ထ

The first time Eric identified himself as a CLEA agent, BB hung up, but continual ringing – and a voice message saying he would call round at her home address – finally got a response. 'Stop calling me,' she demanded.

'I will after you've answered my questions.'

'I've not done anything wrong. I don't have to answer anything.'

'I'm looking into who killed Katy Jones and I think you can help me. That's all I care about,' Eric responded.

'That's it?'

'That's it,' he promised.

'Okay.' BB paused. 'Meet me at Alli's in Sector 3 at 9am tomorrow. It's opposite Train Station 3.2.' She hung up.

Eric was surprised; it was rare that he was dictated to in such a way.

ထ

Eric walked into Alli's just before 9am. Looking around, he couldn't see anyone who might be BB. The place looked tired, and he feared the dark colour scheme hid more than just dirt. He slid into a booth that faced the entrance; the table was sticky and he wondered when it had last been cleaned.

'Can I get you anything?' a waitress asked.

'Coffee?'

'Anything else?'

'I'm waiting for someone.' She came back a few minutes later with two cups, one of which she filled.

'Thanks,' Eric said. He thought the waitress muttered something rude under her breath before she left.

Eric waited a long time, drinking his coffee and hoping the cup was clean. He was about to ask for the bill when a woman walked in; she looked nervous and her face was scarred. Eric knew BB's partner had slashed her face with a broken bottle before she had stabbed him – it had been in the arrest record.

She came straight over, her nervousness clear. 'You Eric Badu?'

'I am.'

'Show me your identity.'

Eric pulled his badge out of his pocket and held it up. Reassured, she nodded and slipped into the chair opposite him. 'What do you want to know?'

'What work you gave to Katy Jones and how you passed it on to her. Her ex-partner says she didn't have a phone. We need to know where she was and who she was with before she died.'

'She had an old phone of mine. There was no credit on it, so she couldn't send messages or make calls and the like, but she could take jobs through the app on it,' BB said. 'I can give you the numbers and details of the people she worked for, but I don't think it will help. She mainly did ironing or cleaning. I brought these with me.' She pushed over some handwritten notes. 'These are the people that she would have done work for and the dates.'

Eric looked for anything relevant and paused when he saw Katy had been cleaning a flat on the date of the new moon. 'Did Katy regularly clean this flat?' he asked.

'Yes, twice a month for about six months. There were no complaints,' she replied. 'I didn't get her killed, did I? Everyone who wants to use the services has to be recommended by someone who is already part of the agreement. I don't accept just anyone.'

'No, her murder had nothing to do with your business,'

Eric reassured her. 'But we need to learn her movements on the night she died. We'll have to contact your customer to get more details.'

'Was it a domestic?' BB asked, touching the scar on her face.

'No, but Katy's death has been linked to other murders. We're looking for connections.'

'I don't like abusers, Agent. If there is anything else I can help you with, please let me know.'

Chapter 11

Johnson paused as she left the court and looked around, convinced that someone was watching her, but no one stood out. She had mentioned the man at the vigil to Michelle, but there was no CCTV in the area so there was no way to ID him. Assuming she was just a bit on edge, she shrugged her shoulders, got into her car and drove straight back to headquarters.

As she walked in, she rang to check in with Eric. 'I've just left BB – I should be back in an hour or so. I'll meet you at Michelle's desk,' he informed her.

Johnson looked at the time and decided to see Michelle then, once she and Eric had spoken, she could give Inspector Kerten the whole picture.

'Johnson!' Her name rang out as she got to her desk. As she looked up, she saw Inspector Kerten coming towards her. 'What have you got for me?' Okay, she would be updating him now.

She quickly summarised what she knew about Eric's meeting and said that she'd got a search warrant.

'Well done,' Kerten said. 'File a resource request – we'll need to search all the premises at the same time. Let me know the date allocated for the operation. I also want to know what Eric has found out, so make sure I get an update when he returns.'

'Yes, sir.' She knew why Kerten was nervous. CLEA had released limited details of the murders to the news to get ahead of Danny's social media campaign. There wasn't much interest yet; murders were common, and details of the bodies had not been disclosed. However, it was only a matter of time before either the reporters linked them to Danny's social media posts, or someone else tipped them off. When that happened, the media frenzy would start. CLEA had to ensure it was on top of the investigation.

Michelle wasn't at her desk and there was no sign of her usual food supply, so Johnson assumed she was catching up on sleep. Johnson sighed; she looked at other researchers and analysts and thought about asking them for help but decided against it. She doubted Michelle would be absent for long and the analyst would want to redo the work.

She turned back to the desk – and there was Michelle with a new box of pastries. Somehow, she had returned while Johnson's focus was elsewhere.

'How did it go at court?' Michelle asked, as if she had been there the whole time.

'I got the search warrants I needed. Thanks for the research – all the premises are covered. Do you have floor plans for these addresses so I can work out how many people I need to search all the locations.'

'Help yourself,' Michelle said as she dropped the pastries on her desk. She sat down and searched for the information. 'The work premises should be easy because floor plans are part of the legal requirement for a business licence. The home addresses might be harder, although I can access the original plans. It depends on what work has been done in the meantime.'

Johnson knew what she meant. In many buildings walls were removed to create a bigger living space or, more commonly, added so that a single property became several small bedsits.

She dragged over a chair, sat next to Michelle and

reached for a pastry. She couldn't remember the last time she had eaten.

∞

It wasn't long before Eric joined them. 'Any success?' he asked. Johnson filled him in about the warrants. 'Good result with what we had,' he congratulated her.

'Thanks. How did you do?' she asked.

'Depends on what magic Michelle can work for me,' Eric replied. 'BB was able to give more details about Katy's last few days. Katy had a regular cleaning job and she was there the afternoon we believe she had died – the couple she worked for confirm she left at 6pm. They said she wasn't behaving any differently – she arrived, did her job and left, saying she was heading home.'

'Do you have the address?' Michelle asked. When Eric gave it to her, she glanced at it. 'It is some distance from where Katy lived. Leave it with me and I will see what I can find for you.'

'Cheers, Michelle.' Eric turned to Johnson. 'Next steps?'

'Update the inspector then complete your resource request,' Michelle answered on Johnson's behalf. 'Just sending over the information now.'

Johnson thanked Michelle and groaned slightly; she was so tired that everything ached. She stood up and went to her own desk, while Eric went to update the inspector on his conversation with BB.

∞

Requests for extra resources were not complicated but you had to fight for every person. Johnson always bid for a few more people than she needed knowing that the number would get knocked down. She couldn't complain; they could pull on extra resources and specialist skills when required. They might not get them straight away, but she knew from experience that it was a hell of a lot more than the sector police got.

Her original request was rejected so she resubmitted it with revised numbers. It came back with a date that concerned her. She really resented having to call Inspector Kerten for help.

⚭

Demonic sexual predator hunting mothers and female key workers

The following morning, several news agencies reported on the series of murders, stating that the victims were all females, upstanding members of the public and had had symbols carved into their bodies.

As Michelle read the articles, she knew it was only a matter of time before the demonic aspect was leaked. Her fingers itched to get onto the dark net. The previous press release had been so limited that it had not brought any meaningful information, but with the mention of 'demonic' she could use that term. She also hoped the news would cause comment in the various groups she monitored.

Logging on, she navigated through different web pages. There was the odd comment about the deaths, but most were questioning what had been done to the bodies and if it was something that they should try. She was about to log out, thinking she would try again later, when a comment posted by @ourlordeggracon caught her attention: _There's more to this than you think._

There was a stream of eager questions wanting to know what the poster meant, but there was no reply.

Michelle made a note of the user and where the comment was posted; there was something familiar about the name, but she couldn't place it. Frustrated, she explored the dark net for more information but there was nothing. Either they had never posted before, or they had deleted any previous comments. She logged off and tried the more conventional systems but nothing came up for the name Eggracon. Maybe something further would appear once the news had been out there for a while.

∞

Johnson woke up to see the headline. She'd known this was coming but it was still shocking to read it without warning. She rolled out of bed and rang Eric. 'Have you seen the news?' she asked as he answered after the first few rings.

'Just now. I was about to call you. Meet you at headquarters?'

'See you there.' She hung up and quickly washed and dressed before leaving for work. When she arrived, she saw Eric just ahead of her and called out to him.

'Have you heard from Inspector Kerten yet?' he asked.

'He sent a message saying he wanted to see me as soon as I got in. I'm heading to his office now.'

'Want some company? He was too busy to talk yesterday when I went to find him so he might want an update now.' Eric knew Johnson was the lead in the investigation but he was annoyed that Kerten had not summoned him too.

'The more the merrier,' she said.

Kerten was on the phone but he waved them in when he saw them. They sat and listened to him reassure the caller that CLEA was doing everything it could before hanging up. The phone immediately rang again, but he ignored it. 'It hasn't stopped since I got in. I'd hoped for time before the media realised that there was more to the murders.'

'At least they are running with the suspect as a sexual

predator,' Johnson pointed out.

'I can assure you that, as far as the sector governor is concerned, that is *not* better, Johnson. And it is a *demonic* sexual predator,' he rebuked her.

'A sex pest of any kind is someone people understand and can protect themselves against. It might make it harder for the suspect if women are careful. If – or when – the truth is released, people might not be so cautious. They won't identify with the threat or they may think it's fake news.'

'Point taken. Have you got a date yet for the resources for those search warrants?'

'Not yet,' Johnson replied. 'I called to chase it after we spoke yesterday, but was warned to expect a significant delay due to demand.'

'I'll escalate it to the governor. He's demanding that action be taken quickly, so he can help you get the resources you need. Eric, thank you for coming – sorry I didn't get the chance to talk to you yesterday. What can you tell me about BB and the family Katy cleaned for?'

Eric recapped before adding, 'Michelle is trying to find Katy on CCTV cameras to learn what route she took home, then she'll check for vehicles and cross-reference them against the information we have for Amy Hood.'

'Good. What about forensic evidence?' Kerten asked.

'There was nothing from the older cases, and we're still waiting for the results for Amy and Jenny. But both scenes were compromised before Matt and his team got there,' Johnson said.

'Make sure I get regular updates. I have to brief the governor and director at 1200 and 1700 hours from now on, so I need to know everything you are doing. I know you'll be busy so I don't care how you update me – it can be a meeting, call, text or email. Just let me know what you have, good or bad.'

Chapter 12

Michelle packed her bag and logged off her computer. Johnson and Eric had already left for the day. They were struggling to find new leads for her to research, though they were out daily making enquiries with not just the friends and family of the victims but the neighbours as well. While they waited for their resource request to be approved for the searches, they were looking for anyone who might have seen something.

So tonight was a good night for Michelle to try something else.

At home, she pulled up the floorboard, reached into the hidden compartment and took out the laptop to reach the clothes and other items beneath it. It was a long time since she'd last worn them.

After she got changed, she looked at herself with disgust. She hated these clothes, hated the idea that this was what a demon would like. A demon wouldn't care what you wore; why would they? After applying a thick layer of makeup to complete the look, she pulled on a coat and set off for the demonic club to which she had received an invitation.

∞

The entrance to the club was hidden in an alcove down a small alleyway. She knocked on the door and a slot opened; she gave the password and was let in by a male dressed in a black robe. How she hated the theatrics.

Walking down the dark hallway and into the room at the end, she made sure her face was neutral. The area was dimly lit and smoke wreathed the floor. She pushed through the crowd towards the bar and ordered a drink. She wasn't sure what was in it; they were all themed cocktails. She took a small sip and had to admit it wasn't bad.

'I've not seen you here before,' a man said, coming up beside her.

'I used to come years ago but I moved out of the sector. Now I am back.'

'To our benefit, I'm sure.' He placed his finger on her neck then ran it down to where her corset covered her breasts. When he paused, she grabbed his hand and gave it a sudden twist. He cursed with pain.

'I am not a submissive, but if you like a bit of sado-masochism I will be happy to oblige,' she snarled, twisting his wrist further.

'No, I'll pass,' he ground out. Michelle let go of his hand and he walked away.

'I do like a lady who knows what she likes.' Michelle turned and saw a small group of people standing behind her.

'I think it is important to make it clear from the start,' she said. 'It helps avoid wasted time and disappointment.'

'We are always looking for someone new to join our little party, but we don't like to be hasty. Join us for a drink?'

Michelle smiled and joined them. The rest of the evening went smoothly. At first, the conversation was general, as if they were testing her on her knowledge to make sure she really was a demonic follower; once she had answered to their satisfaction, the discussion turned to the recent murders. Everyone was keen to see what the rest knew, but actually no one knew anything.

Frustrated, Michelle took a risk and mentioned the post she had seen from @ourlordeggracon on the dark net; though one other person in the group had seen it, they did not know who it was.

She left a few hours before dawn. She had expected something but no one knew anything about who was responsible for the killings, though there was a lot of speculation. Standing outside the club, she looked at the time; she could get home and change before going to work.

As she started to walk out of the alleyway, someone grabbed her from behind and put a hand over her mouth. 'I don't like being made a fool of, but I'll give you a chance to pay me back,' a male voice whispered in her ear. He started to drag her out of sight and she let him.

At the end of the alley, he turned her and threw her against the wall. Michelle saw it was the man from the club. He stepped forward and pulled his arm back to hit her, but she ducked and punched him in the gut. As he doubled over, she put her hands together and brought them down forcefully onto the back of his neck. He crumpled to the floor.

'I thought I was in for a good fight. How disappointing,' Michelle said. She bent and went through his pockets to find his ID; she would run some checks on him. She read the name then dropped the ID before stepping over him and walking away.

∞

Johnson had to admit that the media attention made getting the resources easier. Kerten had briefed the director of intelligence, Maria Garcia, who had argued with the governor that if he wanted results he would have to find money for overtime. Two days later, in the early hours of the morning, she was standing outside the home address of Charlie Ward; Eric was with the team searching Henry Ward's address, and Inspector Kerten had taken the business location.

Johnson waited as the rapid-entry team forced the door and went in, guns raised, shouting, 'CLEA, stay where you are! We have a warrant.' She had done enough of these searches to know that the team would move in quickly and efficiently to detain anyone they saw. A lack of shouting meant the premises were either empty or the occupants had followed orders as the team had entered.

It wasn't long before the place was declared safe and the search team went in. Johnson followed them. The apartment was small; the central area served as a living room and kitchen, and there was a separate bedroom and bathroom. Charlie Ward was sitting at a small, rickety table under the watchful eyes of a couple of CLEA agents. He watched quietly as the officers rifled through his belongings. He knew the process.

'Mr Charlie Ward?' Johnson asked.

'Who else do you think I'd be? You going to explain what you're looking for?'

'We're looking for evidence relating to the murder of the Reverend Jenny Adamson. CCTV footage shows you and your cousin parked outside her church. She was in the church before you arrived, and the next time she was seen she was dead. With your previous for burglary at that address, I'm sure you can understand our suspicions.'

'Whoa, stop! You think I had something to do with Jenny's murder? Never. You won't find any trace of her here.'

'What about in your van?'

'Probably, yeah. She's been a passenger several times. So what?'

'You aren't under arrest at the moment, so you don't

have to tell me anything. However, if you wish to give an account of how you knew the reverend and what happened the night she was killed, as well as why you think we will find traces of her in your van, then I'll need to inform you of your rights and record the interview for your protection. I can't do that here.'

'Yeah, whatever you need. I've nothing to hide. Jenny was good people. I would never have hurt her.'

⓪

Leaving the team to continue the search, Johnson took Charlie Ward back to CLEA headquarters. Once they had settled in an interview room, she spoke. 'You are not under arrest. You have the right to leave whenever you wish unless anything you say incriminates you, then you will be arrested. You are entitled to talk to a solicitor.'

'The only thing a solicitor will do is charge me money to tell me not to say anything. But I want you to understand that I did nothing to hurt Jenny.'

'Tell me how you knew her.'

'I'm not proud of it, but as you know we burgled the church, me and Henry – we were desperate. I bet you've looked at my record and you know I've form for it. After the last time me and Henry went down, well, Henry got himself a little one. His missus said she'd leave him if he got into trouble again and would never let him see his kid, so he went straight, so did I. Then Henry's little one was sick, and we needed cash to pay for the medicine the doc said he needed. We didn't have it, so yeah, we burgled the church. We didn't know how to get it legal.'

'Why the church? Why not somewhere else?'

'We were driving around wondering what to do, when we saw someone leave the church and the door didn't close properly. We thought we'd try our luck and see what we found,' Charlie explained. 'We picked up the

109

donation box. I left but Henry wanted to see what else he could take. He said he put a few bits and pieces in his pockets, but then someone saw him. He was scared of getting caught with what he had on him, so pulled out what he'd put in his pockets and ran out.

'When he pulled the stuff out, I guess he dropped his wallet because the next thing I know, the reverend is knocking at his address. I was there when she came. She saw the sick baby, and Henry and his missus crying. She told him not to worry and paid for everything. Agent, I swear we'd never hurt her – we owe her too much.'

Johnson nodded; that explained why Jenny had refused to press charges against them. She made a note to check if Henry Ward had a baby that had been sick. 'What happened the night she was murdered? Why were you at the church?'

'As a thank you for what she did, we helped her out when she needed it. She collected old clothes, furniture, bits that people didn't need any more. If they were big items, we kept them at our business for her, sometimes cleaned the furniture up a bit so she could give it to people who needed it. That's why we were there. She had some bags of old clothes and wanted a lift to an estate to hand them out. We dropped her off and went home. That's it, I swear.'

'What estate?'

'The Utofia,' Charlie admitted. 'Don't get me wrong. We didn't want to leave her there. We told her it's a bad place, but she said that the women who needed her wouldn't come out and get what they needed if they saw us. It wasn't the first time we took her there – she went every month. She never had any trouble when she visited.'

The Utofia was one of the worst estates. Originally called Utopia, it was supposed to be a shining example of the future, a better way of living. The design had been flawed; the various pathways that had given it a pleasing look were a godsend to criminals, creating a maze they could quickly get lost in. Those who lived there had started calling it Utofia to make it clear it was not perfect.

'Do you know who she met there?' Johnson asked.

'No, she never said, but I can show you where I always dropped her off,' Charlie volunteered.

∞

Before she accepted the offer, Johnson went to find out what had happened at Henry Ward's address. As she left the interview room, she turned on her phone to see a message from Eric. He said that Henry also wanted to talk.

She messaged back, asking what interview room Eric would be in; when there was no reply, she logged a request to see what room had been booked. While she waited for a response, she went to see Michelle and passed on the details Charlie had given her about previous trips to the estate and Henry's son's illness.

'I will see what I can find out,' Michelle promised as a notification on Johnson's phone came through giving her the room Eric was in.

Johnson went into a side room where she could hear Eric's interview, but there was not much to learn; he had finished asking questions and was telling Henry he would check out his account.

'In here,' Johnson called as Eric walked past the room she was in.

'How much did you hear?'

'Nothing – I've only just finished questioning Charlie Ward. What did Henry tell you?'

Eric recapped the interview. When he finished, Johnson said, 'Charlie told me the same thing. When I saw the CCTV, I was convinced that they were involved but now

I'm not so sure.'

'I agree. I was going to ask Michelle to check to see if she could find out if Henry's son was sick.'

'Already ahead of you,' Johnson said.

∞

Michelle confirmed that Henry's son had been sick and his medication had been paid for privately by a third person. She couldn't confirm who was behind the payment as it had been made in cash.

Having had that part of the Wards' account verified, Johnson and Eric updated Inspector Kerten. He agreed it would be useful to let the cousins show them where they had dropped Jenny off. 'Look out for any CCTV and possible witnesses. We don't have enough to hold them at the moment, but if enquiries prove any further involvement we can bring them in again.'

Eric went first so Henry could get back to his family. Johnson updated Charlie, so he was aware of what the delay was. He thanked her for letting him know and said that anything to get Henry back home quickly was good.

Out of curiosity, Johnson reviewed the intelligence on the cousins. As Charlie had said, they'd been keeping clean since they were last released from prison, other than the burglary at the church. They had only done a few months. Henry's girlfriend finding out she was pregnant seemed to change everything for both cousins, who were very close.

When Eric and Henry returned, Johnson went back to Charlie. As she walked into the room, he asked, 'Is Henry back?'

'My colleague is dropping him back with his family now. Are you still willing to show me where you took the reverend?'

'Of course.' He didn't need to ask why it required him

and his cousin to go separately; he knew that the agents wanted to ensure there were no discrepancies in their stories.

��

After Johnson dropped Charlie home, Eric was waiting for her with Inspector Kerten. In front of them was a map of the estate. 'Well?' Eric asked.

'Charlie said it was this area by the north entrance.' She pointed on the map. 'He said they always dropped her off at the same spot and helped her unload the bags of clothing. No one came near them, and he couldn't remember seeing anyone suspicious. They drove straight off.'

'Henry said the same thing, except he noticed several people watching from the flats. He admitted it made him nervous, but it was the same each time so he didn't think much about it. He couldn't remember the exact place, but these here,' Eric pointed to two blocks of flats, 'are the most likely ones where residents would have a good viewpoint.'

'How sure are we that they are telling the truth and have nothing to do with the murder?'

'Henry's alibi isn't strong – he said he was with his partner and child. She has confirmed it. She could be lying for him but I don't think she is,' Eric said.

'Charlie was in a pub with several friends,' Johnson said. 'Michelle is checking to see if any cameras caught him there and also checking the charges to his bank card.'

'Was anything found in the searches?'

'No, the properties were clean. Matt and his team did swabs for DNA at each location, but we'll have to wait for the results. I expect we will find the reverend's DNA in the van and business property.'

'What are your next steps?' Kerten asked.

'Michelle is looking at the van's movements to see if it regularly went from the church to the estate or near where any of the murders took place. It will help to verify the Ward cousins' account. She's also checking to see if Jenny was seen by any cameras in the area to see where she went if she left the Utopia,' Johnson said.

'We need to talk to people in the estate to find out if they saw anything when Jenny went missing,' Eric added.

'Good, remember to keep me updated,' Kerten ordered.

Chapter 13

AN EMAIL CAME through for Michelle from the pathologist's office. They'd had a body brought in a few days ago in advanced state of decay. It had been found in an overgrown patch of land near a car park and had been fed on by various rodents.

The emailer said she was concerned about the similarities in the news between this and the previous murders, particularly about location and estimated date of the death. The death was due to be reviewed shortly; if it was declared the result of suicide or natural causes, the body would be disposed of with no autopsy and no further investigation. The death might be written off unless the CLEA thought the case was connected. Attached to the email were copies of the original call and investigation.

Opening the attachments, Michelle read the details of the death. The original call had been made to the sector police because the local homeless people were complaining about the smell. Because the homeless community moved around a lot, nobody knew how long it had been there for; it wasn't until the smell made the area undesirable that it was reported.

The responding unit had found a decomposed body. No one had thought anything about it and the report said nothing about the body being tied down. Michelle didn't know if that was because the local wildlife had chewed through any ropes and the attending officers had assumed the victim was another homeless person, or if they just didn't care.

The body was finally identified through dental records as Olna Farmer. Officers had made enquiries and discovered that her baby had been found dead from neglect at her home address a few weeks earlier when the landlord had gone to the flat to demand his rent. It had been reported to the sector police and an arrest warrant had been issued for the mother. The informant at the morgue was worried it would be assumed that Olna had killed her baby then herself.

When Michelle plotted the location on her map, her heart sank; though it did not fit in with the deaths of Katy, Carol and Jenny, Olna could well have been the first murder in the pentagram of which Amy was the second victim. Although the date of death could only be estimated, it could fit. However, Olna's soul would be tainted and no good for the ritual if she had killed her child.

Michelle sighed. Either the murderer did not know about the baby's death, which would make Amy the first in the pentagram, or the baby had starved to death because his mother had been killed.

A limited investigation had been conducted into the baby's death once the sector police realised its mother was missing and Olna had been listed as wanted. No reliable time of death had been recorded for the baby because it had not been deemed necessary to do an autopsy. Olna could have died first; it wouldn't have taken a newborn long to die with no one caring for it.

Michelle was concerned about what had happened to Olna. She couldn't authorise an autopsy, but Inspector Kerten could if he declared it a CLEA case. She wasn't sure she could convince him on her own, so she sent it to Johnson with the header of 'Urgent – another victim?'

Johnson saw Michelle's message as she arrived at headquarters. Her first question was how did they know Olna had let her baby starve? What if the baby had died because the mother had been murdered? There wasn't enough information to know if the murder was linked even though both the location and approximate time fitted.

Johnson sent the file to Eric and told him she would be raising it with Kerten. Normally Johnson resented the twice-a-day updates, but sometimes they had their uses. She went to her Kerten's office and briefed him about the death.

'I'm not convinced,' he said, reading through the report.

'The death ties in with location and time. The sector police didn't do any forensics at the scene and we won't know if it is linked or not unless an autopsy is carried out, Michelle has identified enough factors to cause concern.'

'Alright, I'll raise it at the meeting. How sure are *you* that it is linked?'

'Based on the evidence, not very because there has been so little investigation. But I trust Michelle, and if she thinks it's linked then it's linked.'

'I doubt that will be enough, but I'll let you know,' Kerten said reluctantly.

Johnson had to be happy with that. When she had returned to Michelle's desk to look through the information in the report, her phone bleeped with a text from Kerten. *Director is not convinced. Does M have anything else?*

Michelle said, 'I cannot explain it to you, I just know it is linked.'

Johnson felt she was not getting the whole truth. 'How sure are you?'

'Very. I know the intelligence we have does not support

that, but trust me, please.'

M is convinced, will support. Will keep investigation myself if proved otherwise, Johnson texted in reply. One of the problems they faced if CLEA took on a case and then decided it was not in their remit, the sector police were never happy about it being handed back and that increased tensions between departments.

Okay, standby, Kerten responded.

Johnson hoped Kerten could sway the director despite the lack of evidence. Having looked at the limited investigation, she didn't believe Olna had let her son die of neglect and she wanted justice for her.

It's ours. Be right!!! Kerten texted.

∞

'Thank you for coming,' the pathologist said when Johnson arrived to watch the autopsy. 'I'm glad CLEA took on this case. When the file came in originally, I tried to get the sector police to look into it because nothing about it sat right with me, but they refused. Then I saw the details of the series of murders in the news and on social media, and I wondered if it could be connected. It's a sad state of affairs when it's so easy to write off a death without any investigation.'

'I share your concerns,' Johnson said. 'From what I've read, there is no solid timeline between Olna's and her child's deaths. Linked or not, her death deserves answers.'

'I see so many that deserve that and will never get it,' the pathologist said. 'I'm sorry, that's not on you but on the system and society. I hope you can find out what happened to her; for some reason, everything about this death feels wrong. Do you ever sense that?'

'Around this case, definitely,' Johnson confirmed. 'I hope that you can give me some answers to the many questions I have.'

The pathologist led her to the table where the corpse had been laid out. When Johnson saw the body on the table, it was all she could do not to vomit. She had seen many remains during her career, including decomposed ones, but none like this.

'Sorry, I should have warned you,' the pathologist said. 'The remains are worse than they should have been for the time of death.'

Johnson was not sure he could determine anything useful. She had to have faith in Michelle.

'Let us begin,' the pathologist said.

◑

Eric read the report Johnson sent him and had the same concerns about the investigation. A short while later, another message came through from her: *Kerten has taken it on, going to the autopsy. See what you can get out of sector.*

On it, he replied, thankful that Johnson had taken the autopsy. He contacted the sector police first and asked to talk to the officer who'd found the body but was told he was unavailable. Attempts to get further information were unsuccessful; as far as the sector police were concerned, the case had been closed when the body was identified. They hadn't even bothered to wait for the formal closure report from the pathologist.

Eric tried to argue that CLEA had taken on the investigation but was told that the case had been closed and filed. It would take time to locate and send over any information that was not stored electronically; once a case was closed, it usually stayed closed.

Eric didn't miss the implication. He sent an update to Kerten to see if he could get the sector police to cooperate, then drove to the place where the body had been found. Michelle had commented on the importance of the location, though Eric wasn't sure why.

Parking nearby, he got out and walked to the patch of greenery. It was neglected, the grass was overgrown, and weeds and plants had merged into a tangled mess.

As he walked through the park, he tripped over rubbish hidden in the undergrowth. There was trash everywhere. Stepping carefully to avoid broken glass and torn metal, he saw signs of a homeless encampment. He checked the report on the original email; there was not enough detail for him to identify where Olna had been found.

He walked over to a cluster of old tents; a rustle of canvas indicated that at least one person was there. 'Hello!' he shouted, 'CLEA. I just want to ask some questions.' There was no response.

'I need to know where the body was found the other day.' Again no response. 'If I can't pinpoint the exact location, the CLEA forensic team will empty the park to make sure we cover the whole area.' That meant the homeless would be moved out of the park, and their tents and meagre possessions seized.

A zip was pulled up on one of the tents and a head poked out. 'It was over there.'

'There's a lot of ground "over there".'

Someone crawled out of the tent – Eric wasn't sure if it was a young man or woman. Their hair was long and matted with dirt, and their clothes old and baggy. They walked in the direction they had pointed to and Eric followed. 'The body was here.'

Eric looked around. 'You sure?'

'Yeah.'

'Were you here when the body was dumped?' The question was met with silence. 'I'm just looking for intelligence. I'm not pointing fingers at anyone.'

'I dunno when it was dumped. I ain't been here for

long. There are always noises in the night. I don't want to get involved. I only knew the body was there when the smell... Sorry.'

'I understand. Thank you.'

'Do you have any cash? It'd be good to get something fresh to eat.' Eric was about to refuse. 'I don't do drugs,' the person said and pulled up their shirt sleeves to show arms clear of track marks. 'Just want a hot meal, honest.'

Eric pulled out a few notes and handed them over. It was only enough to buy a meal or two, but the person grabbed it and ran off.

He looked around; there were no signs of the victim that had lain there. He pulled out his phone. 'Matt, it's Eric; I don't know if you can help but...'

Chapter 14

THE AUTOPSY CONFIRMED a cut to the throat. Olna also had an old injury to her right wrist and the bone had broken at the time of death, indicating she had fought against restraints. It was impossible to say what the abdominal injury had been because of the rodent activity. It looked like the murder could be linked.

Johnson had hoped for something more definite. She called to see how Eric was doing. 'Slowly,' was his first response. 'The scene was heavily compromised –the area is used by the homeless and as a rubbish dump. Matt has arrived to see if they can retrieve any forensics.'

'Any luck with the sector police?'

'None. They have no interest in reopening the case or sharing information. Once Matt is happy, I'll go over to Olna's place. How was the autopsy?'

'There was a lot of deterioration to the body but it was definitely murder – her throat was cut. There's enough to make it likely that her death is linked.'

'Can you send the report over when you have it? It might shake the sector police enough to talk to me without me having to apply for a warrant for additional files and evidence. If they have any, which I doubt. It will force them to admit they did no investigation.'

'Will do. Let me know how it goes with Matt and tell him I said hi.'

'Eric!' Johnson heard Matt shout.

'Got to go, Johnson.' Eric hung up.

Johnson cringed. Say hi to Matt – what was she, a teenager?

'What have you got for me?' Eric asked, walking over to Matt.

'Honestly? Trying to find anything here will be almost impossible. We've taken soil samples. I want to load up everything and take it back to examine in our lab.'

'Will it take long?'

'Ages – we'll need equipment and trucks to collect everything. You don't need to stay – I'll update you if we find anything interesting.'

'Great.' Eric turned to go then paused. 'Johnson says hi, by the way.' He had almost not bothered to pass on the message, but when he saw Matt smile he was glad he had. Who would have guessed that beneath Johnson's cold exterior she had a soft spot for Matt?

Eric was glad to leave the scene; the stench had started to get to him and he was convinced it was still clinging to him when he got into his car. There was nothing he could do about it, so he drove to Olna's home address.

When he saw the run-down estate, he was not hopeful about getting the residents' cooperation. The place was a maze and the numbering of the flats didn't seem to make sense. He wondered how the sector police managed to negotiate the area, then realised they probably avoided it as much as possible.

As he got out of his car, he saw a drug deal going down. The moment the pair noticed him, they started to advance; they'd seen his suit and thought he would be an easy target to rob. Eric pulled aside his jacket and showed his badge and the gun clipped to his belt. They paused for a moment, wondering if it was worth it, then one of them ran forward hoping to get to Eric before he drew his gun. He stopped about a foot away as Eric pointed the gun at his head. For a second, both kids stood there before turning and running off.

Eric knew he had no hope of catching them; they knew this estate and he didn't. There was also a chance they would ambush him, steal his gun and use it against him. He didn't like ignoring a crime, but he had bigger priorities.

He eventually found Olna's flat and knocked on the door. He had no idea who was living there now. As the sector police had closed the case, the landlord would have cleaned it up and rented it out as quickly as possible. When he got no reply, he knocked again. He heard noises inside, and through the side window saw someone approach, then the door swung open.

'What d'you want?' an irate female demanded.

'I am Agent Eric Badu. I'm looking into the death of Olna Farmer, who lived here...'

'I only moved in last week. I know nothing about any previous tenant,' she interrupted and went to close the door.

Eric put his out his hand and stopped her. 'I would really appreciate it if I could come in and look around, see if anything was left behind from when she lived here.'

'You got a warrant?'

'No.'

'Then get one.'

'Please...'

'I don't care. I hate government types – but I'll tell you this. The place was empty when I moved in. If you want to know what happened to her stuff, talk to the landlord, Teddy Jones. He might be able to help you.'

She tried to close the door again and this time Eric let her. He sent an email to Michelle to see if she could find out who Teddy Jones was, then knocked on the neighbour's door. The curtain twitched and Eric knew someone had been listening.

An elderly woman opened the door. 'Is there anything I can help you with, Agent?' she asked, reinforcing his suspicion that she had been snooping.

'Could you tell me anything about your previous neighbour, Olna Farmer?'

'Of course. Would you like to come in?' she smiled.

'Thanks.' The flat was very tidy but Eric could see nothing personal on display, no photos or souvenirs of past experiences.

'Please sit. I'm Annie. Would you like a drink? I can put the kettle on, it would be no trouble.'

'No, thank you.' Annie looked disappointed. Eric knew he should have accepted but he didn't want to stay long; something about the woman put him on edge. 'What can you tell me about Olna?'

'I thought she was such a nice young lady, but after what she did to her poor baby...' Annie shook her head in disgust.

Eric thought she would continue, but she remained silent. 'What happened?' he prompted.

'I don't know for sure. I assume she had some sort of breakdown. She seemed like such a good mother.'

'Really? Tell me more.'

Annie was relishing the attention. 'Well, she was normally so good at looking after her little one, but I think she was very isolated. No one ever came to see her.'

'So what changed?' Eric asked.

'I think she just gave up. One day, the baby just cried and cried. She took him out for a walk but the crying started again when they got back. I knocked on the door. She didn't reply, but I know she was there.'

'How?'

'Well, I saw someone moving around, just a shadow

through the window and I assumed it was her. I didn't want to call the authorities – I didn't want them to take the little one away from her, you understand.'

'Of course. Do you know how long the baby cried for?'

'I don't know. Definitely throughout one night, but I had to visit my daughter for a few days. When I got back, it was quiet so I didn't think anything of it until people showed up.'

'What people?'

'People from her work came to see her, but she didn't answer the door to them. Then the landlord came around a day or two later looking for rent she owed him. She'd never been late paying before. He let himself in when she didn't answer and found the baby. It was so sad. I heard that she killed herself after her baby had died. Is that true?'

'No, she was murdered.'

'Murdered?' The gleeful tone Annie had adopted while telling her story faltered.

'We think she might be part of a linked series of killings that's been in the news. If she is, then at some point she was followed, abducted and killed. Do you know if she ever went out without her baby?' Eric knew he sounded abrupt but Annie's attitude grated on him.

'Never,' Annie said. 'She never left Alfie on his own, not with a sitter, not with anyone.'

'Can you talk me through the day you heard Alfie crying?' Eric asked. 'Do you remember what day it was?'

'I'd need to check. It was over a month ago.' Annie got up, retrieved a diary of some kind and looked through the pages. The date she gave was the same day Carol Jenkins had been murdered.

'It was about 6pm when she went out with the baby. I didn't see them come back, just heard them return, but the crying started again at about 8pm. I knocked on the door and saw Olna in the flat. After that, as I said, I had to visit my daughter.'

Eric watched as Annie started to think through the events. 'What did you see when you knocked on the door? Was it definitely Olna?' he pressed.

'I, I...' she stammered. 'No one else was ever there. I never thought...'

'Is it possible it wasn't Olna you saw?' Eric asked.

'Yes. Oh God,' Annie said. 'I saw a shadow moving around through the side window and I just assumed it was her, that she was having a bad day, which is why she didn't answer the door.'

'There was no way you could have known it *wasn't* Olna.'

'But if I had called the authorities and not been worried about getting Olna into trouble, then maybe poor Alfie would still be alive.'

'We have no way of knowing that,' Eric responded, but he knew the answer. The baby would have been found and the investigation would have warranted more attention from the start. However, he could understand why Annie had kept quiet. Babies taken in by the authorities often failed to thrive; the chances were that if they had come for Alfie, he would still have died – it would have just taken longer. Poor Alfie had no future whatever happened.

'Do you know where Olna went when she took the baby for a walk?' Eric asked.

'Oh yes. There are not many places to go around here.' Annie was sobbing now as she started to tell him where Olna would go. It was a place near to where her body had been found.

∞

Eric left the estate feeling nauseous; whatever the murderer's agenda was, he had probably been watching Olna for a while and learned her habits. He had abducted Olna when she was out walking her baby and held her captive, then returned her baby to the flat to die slowly from neglect. He had tried again to get into Olna's flat, but again he was refused by the new tenant. A warrant it would have to be.

He messaged Michelle with the information he had gained, hoping she could do something with it.

Chapter 15

A few days before the New Moon

JOHNSON, ERIC AND Inspector Kerten were sitting around Michelle's desk. They were all aware of the date and what could happen soon.

'Is there anything we've missed?' Inspector Kerten asked.

'I don't know,' Johnson replied. It had been days since she or any of them had been home to sleep. 'The forensics have come back on all the crime scenes. There's nothing that can help identify a suspect, though Matt did find traces of rope at the scene of Olna Framer's murder.'

'We wanted a warrant to do a forensic sweep of Olna's home address because we think the killer returned the baby there, but it was denied due to the length of time,' Eric added.

'I spoke to Teddy Jones. He's a scumbag landlord, but he isn't linked to any of the other murders and has an alibi for the night Olna was murdered,' Johnson added.

'How good is his alibi?' Kerten questioned.

'He was in a sector police cell for being drunk and hitting his wife.'

'Doesn't get much better than that.'

'I tried to track Olna on CCTV from when she left her home but failed. All of the CCTV footage had been overwritten because of the time delay. I looked at her social media but there was very little there. She rarely posted or interacted with anyone,' Michelle said.

'We spoke with Olna's work,' Eric continued. 'She wasn't close to anyone there. The manager only went around to her place because they hadn't been able to get hold of her to discuss her return to work from maternity leave. She assumed Olna was out and planned to return the following day,'

'That doesn't give us much. What about the enquires into Jenny Adamson?' Kerten asked.

'We did extensive door-to-door enquiries on the Utofia Estate, but no one was talking to us,' Johnson replied. 'So we asked Danny Jones to reach out to those on the estate that Jenny might have helped and get the community involved. There haven't been any additional leads so far. We interviewed everyone connected to Katy, Jenny, Olna, Amy and Carol – no one could give us anything.'

'I checked CCTV and ANPR records,' Michelle added. 'There is nothing that connects the crime scenes to help me narrow down any suspects. I checked all the victims' social media accounts but there was nothing. I checked for connections between the women – nothing.'

'How can nothing connect the victims? We have five dead bodies,' Inspector Kerten protested.

'There are at least two different murderers. The locations and times of death of Jenny and Amy make it impossible for the same person to have killed them. Plus the autopsies indicate both right- and left-handed suspects.'

'Two murderers might explain why some victims have their belongings left on them and others don't,' Kerten added. 'Do we think they are working together?'

'We believe so,' Johnson admitted.

'So if the killers act true to their MO, we can expect two more bodies next week,' Kerten said.

'Possibly. Olna and Carol were killed two months ago,

Amy and Jenny last month. So far we haven't found a second murder that matches the series for Katy being murdered.'

'Which could mean we've missed someone,' Kerten pointed out.

'I think we need to consider if there is an internal problem. To have five murders and nothing sitting right – the killers must know how we investigate,' Johnson said.

'That is a heavy allegation.'

'I know, but we've run out of leads and there's nothing for us to go on. There is never *nothing*,' she said, frustrated.

'I'll consider your views but I want to make sure of our facts first. Michelle, what have you found on the dark net?' Kerten asked.

'Nothing useful, I am afraid. There was an interesting comment at the start from a user @ourlordeggracon, which implied some knowledge, but I could not track the account and no further comments have been made. Otherwise, there is a lot of interest and conjecture but no one is taking credit.'

A depressed silence fell. Taking a breath, Michelle continued, 'However, I think I have a pattern for the murders.' She wasn't sure what her colleagues would think about what she had to say.

She stood up and retrieved her map. 'We know that two murderers are involved from the autopsies and the times of death. I plotted them onto the map and I noticed a possible pattern.'

She drew a pentagram; it was clear that three murder locations hit three points. 'There are not enough deaths yet to confirm the same pattern in the other sector, but ...' She marked out the second pentagram, which showed that two points matched. 'These are the areas where the murders have either happened or are most likely to happen.' She circled the remaining areas.

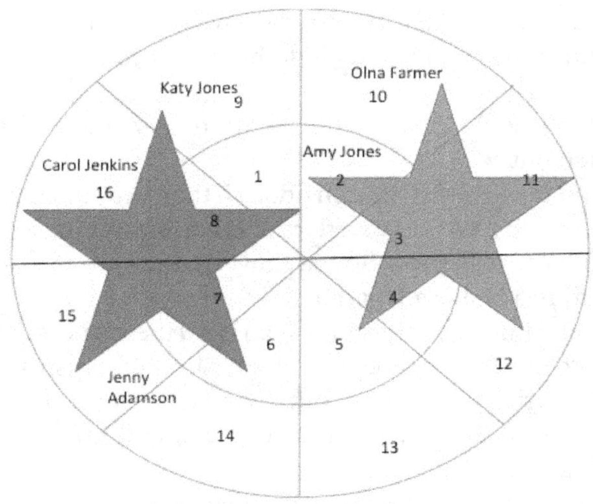

Michelle's revelation was met with silence.

'How did you get two pentagrams from this?' Inspector Kerten asked finally, waving his hand at the map.

'I looked into demonic ritual because of the carvings on the victims' abdomens and pentagrams came up regularly, so I applied the pattern to the locations of the murders. Based on the deaths we have, it fits.' She was lying, but she couldn't tell them the truth.

'It's tenuous,' Inspector Kerten said.

'Do we have anything else?' Johnson asked.

They didn't, and they all knew it.

Johnson looked at the map and remembered Michelle's comment when she had asked them to investigate Olna's death; she had said the location 'fits', and they had thought that was to do with it being a park area. Had she already identified the pentagram?

'I'll talk to the sector police in those areas and see if I can get any resources to help them patrol. Send me the most likely areas for the next murders,' Inspector Kerten said and left the room.

Johnson and Eric stared at Michelle.

'What?' she asked.

'The location "fits" – that's what you said when Olna's case arrived on your desk. It wasn't just because she was killed in a park, was it?' Eric demanded.

'No, it was a start of a theory. It is *still* a theory. If I am wrong and there is no pattern, then we may be deploying resources away from where they are needed.'

'God, I hate this,' Eric said.

'I can't believe we have five deaths and no leads,' Johnson said, frustrated.

'These are the most likely locations where the next murders will take place.' Michelle circled park areas. 'These areas are where the victims are most likely to be taken to and killed. This is where you need the resources.'

'I'm sorry, I don't see it. What you are suggesting is very precise – it's more than something you read on the dark net. What led you to this?' Johnson demanded.

'There were a few random comments on the dark net. Nothing generated any leads, but I thought I would see if it would fit. The rest is just geometry and geography.'

'It could be just coincidence, though?' Eric asked.

'Yes,' Michelle admitted after a pause. She couldn't explain how she knew without being thought mad. 'But I do think it is valid.'

'Alright,' Johnson told her. 'I'll make sure Inspector Kerten knows these park areas are where the sector police need to pay the most attention.'

∞

Eric and Johnson didn't go home for the next few nights. They went through all the evidence and intelligence they had but were no further forward. 'Someone always knows something,' Johnson said, on the night of the new moon.

'I know, and I think you're right about an inside person. I've never known so many dead ends in an investigation.'

'I would have been happier if a press release had been authorised for tonight. That way, women could be aware and take precautions.'

'It would have caused panic!' Eric protested. 'People would have demanded answers, and we have none.'

'I'm sick of waiting. Want to go out and patrol the areas Michelle marked out?' Johnson asked.

'God, yes!'

They grabbed their ballistic vests and their guns and headed out to search the areas Michelle had pointed out and look for anything suspicious. They knew it was a long shot, but they couldn't sit back and wait for the reports to come in.

Eric thought they would have the most luck concentrating on the first pentagram Michelle had identified. 'To try and cover all the possible locations Michelle detected is too much. If we look at the first pentagram, there are only two sectors – 1 and 6 – so we stand a good chance of finding one of the murderers,' he pointed out.

Johnson couldn't disagree with his logic but, knowing that meant the second victim had less chance of being found in time, she struggled to deal with it.

'Kerten will have the CLEA out supporting sector police. We aren't abandoning them,' Eric said, correctly reading the expression on her face. She hoped he was right.

⅖

Eric and Johnson arrived in Sector 6 and went to the park that Michelle had highlighted. They got out of the car, grabbed flashlights and began to walk around looking for anything untoward. They saw several homeless people huddled into the limited space available and Eric made a note. There had been a homeless campsite near where Olna was murdered.

The person he had spoken to had denied being there when the murder had occurred and Eric had assumed he or she had only recently set up camp there. Eric's attention had been pulled away when Matt and his team arrived. When he'd returned to the camp after Matt had started work, the homeless person had disappeared, presumably because they wanted no involvement in the investigation. But what if they had disappeared for another reason?

If someone had been camping there, how had they not been aware of the murder? Eric imagined the victim must have screamed so there would have been noise. Had he missed a lead? Homeless people were nomadic, but what if 'I wasn't here' meant something more?

He and Johnson were about to leave when they saw another flashlight ahead of them and walked towards it. 'Sector police, who goes there?' a voice called out.

'CLEA,' Eric shouted back.

'Good to see you out here are well,' one of the sector officers said, as if they had expected CLEA agents to take the case and not patrol themselves.

'Stay safe,' Johnson said.

'Stay safe,' the officers responded as they passed by.

'Wasn't it obvious? Staying safe?' Eric asked, once they were out of earshot of the officers.

'Sector police consider it good luck,' Johnson replied. Eric didn't ask how she knew that.

Happy that the place was too populated for anything to happen that night, they moved on to the next park in Sector 1. It had a large homeless camp and, as soon as they got close, the occupants came to look at them. 'Why you here?' someone demanded.

'We are looking for a potential murder victim,' Johnson responded.

'Ain't no victims here. Look if you want.'

A walk around the park, followed by the homeless, quickly reassured them that it was unlikely anything would happen; there was no privacy for a murder.

Not wanting to waste time, they went back to their car. 'There are one or two small green areas to check, or do you want to go over the parks again, or move onto Sector 6?' Eric asked.

'Let's move on. There are too many people in the Sector 1 parks for anything to happen without witnesses.'

As Eric drove off, Johnson looked at the time and her heart sank. 'It's gone midnight,' she said.

'It might not be too late,' Eric replied. 'We don't have an exact time of death for any of the victims.' But they both knew it was unlikely that the next victim would be found alive.

They travelled to Sector 6 without speaking. As Eric drove, Johnson contacted Michelle.

'I have nothing for you. I am sorry,' Michelle said. 'As soon as I find anything, I will let you know.' Johnson thanked her and hung up.

Arriving at the nearest park in Sector 6, Eric and Johnson looked around. It was also full of homeless. The second park they visited, however, was empty of people. Johnson heard Eric give a resigned sigh and suspected that he felt the same way that she did.

'We're going to find a body, aren't we?' Eric said.

'I think so.' They walked around looking for clues, but there was nothing.

'Michelle must have been wrong in identifying where the next bodies would be,' Eric said.

'Or we had the day wrong. Or the extra patrols put off the suspect, or the news coverage meant the intended victim was not accessible,' Johnson reeled off the possibilities. There had been a lot of discussion about releasing the dates of the murders. Eric and Johnson had been for it, thinking it would allow people to take their own precautions – and anyway, it would only take two more deaths for the media to make the connection themselves. As a result, a news release had been issued the night before but with limited details.

'I hate this,' Eric said. 'I think a murder was planned. I think this is where it would have taken place but one of our tactics prevented it.'

'Let's just hope we stopped it and didn't force it to another location,' Johnson warned.

'If the murderer has chosen a different location, they could be anywhere.'

'Let's get back and see what reports Michelle can find.'

Johnson couldn't stop worrying. Had they pulled resources away from the relevant area and made the murderer's job easier?

∞

As expected, Michelle was at her desk, not on the main computer but working on a laptop. It was the first time they had seen no food in easy reach, a sure sign that she hadn't left the office for some time.

With a tired sigh, Johnson lowered herself into one of the chairs. The way Eric lowered himself into the other one suggested he wasn't faring any better.

'I assume you found nothing,' Michelle said without looking up.

'That's why we're back here,' Johnson said sarcastically.

'Stupid question,' Michelle replied, taking no offence.

'What are you looking at?'

'The dark net. I am trying to find any chats about a new murder. It is surprisingly quiet.' She paused her search and turned to look at them.

'Do you think we stopped it?' Eric asked hopefully.

'No. I expect two murders tonight. I think the bodies have not been found yet and the killers are keeping quiet on the dark net. They are being very careful.'

'I think the murder was intended to happen here.' Eric pointed at the park in Sector 6. 'It was the only area we saw that matched the MO but had no homeless people, though they'd been there recently.'

'I didn't see any homeless when I went to the scene of Amy's murder,' Johnson said.

'Do they normally congregate there?' Michelle asked.

'From the rubbish in the park, they had definitely been there recently,' Johnson replied. 'I didn't think anything about it at the time, but now it seems strange. I think we need to go back and have another look.'

As the monitors came back to life, Johnson and Eric looked at the searches Michelle was running. No results had been returned. She opened up a new tab and started to input data. 'There was a homeless drive taking place the night Amy was murdered. Free food, a bed for the night, and clean clothes in the morning if they stayed over,' she said.

'Was it the same where Jenny was killed?' Eric asked.

'No, but that was a conservation area. The rules there make it inhospitable for the homeless.'

'Can you check against the other murder scenes?' Eric asked.

'Already on it,' Michelle said. 'I cannot believe I missed it. There are similar homeless drives in the other areas.'

'Any for tonight?'

'For Sector 6, yes. I will need to check for the second pentagram.'

'Damn. Are there any reports of a crime yet?' Eric asked.

'Not yet. Multiple tasking returns are coming in from patrols around the parks for both areas, but no evidence of a body,' Michelle replied.

'So we can hope that we prevented the murders.'

'I would like to agree with you, but I doubt it. I expect they found somewhere else to kill,' Michelle said. Something came back on a search as she spoke and she was distracted. Eric and Johnson waited.

Michelle walked to the map. 'There was a "support the homeless" drive here.' She circled the area. 'There are two park areas covering the project, but one is more prominent than the other. I would check for a body here for the second pentagram.' She marked the area with an X.

Chapter 16

Sector 5

'This is a waste of bloody time,' Officer Jackson muttered when the task was sent through.

'There are worse calls to take,' his partner Wilson pointed out. They had been sent to search a park within their sector to look for evidence of a murder.

'You're new. This park is a trash dump and a homeless wasteland. Walk carefully, otherwise you won't want to know what you'll be cleaning off your boots.'

They got out of the car to walk around the area. As with other open spaces, there were a lot of homeless but this was worse than the others. The smell of rubbish and human waste hung in the air. Officer Wilson understood what Jackson meant. 'How can the CLEA be so sure that there is a body here?' he complained.

'I bet the CLEA read the patrol returns and saw we hadn't patrolled here. They're making us pay for not following their "orders". Bloody CLEA.'

'Yeah, there must be a body,' Officer Wilson said sarcastically. Then he stopped, put out his hand out to stop his partner and pointed.

'Damn!' Jackson said when he saw what was in front of them. They had thought that CLEA had been unreasonable with their request for the extra overnight patrols; the supervisors hadn't made the overtime mandatory, so the number of additional officers was not enough to patrol all the park areas. Now they were looking at a woman with her throat cut and a symbol cut in her abdomen.

'Control, we've found a body; it fits the MO released by CLEA,' Officer Jackson called up on his radio.

'Make sure you maintain a crime scene. Do you need a second unit to assist?' the response came.

'No, we'll be fine as long as CLEA get here soon. We'll need a break at some point, you understand.'

'The message has been sent and acknowledged. A unit should be there shortly,' the control room operator stated.

'I'll believe that when they get here,' Jackson muttered.

'Have you ever seen anything like this?' Wilson asked as he inched closer to the body.

'God, no! This is just wrong.' Jackson had been in the sector police for nearly thirty years, but this was weird even by his standards.

Wilson pulled out his phone and took a picture of the body. 'What are you doing?' Jackson demanded.

'My friends aren't going to believe this if I can't show them. They think the news articles are propaganda to cause fear.' Wilson started to forward the pictures.

'You idiot! This is an active investigation – you can't share anything. You better delete those pictures now. If the boss or CLEA find out, they'll have our jobs.'

'Sorry, doing it now,' Wilson replied, not mentioning that he'd already forwarded the pictures. He just hoped they wouldn't come back to haunt him. He guessed that he could say that someone else had taken them if they appeared on the internet – after all, the body had been there for a few hours. And he needed this job.

∞

'The Sector 5 police have found a body – the notification has just come through. Based on the information received, it is probably linked,' Michelle told Johnson and Eric as they sat together the following morning.

Eric and Johnson had stayed out until 1am searching for a body, then gone home to sleep before coming in again to see if anything had been reported. Michelle was updating them with the tasking returns and further requests when the message came through.

Johnson stood up and grabbed her jacket and bag. 'Will you let Kerten know so we can take on the case?'

Michelle nodded.

'I'll give Matt a ring and see if he can meet us there,' Eric said.

'I will make sure the sector police preserve the scene for you,' Michelle shouted after them as they left the room.

'Thanks,' Johnson called back. Experience had taught them that once CLEA took on a case, the sector police tended to withdraw unless ordered otherwise.

∞

Johnson and Eric were disturbed by the number of people present at the scene, many of them trying to take pictures. 'This is worse than when Amy Hood was found, and that was a nice park with a large footfall, not a small wasteland like this,' Johnson said.

'A lot of these people are police officers,' Eric commented as they got nearer.

Johnson realised he was right. Not many of the officers seemed to be working; they seemed more interested in their surroundings than keeping members of the public away.

'What the hell is going on?' Eric asked, not expecting Johnson to know the answer.

'I've no idea; I'll see if...' She stopped as her phone rang; it was Michelle. 'I've a nasty feeling we're about to find out. What have you got for us, Michelle?'

'A photo of the murder scene has appeared on social media.'

'From whom?' Johnson asked.

'I am still trying to find that out, but it is being shared quickly and the media sites are being slow in removing the images.'

'Damn. Thanks for the heads up. When you find out who posted it, let me know.'

'That explains the crowd,' Eric said. 'With so many officers here, what do you want to bet that it circulated around the police first?'

'Which would indicate an officer took the picture. I'd better let Inspector Kerten know.' As Johnson called Kerten, Eric walked towards the crowd.

'Though it is great to see so many officers here, I'm surprised you're not maintaining the crime scene and keeping people back,' he shouted as he showed his CLEA identity. 'You should only be here if you have a policing purpose. If you're here to maintain the scene, push the public back and stop people from seeing the body. Anyone that leaves will be reported.'

The joking among the officers stopped and they turned to look at him. They knew what that meant: by being there unofficially, they were breaching professional standards. Even if they were there legitimately to maintain the scene, their details would be recorded; if anything about the body leaked, CLEA would know who'd been there. If anyone had already left but it was found that they *had* been there, they would be charged with misconduct.

Reluctantly the officers spread out, put barriers in place and shouted at people to get back.

Johnson joined Eric and looked at him questioningly. 'Since the officers are here, I thought they should be working,' he said. 'At least we have enough of them for the crime scene. What did Kerten say?'

'Nothing polite. We need to keep updating him and he will inform the chief constable of Sector 5. Otherwise, he'll talk to Michelle and monitor the situation from headquarters.'

Johnson looked at the body; the wounds and the setting were very similar to what she had seen at Amy's crime scene, though this park was much smaller and the victim had bruising around her mouth. Johnson assumed the murderer had tried to keep her quiet; though there was no homeless population, he was obviously not confident about who might hear from the roads and houses nearby.

'Bloody hell,' Eric cursed. Though he had read the autopsy reports, he had not seen any of the bodies up close.

'I know.' Johnson sighed as she squatted near the body. The cut across the victim's throat was so deep that it had almost decapitated her. This was a new level of violence.

'I'll see if anyone knows anything.' Eric walked away as quickly as he could.

The pathologist's van arrived a short while later to collect the body. Eric was happy to stay at the scene. 'Can I join you in the van?' Johnson asked. 'We only have one car and my colleague will need it.'

'Please yourself.' She watched as the team cut the restraints and broke the victim's limbs to place her arms beside her body because rigor mortis had set in. They put her in a body bag.

Johnson contacted Kerten to ensure that CLEA had officially accepted the case so there was no delay with the autopsy. He forwarded her the notification in case there was a challenge when she arrived at the mortuary.

She couldn't remember the last time she'd travelled with a body in the back of the van; she normally followed in her own car. She didn't know what to expect, but there was very little communication and the mood was sombre.

When the van arrived at the mortuary, she followed the team inside. 'Agent,' the pathologist said, walking up behind her. 'I understand that this body is part of the series of murders I've read about in the news.'

'Unfortunately that's true.'

'Then let's see what evidence we can find,' she said, unzipping the bag.

∞

Eric thought he'd seen everything until he saw the dead body in the park. He had read the reports but not really grasped the damage to the bodies. He'd had to pull back and leave Johnson to oversee the body and autopsy.

Johnson seemed unfazed; Eric knew she had dealt with similar scenes before, so he had not volunteered to replace her but remained behind to talk to people. Even so, he felt guilty that she had been to all the autopsies so far.

He knew that the people in the crowd would have questions about the murder, but he was used to dealing with that. Many of the people were nodding approval at what was being asked and listening for the reply. 'A body has been found,' he confirmed. 'We don't know who she is but we need to identify her. It is too early to know if this is linked to the other murders, but we are exploring all possibilities. The more information we can gain, the better we can direct our investigation. We know she was found by sector police, but did anyone see her beforehand?' Silence.

'There don't seem to be any homeless here at the moment. Was it the same last night?' Silence.

'Do you know if anyone else could have seen or heard anything?'

'I doubt it,' someone said. 'There was a kick-ass party just across the road.' Others quickly shushed him. 'What? It's not as if it's a secret,' he protested. 'They could find it on Hookup.' Some of the crowd looked disappointed, as if he were giving away their teenage secrets – maybe he was, because the party had not been mentioned before.

'Where was the party?' Eric asked, but the crowd was starting to disperse. They weren't going to get any information from him and, with the body gone, there was nothing left to see. Eric knew that those who had heard about the Hookup party must have thought there was a link so he sent a quick text to Michelle asking her to make enquiries.

He was left waiting with a lot of resentful sector officers so he was relieved when Michelle called him back a short while later. 'I cannot say for certain whether this Hookup party was connected or not,' she told him. 'There were similar parties every week in several sectors. The site lets people know where they are. The killers could monitor this site and similar ones to find the locations. I cannot find any indication that they have been set up on purpose, but I will see if I can find any links.'

Eric felt like cursing but he thanked her and hung up. Matt arrived with his team a short time later, and the sector police had been arguing about having to stay on. He had even received a call from the sector commander, demanding to know why so many of his officers were still at the scene. Eric pointed out that they had all been present when he arrived; that would need to be investigated because it was unusual.

The matter was out of Eric's hands until a CLEA team arrived to take all the officers' details. He suggested that the commander direct his complaint to the supervisors at CLEA if he disagreed with the legislation and agreed protocols.

The commander ended the call abruptly when Eric informed him that Inspector Kerten was talking to the chief about the photo of the body that was circulating on social media. Eric bet the commander was demanding answers from the duty officer; this was one case in which trying to bully CLEA away from correct processes wouldn't be desirable if the media found out.

'Is it me, or are there more sector police here than normal?' Matt asked.

'It's not you. It's... Never mind – they're here and that's all that matters.'

'Fine. We'll be here for hours. My team can take over so the police can go once we're set up.'

'Can your team record the details of everyone here?'

'We always do, but it's normally only two or three officers at best. Logging everyone's details is going to take time.'

'Give me an evidence log and I'll give you a hand.'

'No, it's fine. I'm sure you have plenty to get on with.'

Eric thanked him and stepped away to update Kerten that Matt and his team were there. 'Good,' Kerten said. 'How are the officers at the scene.'

'Resentful.'

'I've had their commander on the phone wanting some of them released. What's your view?'

'Matt doesn't need them. Once their details are recorded on the evidence log, they'll be free to go.'

'I'll let the commander know. He has requested a copy of the log so he can start an internal investigation. The quicker we get ahead of this, the better.'

Eric could imagine the conversations Kerten was having and did not envy him. Confident that the scene was being managed, he left the park. The nearest estate was just across the road; hoping someone would have heard something, he started knocking on doors. Many residents refused to answer; those who did responded out of curiosity about what happened.

The consensus was that there was always a lot of noise from the park – and various parties – but they had not noticed any difference last night. Eric left, disappointed with the lack of answers. As he walked back to his car, a text came through from Johnson.

Autopsy will be finished soon; meet you back at the scene or HQ?

At HQ, heading back there now, he replied.

∞

Michelle wasn't at her desk. A note stuck to her monitor said she had popped out for food and would be back shortly. Eric was about to lean back and close his eyes when Johnson walked in, looking wrung out. She pulled up a chair and collapsed onto it.

'I'm sorry,' Eric said. 'I saw the body and...'

'And you struggled to deal with it?' Johnson finished for him.

'Yes, I couldn't support you...'

'Stop!' she told him. 'I don't need your support with the dead any more than you need mine dealing with grieving families. I can deal with dead bodies. People I can't handle, but you can. We need to work on our strengths and not apologise for them, okay?'

'Okay.'

'Where's Michelle?'

'Gone for food.' He showed her the note.

'Thank God, I'm starving.' They both closed their eyes and slept until she returned.

Chapter 17

MICHELLE SAW ERIC and Johnson sitting at her desk, asleep. The dark circles under their eyes were evident and she paused, reluctant to wake them. Then she put the food down and shook them both awake.

Johnson was immediately disturbingly alert and for a second Michelle thought she would hit out. Something in her past had her on edge. 'Sorry,' she said as Michelle stepped back.

'It is fine.'

Eric was different; he was hard to wake but he was at ease and simply apologised for falling asleep.

'Sorry to wake you both,' Michelle said. 'I have brought food.'

'Thank you so much,' Johnson said. She and Eric gladly reached for it and started to eat.

'I do not have good news, I am afraid,' Michelle continued. 'I have been looking at what CCTV exists around the park and I should have the files tomorrow to view. I ran the few vehicles we have from the previous murders through ANPR, but nothing useful has come back. I have been trying to trace where the crime scene photo came from, but the social media sites are not being helpful. I will continue to try and locate the source. What do you know?' she asked, her hands ready to type, hoping they had something new for her.

'The autopsy confirmed the symbol carved into the abdomen was the same as the other murders, that the victim was bound and her throat was cut. That was the cause of death,' Johnson said.

'Not much I can do with that,' Michelle pointed out. 'Any names, times, locations?'

'The pathologist looked for marks or scars that could be checked against the person database, but there were none. DNA came back as negative, so she has never been arrested before. They have applied for dental records,' Johnson stated. 'No property was found on her, so I don't have an identity yet.'

'No one at the scene knew who she was,' Eric said. 'Most bystanders were not willing to talk. The only thing I found out was that there was a "kick-ass party" last night, organised through an app called Hookup,'

'I know about that and am working on it. Anything else for me?'

'Sorry, it's the best I have. Enquires in the nearby estates proved negative.'

'What is Hookup?' Johnson asked.

'It is an app advertising events and parties, among other things,' Michelle said. 'The party last night started at 2200 hours and doors closed for further admittance at 2300. There are a lot of comments about why it was so early. Normally they start at midnight or later after the legal nightclubs closed.'

'So why would people go with such an early start time?' Johnson asked.

'They were advertising a well-known band and said they wanted everyone in before the performance,' Michelle informed them.

'Okay, we need to ensure that the event went ahead. Can you search where else the band has played and the entry and performance times?' Johnson asked.

'Of course. I will also check to see if other bands were asked to play early as well.' Michelle's hands were typing rapidly. 'This could take some time. Do you want to take a rest? I will let you know when I have anything.'

'I don't know. If you are right, there is another body out there,' Eric said.

'The parks in Sector 6 have all been checked. I am sure there is another murder, but I do not know where it happened. You cannot help just now, but when the body is found or more information becomes available it will be beneficial that you are rested.'

∞

Trying to find information from Hookup was harder than Michelle expected; both her texts and calls went unanswered and there was no email associated with the app. Michelle tried to identify the owner of the phone account from which the notification texts went out, but it was an unregistered mobile with no address or name connected to it. Checks against the number only tied it to Hookup. She could request data on where the number was used, but she suspected it would encompass a wide area and wondered if warrant authority would be given.

'How's it going?' Michelle jumped as Eric spoke. He and Johnson had fallen asleep in the corner while they waited. 'How is it going with Hookup?' Eric asked when she didn't immediately reply.

'Badly.' She explained the enquiries she had conducted while they had slept.

'The area would be huge – unregistered mobiles are more common than registered ones. We're looking for a needle in a haystack,' Eric said. 'Did you find any connection between Hookup and the other crime scenes?'

'The app advertises several events in every sector every day. A few stand out because of the earlier start times, but they happened when there were no murders. It could just be a coincidence that there was one last night near the murder scene.'

'We still need to know for sure, so let's take a different tack.' Eric took out his phone.

'Why do you think you will get a different response?' Michelle questioned.

'You asked formally for more information. I'm asking for details of where the next party is and where bands are playing at earlier start times.' As he spoke, he sent a text: *Any early bands playing 2nite*?

'I doubt the organisers will be there.'

'I'm sure they won't be, but the band's fans will be, people we can talk to about the previous events.' As Eric spoke, his phone pinged with a text message for a party the following night.

'What's going on?' Johnson asked, having been woken by the conversation. Eric filled her in. 'Good thinking, but we can't go there. Everyone will clam up if they even suspect they are being questioned.'

'I was thinking of asking Inspector Kerten if we could redirect some of the covert officers.'

'I like that idea.'

∞

A taxi pulled up outside an address and a couple got out. They paid the driver, took their bags out of the boot and started to enter their property. At the door, they paused. 'I thought you said you locked it?' Karl Edwards challenged his wife.

'I did,' Alex replied, resenting his tone.

'The door doesn't look very locked,' he said sarcastically as he gently pushed it and watched it swing open.

'Why are you blaming me? The cleaner will have been in while we were away. Maybe she left it unlocked.'

'Well, you employed her,' he retorted. 'If we've been burgled, I'll blame both of you.'

Alex clenched her fists in frustration. She kept reminding herself that Karl allowed her a lifestyle she wouldn't otherwise have, a lifestyle she really liked.

They walked into their home. At first, everything seemed normal – until they arrived in the living room. 'Oh my God!' Alex said, looking around. The room was a mess: the coffee table was overturned, cushions pulled off the chairs, ornaments smashed, and smears of blood on the floor and walls. Their cleaner was lying in the middle of the floor.

'Oh, my God! Lilly.' Alex rushed forward, but quickly realised that the girl was dead. She started to sob. 'No, no, no,' she kept saying as she cradled the body.

With shaking hands, Karl pulled out his mobile and called the sector police. 'This is Karl Edwards. I've just got home with my wife, and someone has killed our cleaner. She is dead in our living room.' He gave his address.

After hanging up, he turned to Alex. 'They said to leave the room and not touch anything. You shouldn't have touched her.'

'She had a name, you know,' she snapped back.

'I'm sure the sector police will need it when they arrive. Now put her down and get up.'

'Any idea how long they'll take to get here?' Alex asked as she carefully laid Lilly back onto the floor. She didn't like the idea of leaving her alone.

'No, just that a unit will come as soon as one is available.' Karl walked forward and grabbed his wife's arm then led her outside to wait. He was glad for a reason not to be in the house.

'I can't believe this is happening,' Alex said, continuing to cry.

'You're the one who wanted to go away.'

'How is our going away connected to our cleaner being murdered?' Alex challenged. She didn't think Karl had ever been home when Lilly came to work but Alex had met her a few times. She seemed nice, young.

'I don't know, but you wanted her to continue working while we were away. This wouldn't have happened if you'd refused her a week's work.'

'How do you think I could have foreseen this? Seriously? She needed the money and I didn't want to deprive her just because we were going away.'

Karl was prevented from replying by the approaching sirens.

©

The sector police went into the address and made their way directly to the living room. Officer Taliger touched the body and checked for a pulse. The body was cold, and the air had a distinctive smell.

'Well, she's definitely dead,' he said to his partner, Janis. Bruises and scratches were evident on the body, which tied into the damage in the living room. There had obviously been a fight.

'Poor girl. Some sod tried to burgle the place, she tried to prevent it and this is what she got for her trouble,' Janis said.

'I'll call it in,' Taliger said.

'Imagine what it would be like to live here.' Janis was looking around.

'I know. This room alone is bigger than my flat.'

'What do you say we "search" the address to see if there are any other victims?'

'I think it's necessary, just in case someone is hurt,' Taliger agreed. They didn't expect there to be anyone else but it was rare they were called to this area of the city, and neither of them had ever been in a house before, let alone one this size.

They searched but found nothing out of place; the rest

of the property looked undisturbed. They were jealous of its spaciousness. 'Do you know what they do for a living?' Janis asked.

'No, but I'm definitely in the wrong job,' Taliger joked as they returned to the living room. 'Just the garden to check. Can you believe they have their own garden?'

They opened the patio door, not questioning why it wasn't locked if the family had been away and went outside. The garden wasn't big; their presence startled the birds and they flew off.

'Is that normal?' Janis asked.

'No idea,' Taliger said.

They walked to where the birds were and stopped. In front of them was a second female corpse, tied down, with a mutilated abdomen and a cut throat. 'I think we need to get CLEA down here. Wasn't this the murder they wanted to prevent?'

'Thought it was meant to be in a park?'

'Park, garden – maybe it doesn't make a difference.' Taliger pointed to the body. 'But that is definitely not normal.'

⍟

When Michelle received the report stating the body had been found, she broke away from her enquiries into Hookup. The latest murder was a break from the MO, in that it was in a private garden, but the rest of the details still matched with the ritual. She got her map and marked the location on the pentagram. It fitted.

Knowing that Eric and Johnson were still arranging the covert officer at headquarters, Michelle sent them the details with a notification that they needed to talk. It wasn't long before they both joined her at her desk.

'What information have you got for us?' Eric asked.

'Not much. A body was found that fits the MO, but it

was in a private garden. From the description of the corpse, I believe it could be linked. The sector officers on scene definitely think so.' She passed over the details.

'It certainly looks that way,' Johnson said. 'Out of curiosity, how does it fit in with your map.'

'Perfectly.' Michelle showed them the pattern. 'Not many properties have a garden. The previous killings in parks could have been because a public area was the only space outdoors.'

'If that is the case, this investigation just got harder. I'll see if Matt is available.'

∞

'Why Matt?' Eric asked Johnson as they drove to the scene. He suspected that they had a soft spot for each other, so he thought he'd ask the question and see what response he got.

'He does good work. I always try and get his team, and I also like to stick to the same forensic group in a linked murder. I don't need to explain it to a new team each time – they know the job.'

'Don't you worry about the risk that they might get tunnel vision and miss something?'

She brushed off the question. 'I've thought about it but it hasn't been a problem yet.'

Johnson and Eric arrived at the address; a crowd was already in place and a few local officers were stopping them from getting too close. As they pushed through Johnson paused, convinced someone was staring at her again. She turned and scanned the crowd but saw nothing unusual.

'You okay?' Eric asked.

'Yeah, it's nothing.' She shrugged it off. They showed their ID and were let into the house.

A very young-looking officer was standing watch in

the living room. The body was not part of the MO, and Johnson thought for a moment that false information had been passed to Michelle.

'Who is she?' Eric asked the officer.

'The homeowners said her name was Lilly. She was their cleaner.'

'Where is everyone else?'

'Outside with the other body. I was told to stay here and make sure no one touches this one.'

'I'll go outside and see what I can find out,' Johnson said. 'Can you stay here and maintain this scene?' Eric nodded, relieved.

In the garden, Johnson saw a cluster of officers talking; one glanced up and saw her but ignored her. Johnson was not used to being ignored but she could use it to her advantage. She looked at the body, careful not to touch anything as she crouched beside it. Michelle had raised concern over the change of MO in using a garden instead of a park, but visually this murder was the same as the others. 'Who's in charge here?' she shouted.

The conversation stopped and the officers turned to look at her. One man stepped forward. 'I am. And who are you?'

'Agent Johnson with CLEA. One of your officers saw me, ignored me, and allowed me to come over here to examine the body. How do you consider that acceptable?'

'Only law enforcement can get in here,' he defended himself.

'That isn't a justification. There is a huge crowd outside. You should know, as I do, that means someone could slip in. And I could have been one of your officers, being nosy. Before you say anything, I know this has happened before in this investigation.'

When the man didn't immediately respond, she continued, 'Is someone going to brief me?'

Chapter 18

Matt arrived with his team and looked around the living room. 'They certainly made a mess in here, though it doesn't look like the other scenes. Never mind, we might be able to get forensic evidence for once,' he said to Eric.

'I hope so. We really need a break in this case.'

'I expected to see Johnson here since the body hasn't gone to the morgue yet.'

'She's outside with the second body.'

'There are two?' Matt questioned, 'Never mind. Jack!' he called out to one of his team. 'Stay here and start setting up while I go and see Johnson.'

He went outside. At first, he didn't see anyone and he didn't want to trample blindly forward. 'Johnson!' he shouted.

'Here,' she replied.

Matt turned and saw her standing behind a bush; she must have been squatting by the body. He went to her and looked down at the remains. 'When I saw the body inside, I wondered how you'd tied it to the series. I hoped that you'd stopped the killings when the parks were clear last night, but by the look of it the killer just adapted his MO.'

'Michelle sent us here because she believes these deaths are linked to the others. Sorry, Matt. I forgot to tell you that there are two bodies.'

'It's fine. They'll take us longer to process but we'll get

the job done for you.'

'A superstar as always,' she said, smiling.

'Johnson!' Eric shouted from the house. 'The pathologist's van is here to remove the bodies.'

'Thanks, Eric. I'll be there in a minute.'

'Stay here. It's my turn to go to the morgue.' He really didn't want to go, but it wasn't fair that she always went and he wanted to give her some time with Matt.

'Great. Thanks, Eric.'

'Talk me through what you know,' Matt said.

∞

Johnson finally left the scene at 7am. The temptation to go home, shower and sleep were strong, but it wasn't going to happen. Eric had left her a message saying that the second autopsy was nearly finished and asking what she wanted to do next.

She suggested a debrief with Michelle to decide if there was anything they could task out urgently before they got some rest. Turning on the ignition, she looked at how long it would take to get back to headquarters at this time of the morning and cursed. As she drove away, Matt came out of the house. He smiled and waved at her and she smiled. Her day had just got a little brighter.

∞

Michelle was expecting them; her usual pastries were there, as were a few extras including some rolls filled with beans and sausage and others with cheese and ham, plus large coffees.

'Michelle, I love you.' Eric picked up one of the coffees and sat down.

'I second that,' Johnson echoed.

'I assumed you would need refreshment after a night like this.'

For ten minutes they enjoyed breakfast and a well-deserved breather. Then they brushed off their hands and prepared to work.

'The sector police say that the homeowners, the Edwards, identified the victim in the living room as their cleaner, Lilly Yu. They were able to give her full details,' Johnson said. 'They didn't see the second victim, so she is still officially unidentified, but I think she's a relative of Lilly's because there are facial similarities.'

Michelle brought up a photo. 'I ran the name you gave me. Lilly Yu was nineteen and worked as a cleaner to support herself through university where she was studying mathematics. I believe the second victim is her sister, Rose Yu.'

'It looks like her, but...'

'I know – you need DNA or something to confirm it,' Michelle said. 'However, I did some research. Rose was a medical intern in the Sector 6 hospital. Their parents are deceased and I am still trying to locate their next of kin. I have passed you the details of Rose's work and am compiling a list of her known associates.'

'Thank you, Michelle. From a visual inspection of the body, Rose bears many similarities to the other victims. Matt's not hopeful of finding anything outside because no DNA or fingerprints have been found at any of the other scenes, but inside the house may be a different story. There were signs of a fight and drops of blood on the floor that might lead to a suspect. Nothing personal was found on either victim. When I spoke to Mrs Edwards, she said that was strange because Lilly always brought a handbag. Lilly's keys to the Edwards' home were missing. Sector police say there is CCTV in the area.'

'I have started to check those cameras and the surrounding area,' Michelle said, 'but I would appreciate more information to refine the search. None of the known vehicle registrations or people of interest are coming up and it will take hours to view it all.'

'The Edwards didn't know when the sisters arrived. Lilly had been instructed to clean the property before they returned from holiday. We don't know how long after the time of death the Edwards arrived home, or if the women were held hostage for some time beforehand.'

'Do not the Edwards have a CCTV door camera?' Michelle asked.

'They do, but it doesn't trigger unless the doorbell is rung. Lilly had a key, and the suspect didn't set off it – which implies they were let in,' Johnson replied. She was frustrated by that; high-end properties normally had 24/7 CCTV but it cost money, and Mr Edwards hadn't appeared to be generous with his cash.

'What options does that give us? That one of the victims knew the suspect or suspects?' Eric asked.

'It's a possibility,' Johnson admitted.

'I will have to look at their associates,' Michelle said. 'And check their social media, email and phone activity and see if there is anything of note. You said nothing personal was found – I assume that includes mobile phones?'

Johnson nodded. 'That leaves us with local enquiries to see if the neighbours saw or heard anything. The sector police said they had tried the surrounding addresses but few people answered the door. It will be worth revisiting them. Eric, what happened at the morgue?'

'They started on Rose first, and another pathologist worked on Lilly when a second table became available. There was bruising on Rose's mouth and arms – evidence of a fight – and they'll let us know when any forensics come back. Other than the bruising, the rest of the injuries were the same as for the other victims. The symbol on the abdomen, the cut to the throat, the way she was tied down.'

He went on, 'Lilly was different. She died from a broken neck, but not before being badly beaten. The pathologist is hopeful about finding forensic evidence under her nails because of the blood there. It's unlikely to have been Lilly's or Rose's because no scratches from nails were found on their bodies.'

'We have never had the murderer kill someone to get to their intended victim before. Why now?' Johnson asked. She didn't expect an answer. 'I hate this. I hate that they are so far ahead of us.'

'I say we all get some sleep,' Eric suggested. 'I don't know about you, but I'm so tired it's painful to think. We can ask one of the other analysts to run checks on Lilly and Rose Yu's associates. Depending on what they discover, we can decide our next actions.'

'I can run the checks,' Michelle protested.

'You need the rest as much as we do,' Eric said. 'We all take a break.'

Michelle watched Eric talk to another analyst who then came to take over from her. She hated having to brief someone else but knew there was no way she could refuse without questions being asked. She logged off reluctantly and followed Johnson and Eric out of the building. She would recheck everything as soon as she came back to work.

∞

Michelle went back to her apartment and got dressed before heading back out to the demonic club. She wondered if anything had been said about the man she'd left unconscious on the floor. She had run his ID and found he had previous for sexual assault, which didn't surprise her, but there was nothing that linked him to the case.

'I was wondering if you'd come back,' the bouncer said as he opened the door.

'Is there a problem with me being here?'

'None at all – we always like it when the fights are kept outside.' He pointed to a CCTV camera. Michelle cursed; she had been lax and not seen it. 'I was just about to come out when I saw you floor him. I'm impressed.'

'I told him what I liked at the bar. He should have listened.'

'I like someone who knows what they want.' He grinned and waved her in. Michelle smiled and trailed her hand across his chest as she walked past him.

The club was as she remembered it, but this time she drew more attention and she wondered if the word had spread. At the bar, she was taken aback when she was handed a drink 'on the house'.

A woman approached her. 'I loved the CCTV. I'm one of the owners.'

'I did not expect it to be a form of entertainment.'

'It's not, but he'd been warned about his behaviour and the door staff watch him when he leaves. Normally he toes the line but this time he crossed it. Seeing him taken down so cleanly was a pleasure. He won't be back. What I'm worried about is whether you're going to cause me problems. I like to keep this place safe.'

'My use of force is either fully consensual or in defence. I am not looking for trouble.'

'Then welcome.' The woman walked off. As she sipped her drink, Michelle started to look at the place differently; nothing about the murders tied into here, and she wondered if the other clubs were the same.

She spent the next hour talking and listening but found nothing useful. She didn't think it would be worth returning again.

∞

Johnson returned to headquarters just before 1pm after picking up food on the way in, having felt guilty about how often she had relied on Michelle to provide breakfast, lunch and dinner.

She was surprised to see Michelle already at her desk – with more pastries. She paused, feeling almost self-conscious with her box of food. 'Did you get any sleep?' she asked.

'Yes, thank you, I only just got back in. What have you got there?'

'An offering to say thank you for all the times you've fed us recently.' Johnson placed the box on the table and opened it up. 'But it looks like you got there before me.'

'Oh, they will all get eaten. Thank you.' Michelle went straight for the pastries.

Eric appeared, grabbed some food and sat next to them.

'So, the pathologist has come back,' Michelle said. 'DNA shows that the two victims are close relatives, which strongly suggests that the second body is Rose. Dental will have to prove it, which will take a few days. I have been working on the assumption that Rose is the murder victim. Both women had limited online exposure until recently. They lived busy lives with little time for socialising and neither of them posted regularly. However, after the recent news articles, Lilly expressed concern about the ritual murders. I still have more work to do in that area – I want to identify who she was talking to.'

'I thought another analyst was going to pick up the work,' Johnson challenged.

'They did, but I got in an hour ago and rechecked it. To be honest, there is so little it did not take long.' Michelle could see that Johnson wasn't convinced. 'Check when I swiped in and logged on if you do not believe me.'

Johnson wished she could remember if Michelle was wearing the same clothes as last night; her outfits were always so similar that it was hard to recall the nuances. She knew she was overthinking Michelle's apparent lack of need to sleep, so she moved on.

'We need to talk to Lilly's university friends and Rose's hospital colleagues, then revisit the Edwards' neighbours to see if they saw or heard anything. The sector police checked the addresses shortly after the bodies were found but the people who live in this area have employment that is likely to involve extended hours. Eric, do you want to take Lilly's friends and I'll talk to Rose's? Then we can meet up and make neighbourhood enquiries together this evening.'

Chapter 19

JOHNSON WENT TO the hospital where Rose Yu had worked. She stopped someone in scrubs and asked for the 'chief of general'; the term didn't mean much to her, but from the files Michelle had found she knew that was Rose's boss. The scrub pointed to a stern-looking female looking at medical charts.

'Good afternoon, are you the chief of general?' Johnson asked as she showed her badge.

'Surgery, yes. I'm Doctor Patel. How can I help you, agent?'

'I need to talk to you about Rose Yu.'

'She's not here today,' she said dismissively.

'I know. I need to talk to you *about* her, not to her. Is there somewhere we can talk in private?' The person in scrubs she had spoken to had quickly spread the news and now several people were paying attention to their conversation.

'Of course.' The doctor had noticed the interest that the agent was causing. She closed the chart she was looking at, led Johnson into a nearby office and closed the door. 'What's happened to Dr Yu?' Dr Patel asked.

'I'm sorry but she was found dead.'

Dr Patel processed the information, took a breath, then her professionalism returned. 'Thank you for letting me know. She will be missed – she had a lot of potential. I appreciate being told – but should you not be informing her sister? If you don't have the details, I can get them for you.'

'Her sister Lilly is also dead. I understand there is no other next of kin.'

'I would need to check, but I believe that is the case,' Dr Patel confirmed. 'What happened to them?'

'Unfortunately both sisters were murdered. We're looking for information to assist in our enquiries.'

'My God! Anything you need.'

'We believe Rose was killed as part of the serial murders that have been in the news.'

'I saw on the news that a body had been found in sector 5. It mainly talked about the photos that were circulating. What was she doing there?'

'That is a different investigation. Rose was killed in the garden of her sister's employer in Sector 6, so she was not found until the family returned from holiday.'

'Then Rose's death is my fault? I warned all my female doctors and nurses to be careful and not go out alone that night. She shouldn't have been there...'

'That was good advice, and you are in no way to blame for Rose's murder. I expect the killer had already targeted her and adapted to the change in her routine. Was she due to work that day?'

'Night duty. When she didn't turn up, I was concerned. I tried to call her but there was no reply. I thought... No murder in this sector was mentioned in the media, and it was too soon to report her as missing.'

'What can you tell me about her?'

'Not much.' Dr Patel paused. 'She was here more than eighty hours a week like most interns, so I don't expect that she had much of a personal life outside the hospital. I can introduce you to the other interns – there were a few she was close to, especially those on the same shift rotation. Maybe they can tell you more.'

'That would be useful, thank you.'

'I can't believe this happened to Rose. She had so much promise. She always went out of her way to help others. I told them to be careful, I told them to be careful,' Dr Patel repeated, clearly shaken.

∞

Michelle had contacted the university before Eric arrived, so a warden at the halls of residence was waiting to let him into Lilly's room. It was small and comprised a neatly made single bed, a small wardrobe, a desk with a stack of books, a tablet and an open notebook.

Eric picked up the notebook to see what Lilly had been working on. He flicked through the pages, but they appeared only to contain material related to her studies. He checked the tablet but it was locked and needed a thumbprint or a number code to unlock it. He pulled an evidence bag out of his case and carefully bagged it; maybe Michelle could unlock it. Otherwise it would have to be sent to the lab and that could take weeks.

He continued searching the room. There was nothing under the bed and the wardrobe contained only clothes and shoes. Lilly had lived a very minimal life, Eric thought. He was about to close the wardrobe door when something caught his eye and he pulled out a coat. There was a coloured piece of paper in the pocket, the first name, Janus, and a time and location, but no date. Eric placed the paper in another evidence bag and took a picture of it before sending it to Michelle so she could start researching the details.

Not knowing who the person on the note was, or how they could tie into the investigation, Eric called Matt to see if one of his team was free to come down to the room and check for fingerprints and DNA.

∞

Rose had shared an apartment with a few of her fellow interns from the hospital. Johnson thought it looked like student accommodation.

'This is her room,' Dr Mathers said. He'd been introduced as one of Rose's fellow interns. None of them had had much to say, other than that Rose was nice and worked long hours. Only Dr Mathers knew her outside work.

Johnson learned that Mathers and Rose had studied together at university then joined the same programme for interns. Looking at the male items of clothing scattered around Rose's room, Johnson suspected that was more than just a coincidence. 'Were you not working together the other night if you were on the same shift rotation?'

'We should have been, but Rose had already exceeded her eighty hours for the week. Instead of doing a double shift, she was only coming in for the night shift.'

'If she had exceeded her hours, why was she going in for the night?'

'She'd only do an extra two hours before the working week's clock reset at midnight. She wasn't happy about not coming in at the same time as me, but Dr Patel is strict about the rules – "too many hours equals not enough sleep equals mistakes", she always says. But I told Rose not to come in on her own, and she promised she wouldn't.'

'Do you know how far Lilly lived from here?'

'Not far. Rose and I lived here when we were students at the university. The landlord was going to sell the place when we graduated so we put in an offer and it was accepted. It's near the hospital. Also, Lilly had got into uni here and Rose didn't want to leave the area.'

'It sounds as if they were close.'

'They were. Rose spent most of her free time with her

sister. They lost their parents when they were young – she was very motherly towards Lilly.'

'Do you know why Rose went to her sister's workplace?'

'I imagine she wanted to make sure Lilly was safe and didn't go out on her own. After Lilly had finished work, I suspect she would have come to the hospital with Rose. Rose might have arranged for her to sleep in an on-call room.'

'How can I find out if she'd booked a room?'

'Officially, you can't – the rooms are for on-call doctors or those working extended double shifts. The keys are kept at the nurses' station and they have a copy of the roster, but it's easy to bypass the system.'

'So I need to talk to the nurses who were on duty that night and see if Rose had "negotiated" the use of the room for Lilly.'

'They might not tell you – it's not something they should do.'

'I understand. I'll be discreet. Why the separate rooms if you and Rose were together?' Johnson asked, lifting up the male underwear. 'I assume these are yours?'

'Yes. With the hours that we worked, most of the time the thing we both wanted was sleep. We did enjoy each other's company when we weren't so tired,' he admitted. 'I can't believe she isn't coming back, that I won't see her again. Is there any chance I can see her to say goodbye?'

'You aren't next of kin so you would need their permission. I'm sorry.'

'I understand.' Dr Mathers looked defeated; he knew the girls had no relatives, so there would be no chance. He sat on the bed and ran his hand over the duvet.

'Thank you for your help,' Johnson said. 'I'll keep you updated as much as I'm allowed to.'

'Thanks. If there's anything I can help you with, please let me know.'

'I'd like to get a team in to check the apartment for evidence, but we need the owner's permission or a warrant,' Johnson said, looking at him.

'Of course. Anything you want.'

∞

Johnson pulled up behind Eric's car outside the Edwards' cordoned-off property. Eric met her on the pavement. 'Have any luck?' she asked.

'I don't know. I found a note that I sent to Michelle, and one of Matt's team is checking the room. You?' Eric replied.

'It seemed Rose was with her sister because of our warnings not to go out alone,' Johnson admitted. 'Otherwise, she worked long hours and her free time was spent with Lilly or her sort-of boyfriend. He's given us permission to search their home. Matt couldn't go there after being at Lilly's without the risk of cross-contamination, so he's arranged for another team to attend.'

'So Rose was targeted, changed her routine and the killer followed her to the new location.'

'I agree, but I've no idea how the suspect got in without activating the Edwards' security system.'

'Let's hope that the door-to-door enquires will give us some idea. I'll take the left, you take the right.'

Chapter 20

Johnson and Eric met up after talking to everyone who would open their doors to them. They both agreed there was no need for any deployment that night; there would be greater benefit in going home and getting some sleep to start fresh tomorrow.

Johnson climbed gratefully into bed but regretfully set her alarm clock for 5am so she'd be back in the office early.

She woke feeling cold. When she opened her eyes she couldn't see anything. She searched for the light switch but felt only air. She heard a noise in the distance and shouted, 'Hello?' but got no reply, though she was sure she was being watched. She tried to move but couldn't. In the distance she heard a laugh that sent a shiver of fear down her spine.

She woke with a start when the alarm rang and realised it had just been a dream. She climbed out of bed and rubbed her face to wake herself up before heading for the shower.

⏀

Johnson wasn't surprised when she saw Michelle at her desk as usual. She had asked many times how Michelle pulled the long hours so there was no point asking again, though she wished she knew her secret.

She and Eric approached Michelle's desk. 'I am glad you are here early. I was just about to call you,' the analyst said as they sat down beside her.

'What have you found out?' Eric asked.

'The note you sent through from Lilly's room did not have enough details for me to narrow down any information. The area has no CCTV, and with no date to assist I have no idea which direction Lilly was coming from. But the tablet was another matter. Luckily she was not adventurous with her password and gaining access was easy. I looked through her search history. She had been learning as much as she could about the murders.'

'Why would she do that?'

'I think she was worried about her sister Rose. The searches in themselves were for information, but they led her to a chat group where she asked questions about how to protect someone who was a potential target. The group appeared to be supportive and other people had similar concerns. The name Janus on this piece of paper is the same as the group's admin. That gave me more to work with.'

'Please give us some good news,' Johnson said.

'If you are asking if I think this guy is a killer, I am sorry but no. Do I know who he is? Yes, I do.'

Michelle pulled up the details. 'The person Lilly went to meet was Janus Alman. He is single, has no criminal history and loves a good conspiracy theory. The group was set up when the murders first made the news. Looking at some of his comments online, he definitely wants attention and to connect with like-minded people. I also suspect he is not above exploiting the concerns of females who think they are targets or have a loved one who might be.'

'In what way?' Johnson asked, not sure she would like the answer.

'Lilly expressed fears for her sister, said that she fitted the victims' type. Janus said he understood and that he could help her protect Rose, but he and Lilly had to meet. He sent the details by private message. I logged into her account on her tablet and accessed her messages. You might think it is a massive time-saver to have your device remember your details, but it makes it easy for others to access your data. I do not recommend it.'

Michelle went on, 'I found a date for the meeting. From that, I retrieved CCTV. It does not cover the location, but I saw Lilly enter the area. She arrived and left alone, but she looked upset after the meeting. Janus did not follow her.'

'We definitely need to talk to him. What could he advise her about? Do you think he knows more than he should?' Johnson asked.

'From the chats, I do not think so. Everything he said has been in the news or on conspiracy websites. I think he could be a predator of a different type. These are his details and what research I could do on him.'

Michelle emailed the file to Eric and Johnson then asked, 'Now, do you have anything else for me? What happened with the door-to-door enquires?'

'I found out nothing. The occupants were either not in or they didn't hear or see anything,' Johnson said.

'I got the same,' Eric agreed. 'Some were scared, but no one was forthcoming with information.'

⚭

Johnson and Eric went to Janus's address, a small, boarded-up apartment in a derelict part of the city. 'This isn't suspicious at all,' Johnson said mockingly as she banged on the door.

'Go away!' a voice shouted from inside.

'Janus Alman, this is CLEA. Open the door,' Eric called loudly.

They heard a crash. Johnson pulled out her gun and

went to look for other exit points as Eric kicked open the door and, weapon raised, went inside.

Janus wasn't trying to run: the room was dark and a chair had fallen over. On his wall were pictures of not only Lilly but other women, too. He was trying to pull them down. 'Stop what you're doing and show me your hands,' Eric ordered.

Janus immediately obeyed. 'I'm sorry, please don't shoot me,' he begged.

'Johnson, I've got him. He's unarmed,' Eric shouted.

'Why did you do that to my door? I've not done anything wrong,' Janus protested.

'Then why are you trying to hide evidence.'

'What evidence? I said I've not done anything wrong.'

'You didn't meet with Lilly Yu the other night?' Eric asked as Johnson joined them.

'Whatever she claimed happened, it didn't!'

'Lilly Yu and her sister have been murdered. We need you to answer some questions down at headquarters – and we'll be taking all of this.' Eric indicated the photographs.

'Murdered? It wasn't me.' Janus was obviously shocked by the news.

'I have to remind you that you have the right to legal advice before we question you,' Eric said as he placed cuffs on him. Though it gave him pleasure to do so, he already believed that the complaining Janus did not fit with the type who would murder.

∞

'When did you meet Lilly?' Eric asked as they sat in an interrogation room at headquarters.

'It was three days ago, at her university cafe. But you should know that, right?'

'I want to confirm a few points about the timeline. Tell

me what happened the night you met her.'

'Nothing happened. She wanted to discuss the murders. As I'm sure you know, I have a great interest in crime,' Janus replied.

'What exactly did you tell her?'

'I told her that I believed the killer was disturbed. The new moon is known to bring out mental health problems in those who have never suffered them before, or aggravate those who are already ill.'

'The *full* moon is reported to have that effect on a person's mental health. The murders happened when there was a new moon,' Eric corrected him.

Janus brushed off the correction. 'All phases of the moon affect people differently. I told her that I felt the murderer was preying on women who were being careless about their safety. If her sister was cautious and stayed with someone, there was no risk to her.'

'What led you to believe that?' Eric challenged.

'It's obvious! Who else would do this but some random nutter? Comments have come onto my site linking the murders to a demonic ritual, but who'd believe that?'

'I have to disagree,' Eric responded. 'These murders are planned and there is no evidence to suggest that the perpetrator is mentally ill. When we came to your apartment, you said "whatever she claimed happened, it didn't." What did you mean by that?'

'It was a silly misunderstanding, nothing more.'

'Tell me anyway.'

'I misread the situation and I made a pass at her,' Janus admitted sullenly.

'Define "pass"?' Eric demanded. Janus didn't reply. 'If you don't answer, I'll assume the worst, so you have nothing to lose by telling me the truth.'

'I kissed her and touched her breast. She freaked out and ran away,' Janus admitted.

'Did anyone else know about this?'

'She posted on my site that I was a pervert. I removed the comment. It was an unfair representation of the event.'

'You know a lot about the murders,' Eric said. 'So how do we know that you didn't kill Lilly as revenge for the comments she made?' Eric asked. He was interested to see what Janus's response would be. He honestly didn't think that Janus had murdered the women, but he saw no reason not to make him panic.

∞

'I don't think he did it.' Eric had left the interview room and headed to Michelle's desk, where he knew she and Johnson would be. Frustrated, he threw himself onto a chair. 'I think he's a narcissist. He's convinced he is giving the right advice to frightened women, and if they meet with him he takes that as a sexual advance. He showed no empathy when I told him that Lilly and her sister were dead. When I suggested he might be a suspect, he swung from being aggressive to crying.'

'Any reason to exclude him?' Johnson asked.

'He gave an alibi – he was meeting another woman when Lilly and her sister were murdered. He has warned me that she would also make "false allegations against him" if we contacted her. This is her name and social media handle. Can you find her contact details or an address?' Eric passed over the information and Michelle started typing.

'Michelle and I have been trying to identify who the other females were on Janus's wall. We don't think they are involved with the murders, Janus may have targeted them. We're putting a file together for the sector police and CLEA's sexual offences unit,' Johnson said.

'That's great. I doubt Janus is a murderer, but he's

definitely a predator who needs to be dealt with.'

'We found an offence in Sector...' Johnson started but was cut off by Michelle, who had been paying no attention to their conversation.

'I have an address for the woman Janus was with when Lilly was murdered. Do you want to attend or send the sector police?'

'Send sector. If an allegation is made, it will be their case to start with. I'll make sure they know that they must work within Janus's detention time, so they can't delay their enquiry,' Eric said.

'Make sure they link it to Lilly. If there are any cross-border offences, they could become ours so we need to monitor it,' Michelle pointed out.

'If we can take Janus out of the investigation, we're no further forward,' Johnson responded.

Eric said thoughtfully, 'Michelle can you restore deleted comments? Janus mentioned that he had removed Lilly's comments from his website about him attacking her.'

'The comments do not get deleted, they just get hidden,' she replied. 'The easiest way to see them is to log into Janus's account.'

'What do you mean?' Eric asked.

'If Lilly made a comment in a forum, Janus had access to it,' Michelle said. 'He could hide it so that only he could see it.'

'Why do you think this is important?' Johnson asked Eric.

'Janus said that Lilly commented on his attack on her but he blocked the comment. What if someone saw it, knew where she worked and went to see if she was okay? There may be an indication that the killer contacted her directly, but we won't know without her phone. She might have let him in. But there is no way Janus is going to give us access to his website,' Eric said.

'A warrant it is, then,' Johnson concluded.

◐

The warrant came through quickly, giving them access to all social media sites where Janus was recorded as the administrator. It soon became clear that he deleted any comment that did not fit with his views; any criticism or challenge was removed, as was any show of sympathy from other men. Janus clearly wanted to be the main contributor.

Michelle found the comment from Lilly accusing him of being a pervert; there were several sympathetic responses before Janus had 'deleted' it. On its own, there was nothing suspicious about it but what grabbed her attention was the level of detail Lilly gave about where she and her sister worked.

Michelle's heart sank as she read the information. Lilly could have given the killer all the information they needed to trace Rose, together with her profile and her mobile number. Her phone had not been recovered at the scene.

The killer could have tracked Rose's movements through her sister. Michelle doubted he had communicated with Lilly on social media, but she believed he had seen her posts.

She turned her attention to the dark net. Though there were comments on the murder in Sector 5, there was nothing about Lilly and Rose.

Having completed all the lines of enquiry she could think of, she turned to the other comments on Janus's social media accounts. The warrant had been for access, so it did not bar her from finding evidence that would help prosecute Janus for sexual offences if the victims wanted to come forward.

Chapter 21

OVER THE NEXT few nights, the covert officers went to several early Hookup parties, including one where the band had been playing in Sector 5 when the murder took place. Nothing came from their enquiries. Most bands were looking for exposure and played for free; they liked to play early if they had a paid gig afterwards. The doors were always closed to ensure the performances were not disrupted by late arrivals. The report, emailed to Johnson, asked if she wanted to extend the operation to future events.

Johnson was reading the file as she entered Michelle's office and nearly collided with Eric. 'Sorry,' she mumbled, continuing to read.

Eric smiled to himself and guided her to a chair next to Michelle's desk. Suddenly Johnson cursed. 'I take it it's not good news,' Eric said, sitting next to her.

'See for yourself.' Johnson handed over the file.

'This doesn't help us at all,' Eric said. There was no evidence that the killer was using the Hookup platform.

Johnson forwarded the report to Michelle, who read it quickly.

'Sorry, I do not think Hookup is connected,' Michelle told her. 'I cannot find any connection other than that a party might draw people away from the murder site. All the killers would have to do is monitor the Hookup website. I do not think there is any direct involvement.'

'Then why did you ask us to meet you here?' Johnson asked.

'The victim from Sector 5 has been identified through dental records as Tami Rankin, a primary-school teacher,' Michelle said. 'A missing person report for her was filed as soon as the seventy-two hours elapsed. I have started to look into her life, but it is the same as the others. Law-abiding. I will let you know if I get anything that can help you.'

'Damn. Do you have next-of-kin details?'

'Yes. They are not local.' Michelle passed them over.

Johnson and Eric both cursed; though they had jurisdiction anywhere in the sectors of the city, outside was different.

∞

Tami's parents lived in Regional City, which made visiting them difficult because of local government politics. Most cities operated a free-movement policy and there were no borders to hinder travel, but Regional City was different. It was a considerable distance away and had strict rules.

A decade earlier, it had had the worst crime rate of all the cities, so local government had closed the routes in and forced people to apply for travel permits if they wanted to leave. Doing so had hindered the supply of drugs and weapons, and the gangs had gone elsewhere. As the local crime rate was now the lowest in the country, Regional City had maintained the restrictions but there were rumours that the dictatorial nature of the government and police was not well-received.

Eric's request to the local police to visit the family in person was rejected. Next, they asked for a Regional City police officer to visit them but that was also declined, leaving Eric no option but to call the family to inform them of the death of their daughter. It seemed a cold way to pass on such heart-breaking news, and he had no idea what support the family would have. He knew the sector police always broke bad news by phone because of their limited resources, but experience had taught him that it was always better in person.

He listened to the phone ring. He was about to hang up and try again later when a woman answered. 'Rankin residence.'

'Is this Janet Rankin? Tami's mother?'

'It is, yes.' A note of worry entered the woman's voice.

'I am Agent Eric Badu of Sector City's CLEA. I'm sorry to have to tell you, but Tami is dead.'

Janet started crying as she handed the phone to her husband. He demanded to know what was going on, so Eric had to repeat that Tami was dead and explain what had happened. 'I'm so sorry to break the news to you like this. It's not how I wanted to do it.'

'I understand, Agent. Thank you for telling us.' Mr Rankin was clearly trying to hold it together. 'Tami had such a time getting the documents approved so she could work in the sector city. I know there are issues with crossing the borders; we haven't seen her since she left because of those.'

'Thank you, sir. I know this is a terrible time for you, but I wonder if I could ask you a few questions about your daughter?'

'If it helps you find out who did this to her, ask anything you want.'

'I need to know about her life in the city, who her friends were, where she liked to go.'

'We speak once a week, but she doesn't talk much about what she's doing. She mainly speaks to her mum.' His daughter's death had clearly not sunk in and he was talking about her as if she were still alive.

There was a pause as Eric heard a muffled conversation between Mr Rankin and his wife.

'Tami's not been back to visit for over a year,' Mr Rankin

said. 'My wife can't talk to you right now but I'll get her to call you when she can. I want to help you – I just don't know how.' That realisation seemed to affect him badly.

Before he hung up, Eric gave his contact details and promised to keep updating them. 'I hate breaking bad news on the phone,' he said.

'Thank you for doing that. I...' Johnson started.

'Don't apologise. Remember what you said about the autopsies. We each have our strengths.'

'Were the parents able to give us anything?'

'The father couldn't help. The mother might, but she was too upset to talk.'

'Because they're outside the city, they can't give authority for us to search Tami's home. We'll have to get a warrant,' Johnson pointed out. It was yet another delay.

∞

While they waited for Kerten to get the warrant, Johnson and Eric talked to Tami's work colleagues. Arriving at the school, they showed their CLEA badges then asked the receptionist for the headteacher. 'Can I tell her what this is about?' the woman asked.

'No, but we really need to talk to her,' Johnson replied.

The receptionist gave them a cold smile, clearly unhappy that she couldn't get the gossip, but she passed on the message.

The head came out and invited them into her office. 'How can I help you, Agents?' she asked as she indicated for them to sit in front of her desk.

'I'm sorry to inform you that Tami has been murdered.' Eric quickly explained it was part of the linked series of deaths that had recently been in the news.

'I was worried when she didn't show up to work,' the headmistress said. 'I tried calling her, and one of the other teachers went to her home, but she wasn't there. I never suspected that something like this had happened.'

'Why did you think she had failed to show up? Was she was involved with someone?' Johnson asked.

'Not that I know of, but she recently asked for time off to go back home. She was missing her family. As they couldn't get clearance to enter the city, she wanted to go back to them. I filed a missing person report as soon as we could because no one had heard from her, but I honestly thought she had just gone home.'

'I know this is shocking news, but we will need to talk to the staff who were closest to her,' Eric said.

'Of course. Classes stop for lunch in about ten minutes. I can arrange for the teachers and assistants to come here to talk to you.'

'That would be very helpful,' Eric said.

'If you'll excuse me, I need to check who is on playground duty to make sure they will be available.' She left the room.

'I hate this "seventy-two hours before you can report someone as missing". It makes investigating a disappearance all the harder,' Eric muttered.

'I know, but there used to be so many calls, most of which related to people just getting home late,' Johnson said.

'Then make it twenty-four or forty-eight hours,' Eric retorted.

'I didn't say I agreed with it,' Johnson said as the door opened and three people walked in.

'The headteacher said we needed to talk to you about Tami. I'm Ben, her teaching assistant. This is Marie and this is Molly. Marie is the teacher in Tami's sister class, and Molly is her assistant.'

'What's happened to Tami?' Marie asked. 'The head seemed upset.'

It was clear they had not been told. Johnson asked

them to close the door and sit down, then Eric explained. For a moment there was silence before Marie started to cry, followed shortly by Molly. They clung to each other. Ben was clearly upset but trying to control his emotions.

'I saw the news but I never suspected it could be one of us,' Molly sobbed.

'We're sorry for your loss,' Eric said. 'To try and find out who did this, we need to know as much as we can about Tami's routine so anything you can tell us would be helpful.'

At first none of them said anything, then Ben told them Tami had a fitness class once a week. He didn't know where, but she sometimes commented on 'having overdone it' and her muscles being sore. He also thought she occasionally went out on a 'girls' night', but he had no idea with whom.

'It was with us,' Marie said. 'She wasn't settling in and she was lonely, so every now and then we took her out for a drink. But the last time was about two weeks ago.'

None of them had much more to say. Tami definitely had a set routine and it was clear she got on with her colleagues, but she was not close to them.

Johnson contacted Michelle and asked her to find the fitness class that Tami went to.

∞

Kerten had fast-tracked the warrant and he sent it through to them that afternoon, so Johnson and Eric went straight to Tami's address after they finished at the school. Before these murders, they could have expected to have waited a few days for authorisation, but now everyone was on edge.

When they arrived at the address they couldn't find anyone with a key to let them in, so Eric forced the lock. The flat was a small studio, with one room acting as a kitchen, living room and bedroom. The bed had to be folded away during the day and only the bathroom was separate.

As they looked around the property, they realised how little Tami owned. 'This reminds me of Lilly's place. She also had very few possessions,' Eric said.

'Other than a picture I assume to be of her parents and a few books, there's nothing personal here,' Johnson said. 'Do you think it's relevant?' She couldn't help drawing a comparison with her home; she spent so much time working that she used it to sleep in and little else.

'I doubt it. Some of the other victims had loads of personal items in their homes.' Seeing a laptop on the table, Eric picked it up and placed it in an evidence bag. When someone arrived to make the property secure, they headed back to headquarters.

⓪

Michelle could tell they'd had an unproductive day when they arrived back in her office. 'I take it things have not gone well?'

'Tami was reclusive. The only thing she did was attend a fitness class. There was this laptop at her home,' Eric placed it on the desk, 'but nothing else of note.'

'Let me go through it. Go home and get some rest and I will let you know what I can find.'

They didn't need to be told twice. Michelle watched them walk out of the door then turned to see to the laptop. She went through Tami's accounts, email, calendar, and social media; there were no obvious red flags but, like Lilly, Tami didn't hide what she was doing. Anyone could find out where she was.

Some of the victims had had limited social media access, so the killers must have found them by other means. Michelle would need to unpick their lives.

Chapter 22

JOHNSON WOKE UP to her phone buzzing. She glanced at the time – 5am – before looking to see who was calling. It was Inspector Kerten. That wasn't good.

'Have you seen the news?' he asked, getting straight to the point.

'No, wait a minute.' She turned on the light, put her phone onto speaker and started to search the internet for articles. It didn't take long to find the information. She swore.

'I take it you have found it,' Kerten said.

'Sorry, sir. Yes. How did they find the details so quickly?'

'We'll look into that, but the pressure for a resolution of these murders will increase. I want regular reports. Is there anything that could assist you?'

'Can the seventy-two-hour reporting rule for missing people be changed? Tami and Jenny weren't reported missing as a result of that, and it delayed the investigation.'

'I'll raise it with the director and head of the sector police.'

Once Kerten hung up, Johnson took the time to read more than the headline:

Women are not safe in homes.

The article told how the killer had stalked Rose Yu. Though she had taken precautions that night, the suspect had changed his pattern of offending to kill her.

The article was accurate; though it did not contain many details, it was still worrying how the media knew what they did. The communication unit would have to investigate.

As she pondered the 'how?' she realised a murder in that neighbourhood would always get a different response from the press. Johnson thought of all the people who'd been around the Edwards' house; it would have only taken one indiscreet sector officer, and a reporter could have put the rest together from previous articles and social media posts.

Johnson jumped out of bed and got ready for work. Eric had sent a text saying he'd seen the news and would meet her at Michelle's desk. She was not surprised to see Michelle already there, but there were no pastries lying around this time. Johnson pulled out her phone and sent a quick message before sitting down.

'Have you seen the news?' Michelle asked. 'I came straight here when I saw it.'

Johnson nodded. 'We should have got it out ahead of the story. It doesn't make good reading.'

'Especially with the photo of Tami in the park.'

'What? I've not seen a photo.'

Michelle pulled it up on her monitor. 'It is the one that was on social media.'

'I don't suppose anything has been done to find out who took it,' Johnson said.

'I know that sector anti-corruption unit asked Matt for a copy of the evidence logs, so they know who was there. A number of officers, including the first on the scene, have been suspended. If I find out more, I will let you know.'

'At least the sector police are looking into it,' Johnson said. She would be interested to know the outcome; she wouldn't be surprised if someone was made an example of to remind officers what was expected of them. 'There's nothing we can do about the media now. Eric is on his way in.'

As if he'd heard his name, he appeared with a bag of pastries. 'I heard there was a need. Have I missed anything?'

'Thank you for these.' Now Michelle knew who Johnson had been messaging. 'We were discussing the news article. I have been through Tami's laptop but there is little there. I found the fitness class, a HIIT session at her local community centre, but there is no evidence that she knew anyone there. There is no communication between her or others attending the class.'

'Damn it!'

'That was the bad news,' Michelle said. 'The good news is that I have two suspects for Lilly and Rose's murder.'

'What?' Both Johnson and Eric said together.

'Going through Janus's accounts, I found a deleted comment in reply to Lilly's post expressing concern about what had happened with Janus. The person who posted it wanted to meet her and gave her a phone number if she wanted to talk. She had "liked" the post.'

'And you know who he is?' Johnson asked eagerly.

'Based on the profile name, no – that does not help me narrow it down on its own. The number is for a burner phone that has not been used since. However...' she put her hand up to prevent questions '...we also have two DNA profiles, one of which is strongly linked to the profile name.'

'Spell this out to me,' Johnson said.

'User name @JMSMITH reached out to Lilly. With a name like that, there are many possible users, DNA found under Lilly's nails was from James Martin Smith. I need access to his social media accounts to know for sure that they are the same person.'

'The DNA is more than enough to bring him in. What about the second DNA sample?'

'Jonny Timmons, a known associate of James. They

both have a long history of offending. I have profiles for them both. '

'Let's get some warrants,' Eric said enthusiastically. Finally, they had a break in the case.

⚭

Johnson went to Inspector Kerten's office while Eric typed up the warrant request. Kerten waved her in and noticed the smile on her face. 'Tell me you have good news,' he said.

'We have a DNA match from under Lilly's nails and a method for the killers gaining entry into the Edwards' property without setting off the cameras. Eric is doing the forms for the warrants as we speak.'

'That's great news. I'm about to go into a briefing with the big bosses. Do you need anything?'

'A meeting with a judge and, if the warrant is approved, the resources we need without a long wait.'

'I'll tell you what I can get for you in an hour.'

She was dismissed 'What did Kerten say?' Eric asked when he saw her approach Michelle's desk.

'He'll see what he can do. For now, we do the paperwork and wait.'

'The evidence is strong. Have faith,' Michelle said.

Johnson snorted; she didn't trust the big bosses to make a decision; they would suggest following the current protocols, which meant delay.

She was wrong. They had a meeting with a judge within the hour, and the warrants and extra resources were issued immediately. The latest news article was causing concern, and both the CLEA and the sector police had to be seen to act.

⚭

The next day Johnson was standing outside Jonny's

address with a search warrant and an assault team. Eric had gone to James's address with a second team. Michelle had completed briefings on both suspects that showed their propensity for violence as well as floor plans for the addresses that had been compiled from previous warrants and council documents.

Johnson was now waiting. Both assault teams were checking if anyone was on the premises before moving forward because that would influence how they entered. They also wanted to go into the two addresses at the same time.

'Okay, Agent, hold back until we've secured the premises,' the team leader, Agent Fisher, informed her. He approached the door with his team, then two agents forced it open and released a flashbang. There were shouts of distress from inside.

Fisher's team moved in, ready to fire. 'CLEA! place your hands in the air. Do not reach for a weapon. Identify your location.'

A gun was fired and hit one of the agents, who went down. 'Hostile fire!' someone called.

The CLEA agents returned fire. 'AAHHH'! Stop! I'm on my own,' a man shouted.

'Cease fire,' Fisher ordered before motioning his team to move forward.

The suspect was on the floor with an injury to his arm. An agent moved the gun lying next to him out of his reach. As they restrained him, he tried pull away from the cuffs.

'Stop resisting!' They handcuffed him and got him off the floor, then assessed the wound and applied a compression bandage. Other agents searched the property and confirmed that Jonny was alone.

Another agent checked on his colleague who had been shot; the casualty was already sitting up and cursing –

the round had hit his bulletproof vest.

When the 'All secure!' shout came, Johnson went inside. When she saw members of the assault team helping one of their own, her heart sank; she hated it when agents got hurt but it was part of the job. She would enquire later how he was doing.

Johnson walked up to the man in handcuffs. 'Are you Jonny Timmons?'

'Yes! What the hell?' He pulled angrily at the cuffs.

'I am arresting you for the murders of Lilly and Rose Yu. You don't have to say anything, but anything you do say could be used as evidence.'

Her words were met with silence. Though she expected there was a lot Jonny wanted to say, he wouldn't dare while he was surrounded by armed men. Coward, she thought. She noted the injury to his arm; she would make sure a doctor saw him after he was brought in.

'Agent, you better look at this,' one of the assault team shouted from the bedroom.

She went to see what he had found. On the wall were images of Rose Yu; he had clearly been following her. There were also drawings of the symbol that had been carved into Rose's and the other victims' abdomens, though there were no photos of their bodies, which meant she lacked evidence of Jonny having been at the murder scenes.

She pulled out her phone, photographed the evidence then called Matt. 'I'll need you or one of your team to come to this address. I've a wall of evidence that needs to be collected.'

'I'll be there as soon as I can. I've just had a similar call from Eric.'

'Do you have any details?'

'Nothing much,' Matt said. 'I'm afraid you'll have to talk to him.'

Johnson hung up and turned to the officer who had shown her the wall. 'This will need to be preserved for the forensic team. Don't touch it.'

After she had arranged for Jonny to be transported back to headquarters, she helped the assault team search the house. She found a tablet but little else; she was disappointed that neither the murder weapon nor the type of rope that had been used on the victims was there.

∞

Disappointed at not finding any real evidence to link Jonny to the murders, Johnson left one officer at the scene to wait for Matt and returned to headquarters. Jonny was outside the cells surrounded by several agents; the doctor had already been and cleaned and bandaged his flesh wound.

'I want a solicitor,' Jonny said to Johnson.

'Fine. We'll take swabs and photos while we wait – a solicitor has no say over that, and we can use force if we need to.'

A cell door was opened. Jonny started to struggle as they took hold of him and led him inside, but his hands were held down as his nails were cut and his hands swabbed. The agents took extra care not to 'aggravate' his injury.

When they removed his clothing, they found scratch marks and bruising that were a few days old. Jonny cursed and struggled as these were swabbed and photographed, telling them they'd all rot in hell.

Once they had acquired the evidence, the agents left the cell. 'Let me know when the solicitor arrives,' Johnson said and set off for Michelle's desk.

She texted Eric en route to see how he was doing. *'Just arrived at headquarters,'* he replied.

Kerten was with Michelle. 'Good work, Johnson,' he said. 'I hear your suspect is in custody and Eric is coming in with the other one.'

'Thank you, sir – but why do I think you are here for another reason?'

'Whoever leaked the information to the press about where Lilly and Rose were murdered has given more information.' He showed her the new headline:

Suspects arrested for demonic murders of women!

'Though a leak is bad, would we not have released this information?' Johnson questioned.

'We would have when we had more. This didn't come from us. The language is inflammatory. As a result, a demonstration has been planned outside headquarters later today.'

'Why? Surely the arrests are good news?'

'There is a lot of tension in the community since the news came out about Janus preying on vulnerable females. I found a lot of other reports,' Michelle said. 'Though we have not released his name, several people knew Lilly from her posts and connections are being made online. The cyber unit is monitoring the internet for any intelligence and closing down Janus's accounts. However, now there is interest on social media, more people are posting so the raids this morning were reported.'

'I understand people posting about the raids, but how did they connect them to Janus, the arrests and the murders?'

'People are making assumptions. They will expect us to deny it but if we don't, it will support their story.'

'Why didn't you tell me about this?' Johnson demanded.

'You were busy arresting Jonny and the information would not have benefited you. I have found several women who voiced their anger not only at being targeted

194

by Janus, but also by others who preyed on their fear. I have forwarded details of the culprits to make sure there are no further offences. I also found a planned protest over police and CLEA's lack of action. People are angry. They believe we only act when women are killed in a rich neighbourhood.'

'Damn. At the moment, we can only implicate these men in two murders. We have no idea if we can charge them for any other offences – but if we don't, this could get messy,' Johnson said.

'I need you and Eric to really push them on the other murders,' Kerten instructed.

'We'll do our best,' Johnson promised. 'What happened to Janus?'

'The number of victims coming forward makes it our case, not sector's. I've another team assigned to investigate his offences, so don't worry about him. Get me a conviction on these murders.'

∞

Johnson sat in the interview room with Jonny and his solicitor. Jonny met every question about the murders of Lilly and Rose with 'no comment', but Johnson wasn't worried. With the DNA found at the scene and the pictures at his home address, she didn't need him to admit anything.

Everything changed when she started to question him about the other murders: then he started to talk.

He was very vocal about not having committed them. His solicitor tried to silence him, reminding him of the 'no comment' advice. 'Screw that. I didn't do no others! I ain't taking no blame for them,' Jonny said.

Johnson had to hide her smile; he had as good as admitted murdering Rose and Lilly. He had alibis for the times of some of the other murders; he denied committing the rest but said he'd either been home alone or watching TV or gaming with James.

Johnson left the interview feeling frustrated; though she was confident about getting two murder charges, there was no way she would get a charge for the others. She went to Inspector Kerten's office and was waved in. Eric was already there.

'Eric was about to update me on his interview,' Kerten said. 'Are you here for the same thing?'

'Yes, sir.'

Eric went through what had happened. Once the assault team had restrained James, they'd searched his place and found rope and mobile phones believed to belong to Lilly and Rose. Lilly's phone had a series of messages where she'd told James where she worked and arranged to let him into the Edwards' house.

'He made no comment about the murders of Rose and Lilly, but he was adamant he didn't commit the others and gave alibis,' Eric said.

'Did you find any photos?' Johnson asked.

'No, why?'

'I didn't find any rope or a weapon, but there was a wall of photos of Rose and drawings of the symbol. And I had more or less the same experience with Jonny during the interview. I've nothing against him other than Rose and Lilly – and a lot of enquiries to make to prove or disprove his alibis for the other murders.'

'This isn't the result I hoped for,' Kerten sighed. 'Get them charged with Rose and Lilly's murders and remand them in custody. It will give us time to check their alibis. If they are sound, we could be looking at different suspects for all of the murders.'

Chapter 23

MICHELLE EXPLORED EVERY aspect of Jonny and James's lives. She went through their internet searches, accounts and associates to try and find a link between them and other possible suspects. The MO was too unique; they had to know something about who was arranging the killings. The problem was that they weren't talking, other than to deny the other murders, and she couldn't find any links. She had expected something!

She tried the dark net. As she navigated the usual sites, she saw a post from the previous day that made her pause: *Egraxan will soon walk this earth again.*

Her heart sank. She knew that name and now she realised who was behind the murders. Suddenly, the lack of suspects made sense.

Michelle searched for Egraxan's name elsewhere on the dark net but nothing came back; she knew that he wouldn't be pleased his name had been used. Egraxan was a high-level demon who was very good at manipulation; now he was trying to come through to this dimension.

Michelle remembered the user name, @ourlordeggracon from some time ago and realised she had missed the connection. She had checked several times to see if the user had posted anything new but they never had. Now she cursed her own stupidity; demon names were often similar, so she had not considered the possibility that it had been misspelt. The reference to 'lord' instead of 'master' had thrown her; she had thought it was just some fanatic rather than a genuine follower.

Egraxan had been quiet for centuries and she had forgotten about him until now. If he was behind this, there would be no link between the killers. Each one would have fallen under Egraxan's, or one of his demonic servants', influence and they wouldn't be aware of each other.

Egraxan would seek a particular type of person to influence; he couldn't get someone to kill unless that person was already willing to do so. The problem was that the state of society created a big pool of suspects.

How could she direct Johnson and Eric's investigation without telling them that demons existed? She wasn't sure they would believe her.

∞

CLEA have charged two suspects for the murders of Rose and Lilly Yu.
Johnson read the headline. She should have felt some sense of achievement, but they were no further ahead with any of the other murders – and she was sure there would be more.

It didn't take long for the media to start asking about justice for the other victims. Did CLEA only care about crimes against the rich? Rose and Lilly weren't rich, but the public ignored that; they had been killed in one of the few affluent areas in the city, and that was all anyone cared about.

As the media pushed for answers, CLEA released a standard statement: *We are progressing with the investigation. When more information is known, we will make further statements.*

There was nothing else the communications could say, but people were scared and angry and they needed more.

She raised her concerns with Kerten. 'What do you want them to say, Johnson?' he asked. 'We have nothing to tell them.'

He was right, but she knew there would be problems. 'I don't know, just something *more*. I think this will make people even more angry.'

Overnight, the demonstrations outside CLEA head-quarters spread to all the sectors where women had been murdered. People were protesting against violence towards women and wanting to know what the police and CLEA were doing about it.

Johnson and Eric watched the violent clashes with police on TV. They had driven past some of them on the way in. Demonstrators were still blocking the public entrance to the headquarters' building, though they had left the rear access free.

'I don't know what they hope to achieve,' Eric said as he saw a sector officer push back a group of women. 'I get they want to make themselves heard, but this takes resources away from the investigations.'

'They don't think there is any other way to be heard,' Johnson said. 'This has been a long time coming, and I can't blame them. Better turn the TV off for now, we need to get to the remand hearing.'

∞

Michelle was also watching the news and wishing CLEA could do more to reassure people. As distrust for police spread, and the sector police tried to keep order, it simply gave the criminal element more opportunity. But if the demonstrators knew what she knew, it would be even worse.

There was nothing she could do to progress the case for now, so Michelle grabbed her jacket and left a note saying she was going home to get some sleep. She wanted to change and head back to the demonic club; with the unrest and the mention of Egraxan's name, there might be more talk. It might also stop Johnson going on about how Michelle was always at work and never seemed to sleep, so it could be beneficial in two ways.

⊙

Johnson returned from the remand hearing. The protests had closed some roads and it was impossible for her to get home. She was hungry – and Michelle always had food... When she got to the desk, there were a few pastries and a note: *Gone home to sleep, back 7 AM.*

Thank God, she is human after all, Johnson thought as she collapsed on a chair and fell asleep.

⊙

Though Jonny and James pleaded guilty to killing Rose and Lilly at the first hearing a few days later, they denied the other murders and their alibis were verified. The two men were refused bail while they awaited trial.

When Johnson next met Michelle, there was a whiteboard next to the analyst's desk and Michelle was writing a long list of names on it. 'What's this?' she asked.

'Possible suspects,' Michelle explained. 'Because of the timings of the killings, we know there are different people carrying them out. They are like copycat murders.'

'That's ridiculous! How would that even be possible?' Johnson was horrified by the idea of so many names to investigate.

'I do not like the idea of copycats,' Michelle said. 'But we have not released details of the murders and I do not know how they could have been circulated for others to imitate them. I think there is a mastermind we have not identified enrolling different people to commit each murder.'

As Johnson opened her mouth to argue, Michelle continued. 'I know it sounds impossible but think about it. We cannot tie Jonny and James to any of the other killings. We have a mixture of left and right-handed killers. Some take property, some do not. If the MO were not so unique, we would not have seen the deaths as a linked series.' Johnson said nothing. 'Am I wrong?'

'No, I don't think you are,' Johnson said. How the hell would they find a group of killers rather than one serial killer? And where would they look for the mastermind?

Johnson filled Eric in on Michelle's theory when he arrived a short time later 'Okay,' he said. 'Do we have a suspect type?'

'Yes, but the pool is extremely big,' Michelle pointed out. 'Most on this list are wanted by either by us or the sector police. There are several who are linked to crimes. The list will get longer.'

'There's no chance of us investigating all these suspects on our own,' Eric said.

'I'll talk to Kerten,' Johnson responded. 'With the demonstrations and the level of public interest, I'm sure the bosses will give us resources if only to show that we're doing something.' Though she doubted there would be enough resources to investigate all the names.

ထ

'Should I be worried that you're updating me in person and not sending your usual brief email?' Kerten asked when she went into his office.

'Michelle has a theory – but it isn't good.' She explained it to her supervisor.

'I don't want to admit we have seven different murder suspects out there,' Kerten said. 'But you're right – we can't discount it. If we work on that premise, at least we know we'll have covered all lines of enquiry. However, this stays between us, understood? I don't want it leaked to the media, social or otherwise.'

'Of course, but...'

Kerten cut her off. 'I'll do what I can to get extra resources to bring in all the suspects. Although I have faith in Michelle's abilities, I can't base the request on what you've given me because there's so little to support it. However, I'll suggest that a high arrest record will reassure the public. The senior officers and politicians will understand that argument. Get Michelle to prioritise who she thinks we should target first, and I'll let you know if I have any luck.'

☾

Kerten argued successfully with his bosses, and overtime was authorised for officers to arrest the suspects. Michelle identified several people from their criminal history on the internet and dark net who she thought could be involved. Johnson and Eric managed to process the warrants quickly through Kerten, and the suspects were brought in for questioning. Their homes were searched, their computers and other electronic devices seized, but other than them having a disturbing interest in the murders and demons, there was nothing to tie any of them to the deaths.

Crime rates dropped and the cells were full of prisoners, but Johnson, Eric and Michelle still didn't know if they had arrested any of the murderers they were seeking.

☾

'I can't believe we have nothing after two months working this case,' Johnson said. 'And tonight is the new moon.'

'We cannot know for sure how effective the arrests have been,' Michelle pointed out.

'I know, but none of the suspects I've interviewed

screams "murderer".'

'We should never underestimate anyone. At least we can limit potential victims to certain sectors and professions,' Michelle said. 'It will help focus resources.'

'Unless the increase in police and CLEA push the suspects elsewhere,' Johnson said cynically.

'I do not think so. The pentagram and the victims' professions are very important. When Rose changed her routine, they knew where she had gone and followed her there.'

'I know you're convinced about the importance of the pentagram, but I'm not so sure. If someone wants to kill, they'll do so regardless of location.'

'It came from the dark net chats connected to a demonic ritual. I have said this before.' Michelle was frustrated that she couldn't tell them the truth. 'Trust me, there will be a victim in Sector 1 to close the first pentagram. The second pentagram is harder because the murder will be either in Sectors 11 or 12. One of the victims will be a religious leader.'

'What profession will the last victim of the first pentagram be?' Johnson challenged.

'I think it will be someone in law enforcement.' She saw Johnson's reaction. 'You have the mother, the carer, the religious leader, the teacher. The law-enforcer is missing.'

'How sure are you of that? Have we just sent out a female officer to be killed?'

'I doubt it,' Eric stated. 'With so many CLEA agents and sector officers on patrol, when would a killer have a chance?'

'That's true,' Johnson said. 'And women have been warned to keep safe. Those who are not working should be staying inside.'

'Law enforcement could also include security officers

or lawyers,' Michelle pointed out.

'I really didn't want to know that,' Johnson said, frustrated. 'The suspect could still be pushed into another sector.'

'I doubt it. The victim will be killed in the appropriate place.'

'Considering the increased number of patrols, I can't see how the murderer would have that level of control,' Eric said.

'So go back out there and prove me wrong,' Michelle challenged them. She watched them walk out then continued with her work.

A face came up and she paused; it was familiar for some reason. The man didn't have much of a criminal record and he had come back as low-risk. Suddenly she cursed. She looked back at the CCTV images from earlier in the investigation, then she left quickly, hoping her suspicion was wrong.

⚭

Eric and Johnson left to patrol Sector 1, where their headquarters were. Though they could identify the pentagram that was being formed, they struggled with Michelle's idea of its importance; however, it gave them an area to focus on.

They started at the park areas. Eric left his car at the nearest one to their offices, and they walked the rest of the way. They noticed the tents of the homeless people and the movements inside them. After a while, Johnson spoke. 'If Michelle is right, there are plenty of options for a law enforcement victim here.'

'Including you,' Eric pointed out.

'The thought had crossed my mind.'

'I'll have your back,' Eric promised.

'I expect nothing less,' she retorted.

'If I'm at risk of being collateral damage, am I allowed to know your first name? We've worked together for months, and I'm still calling you Johnson.'

'Is it important to you?' Johnson asked after a pause.

Eric thought he might have hit a nerve. 'It's not, but we work together and I don't know your first name. Even your email address is just P. Johnson. If I overstepped the mark, I'm sorry. You don't have to tell me.'

'It's Patty,' Johnson finally admitted. 'But don't ever call me that.'

'What's wrong with it?'

'I grew up in care homes and my name was a joke. "What's your name?" "Patty." "What, Pat Me?" And that's what they did. So I'm Johnson.'

'I'm sorry.' Eric realised there was a lot he didn't know about her, though he should have realised that her childhood had not been ideal when she'd mentioned where she'd lived when the religious riots were taking place. He knew that he wouldn't have got an answer if he'd asked earlier in their partnership.

'Don't be sorry, just never call me Patty or tell anyone.'

With the homeless in the park, the next murder was unlikely to be committed there. They headed back to the car and drove in silence to an area that tried to pass for a park; it was nothing more than a small patch of greenery. As they got out of the car and, they passed the sector police and acknowledged each other.

'What do you want to do next?' Eric asked several hours later. They had visited various open spaces and they were no further forward.

'If Michelle is right, there's no point going into another sector. There isn't the time, and there's too much ground to cover.'

'The murderer could have gone onto private premises.'

'If they've done that again, we have no chance. There

is a neighbourhood in this sector that is nice enough for properties to have gardens, but I want to make sure the main target areas have been covered because I can't think of what else to do,' Johnson admitted.

Eric drove them back to the first park; unlike earlier, it was deadly quiet. 'Am I imagining it, or have all the homeless gone,' he asked.

Unnerved, they both pulled out their guns and shone their torches around. Johnson radioed and requested additional units, then they quietly moved forward.

Something barrelled into Eric just as he heard a gunshot. He stumbled and fell to the floor, his heart pounding. He tried to work out what had knocked him down, but it had moved on. He rolled to his feet, reached for his dropped torch and, with his gun raised, looked for who had fired the shot.

'Assistance needed Sector 1, shots fired,' he called over his radio and gave his co-ordinates. He scanned the area. At first he didn't see anyone other than Johnson; then he looked down and saw a body next to him.

Johnson heard the shot and turned. She was relieved to see Eric standing up, but then her eyes followed his. Someone was lying on the ground, bleeding. She rushed to Eric's side as he knelt down, turned the body over and saw the bullet wound in the woman's chest...

It was Michelle! Where the hell had she come from?

Johnson pulled Michelle's blouse apart to see where the bullet had penetrated, then applied pressure to try and stop the bleeding. Suddenly Michelle's eyes opened. 'I will be okay. Pick up your gun,' she said.

'No, you'll bleed out!'

'I will be alright. You need to pick up your gun. They are coming for you.' Michelle tried to pull Johnson's hands away.

'Eric has us covered.'

'No, that is not good enough – they will kill him to get to you. Leave me and pick up your gun.' As Michelle started to cough, blood came out of her mouth.

'You don't know anyone is coming for me,' Johnson said. 'And anyway, what are you doing here?'

'I worked it out too late. The man you saw at the vigil for Jenny Adamson – he was on the list. I only saw it after you left.'

'Then why didn't you call me?'

'You could not stop it. *I* needed to.'

'That makes no sense. What do you mean?' Johnson asked but she got no reply.

Michelle's breathing was becoming more and more laboured. A voice over the radio said that a local unit was en route. 'You'll be fine. You just need to hold on,' Johnson promised.

'I do not matter here. It is you they want. Pick up your gun,' Michelle gasped.

'No.'

'This is so entertaining,' a new voice said.

Johnson turned her head. A man had appeared, holding a gun – the man she had seen at the vigil. She heard another shot and Eric cried out in pain before he fell to the floor and dropped his gun.

'You really are making this easy for me,' the man said. A second armed man appeared.

Regretfully, Johnson did as Michelle had asked. She stopped applying pressure to her wound and went for her gun, but she was not quick enough. The first man grabbed her and dragged her away from Michelle. Johnson clawed at his hands then she tried to scream, but he put a hand over her mouth.

Eric reached for his gun and started to get up, then shouted with pain as the second man came up behind him and stamped on his hand. 'You won't get away with this. More units are on their way,' he gasped.

'I'll think you'll find that they've been cancelled and we'll be left in peace.' As the stranger spoke, Johnson heard the cancellation request go out over the radio.

'Now it is time for you to die,' the man said to Johnson.

'No!' Eric shouted. He tried to get up again but was knocked back down.

'Don't worry.' The man sounded amused. 'I'll let you watch your friend's sacrifice to our master before we kill you.'

'And Michelle?' Eric tried to look over at her. Her breathing was laboured. She wouldn't live much longer unless she got help, and help wasn't coming.

'I don't care about her. She shouldn't have been here.'

Why *was* Michelle in the park? She was an intelligence analyst, not an agent!

The air around them suddenly became hot, as if a fire had started. That didn't fit, Johnson thought; none of the victims had been burnt.

'My master,' the man holding her said. 'We didn't expect you.' Johnson tried to turn her head to see who he was addressing but she couldn't move.

'I've come to watch the end.' There was something about the voice that sent terror through Johnson and Eric.

'Master, do you want us to make their deaths slow?' The man tightened his hold on Johnson, making her shout out in pain and fear.

'Please. Having made the journey, I want to make the most of this.'

Johnson was pushed to the ground. Her arms were forced above her head and rope tied tightly around her wrists. The men laughed as she tried to fight them.

'We normally do this while the sacrifices are unconscious, but with the master here this is more enjoyable,' her captor whispered in her ear. She tried to turn her head and bite him but failed.

'Your spirit just makes this more fun,' he taunted her as he ripped open her shirt and trailed a knife down her stomach. She tensed, anticipating the pain.

No one noticed when Michelle's laboured breathing stopped; if they had done, they would probably have assumed that she had died.

'Let her go,' a voice rang out. No one stopped what they were doing. 'I said let her GO!'

The man holding Johnson turned to see that a blood-covered Michelle was now standing. A circle of light appeared next to her and she put her arm through it and pulled out what looked like an ornate stick. When she twisted her hand, two blades appeared on either end of it.

They all went still. Michelle should have been dead.

She addressed the master. 'I have to thank you for coming here today. Your arrogance has helped prevent another death.'

'Who are you?' he demanded.

'I am the last of the Nephilim.'

'But you are all dead!' the master declared.

'Not all, and you are not the "master" – you are only a servant. When I have sent you back to hell, tell Egraxan that he will have to deal with me if he persists with his plans.'

Without warning, Michelle ran forward and swung her blades at him and his head fell to the floor with one swift cut. She immediately started to chant strange words and the master's body started to disintegrate.

'What did you do?' the man holding Johnson demanded.

'I sent him back to hell. Let her go or you will follow him.' Michelle brought the blade to his neck. Johnson wrenched herself free and pulled her shirt closed. 'That goes for you too,' Michelle said to the man who was holding Eric.

'No!' He fired at Michelle. Both Eric and Johnson expected her to stagger back from the impact but she didn't, even though there was a clunk as the bullet hit something.

Michelle moved before he could shoot again and thrust one of her blades through his heart. Then she was back in front of the other assailant, who was now grovelling on the floor and begging her not to kill him.

'What the hell?' Johnson asked.

'I am afraid you will have to be inventive when you write this up,' Michelle said. She moved over to Johnson, who flinched away. Michelle pulled back, a resigned look on her face. 'It is okay. Call it in.'

Eric made the call. 'Control, the cancellation was false. Two CLEA agents have been attacked. We have three – no two – suspects.' He got to his feet and moved towards the place where Michelle had cut off the master's head, but there was nothing there. The body had gone.

'Received. Units are being deployed,' the response came.

'Where is the other body?' Eric asked Michelle.

'You will never find him,' she responded.

'Will we get an explanation about what the hell happened here?' Johnson demanded.

'Yes, but I cannot guarantee you will believe me,' Michelle replied. 'You have to trust me to protect you and stop these murders, but for now I need you to say I was never here.' Sirens were approaching, 'I cannot be seen here and you are safe – for now.'

Michelle ran off, leaving Eric and Johnson wondering how they were going to explain what had just happened.

Chapter 24

JOHNSON WATCHED MICHELLE disappear as the first
sector unit arrived. She didn't know what to think about
what she had seen, but she did know that if it hadn't been
for Michelle, she and Eric would be dead.

Her hands were shaking as called Inspector Kerten to
tell him what had happened. Her call went to voicemail
so she left a message asking him to call her back.

When the police arrived, Johnson could barely answer
any questions. She needed time to think of a story that
would be believed, but for now shock and stress were
good reasons for her not responding. She was worried
about what the remaining assailant would say but he
was almost catatonic. He kept muttering, 'Who could
have done that to you, master?'

The sector police called in paramedics and asked for
more units to seal off the scene. Inspector Kerten arrived,
together with Matt and several other CLEA units. Seeing
both Eric and Johnson covered in blood, he ran over to
them. 'I'm sorry, Johnson, I just missed your call. I tried
to call you back.'

She looked at her phone and realised that the battery
had gone flat. 'I'm sorry...' she started.

'No, I didn't mean it as a criticism. How badly are you
both hurt?' Kerten asked.

'I'm fine, sir, just a bit battered and shaken. But Eric
was shot.' Johnson knew that Kerten could see marks on
her wrists.

'I'm fine – a flesh wound only,' Eric reassured the inspector.

'What about the blood on your hands?' Kerten looked at Johnson as she tried to wipe Michelle's blood off them.

'It's mine,' Eric intervened. 'The wound bled a lot to start with.'

Kerten was not convinced that he was hearing the truth, but he didn't press them. 'Did anyone get away? Is there anyone else we should be looking for?'

'No sir, there were just the two of them,' Eric said. Any CCTV would only show those who had arrived by normal methods. He had no idea how Michelle would explain her arrival and departure. He shook his head. Whatever she was, he was sure she'd find a way around it.

'Once Matt has your clothes and whatever swabs he needs, go home,' Kerten ordered. 'Write your reports after you've had a chance to sleep – and write them separately. If either of you needs additional support, my door is always open and I'll do what I can to help.'

∞

Matt took various swabs of Johnson's body, apologising the whole time, but she reassured him that she knew it was necessary and was glad it was him. When he had finished, she was given a change of clothes and taken home; she would give her statement when she'd had the chance to rest.

Walking through her front door, she had no idea how the hell she was going to explain what had happened, but at that moment she did not care. She stripped off her clothes, walked into the shower and felt temporary relief as the water rushed over her.

She scrubbed at her skin, determined that no blood would remain, and stood there until the water turned cold. Wrapping a towel around herself, she went into her bedroom – where Michelle was sitting on her bed.

'How the hell did you get in?' Johnson demanded.

'Easily. You really should improve your home security, especially after what happened tonight. I can help you with that.'

'What?' Johnson looked at her for a moment as if nothing Michelle had said made sense. 'Why are you here?'

'I wanted to see how you are.'

'Alive – though I'm not sure what the hell happened or where you came from.'

'I have a lot to explain, but I did not think that you would believe me until tonight. You still might not.'

'At the moment I don't think there is anything I wouldn't be open to. Though I'm not sure how I'll explain it in my report without sounding crazy.'

'Keep it as close to the truth as you can. Do not mention me or the demon. Say that you were attacked and fought off the two suspects.'

'Really? When forensics come back with your blood all over me? And look at how that man died? Where did that weapon come from?'

'My DNA is not on file and any tests they run on it will be corrupted. You will probably find the lab will admit to an error in processing the sample. As to the weapon, just say that the man's knife was used against him in the fight.'

'Michelle...'

'This evening has been hell, but know that you are safe. I will not let them get to you tonight, and after that it will be too late. I will explain everything to you and Eric tomorrow – but you will have to keep a very open mind.'

The tension in Johnson's body eased. She had not realised that she was still scared that someone would still come after her until Michelle promised she was safe. 'Thank you.'

She sat on her bed. It was the last thing she remembered before exhaustion claimed her.

⚭

When Johnson awoke, Michelle was gone. She dressed and went to work. Checking her phone, Johnson saw a message telling her the Internal Investigations Bureau, or IIB, wanted to talk to her. She cursed; the IIB oversaw all complaints against CLEA and investigated all deaths where an agent was involved.

One of the IIB agents met her as she entered headquarters and led her into a small office. He asked if she had spoken to anyone or made any notes about the incident and Johnson said she had not. Satisfied with her response, he invited her to make her statement, gave her a pen and paper and watched as she wrote. It was an old-fashioned method, but it ensured that they were her words; a statement on a computer could be changed, but a handwritten one was a lot harder to alter.

Johnson tried to be as honest as possible without mentioning the 'master' or Michelle's presence. She said she had got into a fight with the suspect and he'd fallen onto his knife; she had checked the extent of his injury and tried to do first aid, but it was too late. The rest Johnson filled in as best she could. She knew there would be discrepancies with Eric's account but she hoped they wouldn't be too great.

When she'd finished, she expected to be allowed to leave but the IIB agent stopped her. 'Am I under investigation?' Johnson asked.

'Not that I am aware of, but my supervisor wanted to talk to you once your statement had been written and reviewed.'

'How long will this take? I want to know what the man

who was brought in had to say for himself. I assume someone has spoken to him.'

Before the IIB agent could answer, Inspector Kerten and a woman Johnson didn't know entered the room. 'Sir, please, what is going on?' she asked.

'This is Special Agent Singh,' Kerten said. Johnson didn't need a further introduction; Singh was the deputy head of the IIB. 'We need your phone.' Kerten held out his hand and Johnson passed it over.

'An IIB unit is at your home to examine your computer and any other devices you have. It would help if you could tell us where everything is,' Special Agent Singh said.

'I've a laptop, that's all. It should be on the table in the living room. What is this about? I've not been read my rights or told of any allegations against me.'

'We don't know if there is anything yet,' Special Agent Singh said. 'The suspect who attacked you last night was found dead in his cell. We need to ensure that you were not involved.'

'Dead! How?' Johnson was shocked. 'Did he say anything?'

'At the moment, we need to rule out your involvement in the death. Please stay here until we've finished searching your flat.' Singh turned and left. Kerten gave Johnson a reassuring smile and followed her out of the room.

Johnson sat down and hit the desk with her fists in frustration. She had hoped the suspect would open up new leads. How had he died?

⁂

Left alone in the office with nothing to occupy her, Johnson dozed; so many long days and short nights were taking their toll. When she was shaken awake, she was temporarily disoriented and had forgotten where she was.

'It's me,' Inspector Kerten said. 'You're in an office at CLEA headquarters.'

'I'm sorry, sir, I...' She rubbed her eyes and tried to clear her head.

'No need to apologise. I just wanted to let you know that the IIB are satisfied and you can resume your normal duties. Though I do wonder if you need some time off?'

'No, sir. I'm keen to get back to work.'

'Good, I've read both your and Eric's reports, as well as the intelligence from Michelle. It looks like you were the target in the latest murder and had a lucky escape. There was a death recorded in Sector 12 but nothing in Sector 1, other than the attack on you. I was going to reassign the investigation after what happened to you last night.'

'No, sir. Last night has made me even more determined to find out who is behind the murders.'

'Alright. Eric should also be released shortly. Go and catch up with Michelle; she has been working through the evidence and can tell you what has happened during the last thirty-six hours.'

Michelle! Johnson definitely wanted to catch up with her.

∞

As she walked onto the analysts' floor, she saw Michelle sitting at her desk, as if nothing had happened. Johnson grabbed a chair and sat next to her.

'I am glad the IIB has released you,' Michelle said.

'Did you have anything to do with it?'

'The IIB releasing you? No, why would I?'

'No – the suspect's death in the cell,' Johnson whispered angrily.

'Of course not.'

'Sorry, but after the other night, there is no "of course

not" about it.'

'Fair challenge,' Eric joined them before Michelle could reply. '*Did* you have anything to do with it?' he asked.

'No, I promise. When we get out of here, I will explain everything to you about what I am and what happened. For now, we need to talk about the most recent murder.'

'Alright,' Johnson said.

'Seriously?' Eric questioned her.

'After what we saw, do you really want to discuss it here? Where would we go now? We're expected to work the case and it will be noticed if we disappear so we can talk,' Johnson pointed out.

'Fine,' Eric conceded. He turned to Michelle. 'What have you got for us?'

'Both the men who attacked you have never been arrested before. The one who died at the scene has not yet been identified, but dental records have been requested and we should have a result shortly. The man who was brought in was identified by his fingerprints: Trever Yeller. He was suspected of numerous offences, but there was never enough to get an arrest warrant. He was the one that you saw at the vigil.' Michelle brought up the intelligence on him.

'Why was a warrant never authorised?' Eric asked.

'The crimes were low level – anti-social behaviour, criminal damage and assaults. The victims either did not want to know, or the balance of evidence was low. I expect there will be similar information about the other man.'

'Damn. Those investigations will have to be reviewed and passed to IIB or Sector Professional Standards. For now, we need a search warrant for Trever's address,' Johnson said.

'Agents went to his address a few hours ago. They found some disturbing things, similar to those at Jonny's address. I will go into that in more detail when we talk later – I can explain it better then.' Michelle paused as if expecting some response. When Johnson and Eric said nothing; she continued. 'So far, no murder victim has been found in Sector 1. That suggests you were the intended victim, Johnson. I had worried that they would target another law enforcement officer when they failed to kill you, but all female CLEA and sector police have checked in.'

'The suspects were out of action. Why did you think someone else would be targeted?' Eric asked.

'The men needed to finish the ritual. After the deaths completed the pentagram, then it was done. I could not rule out that they had another victim lined up if they failed to kill Johnson.'

'If they had other options, why risk going into the Edwards' home and killing Rose and her sister there instead of finding an easier target?' Johnson asked.

'The Edwards' home was at the correct location. In fact, it was better than the nearest park,' Michelle replied. 'The bad news is that a body was found in Sector 12. Her name was Andi Wallace, and she was a priest.'

'Damn. Does Danny know?' Eric asked, thinking of Jenny Adamson's curate, who had been very vocal about his friend's death.

'Yes, as does her congregation. Andi's death was not the same as Jenny's. While we never found out where Jenny was abducted and could not track the suspects, we believe Andi was taken from her church. There were signs of a struggle in her office, and her body was found in the graveyard.'

'Bloody hell!' Johnson said.

'Parishioners found her when they arrived for morning service,' Michelle said. 'It has been on the news for hours, so I assumed you found out about it after you were released from IIB detention.'

Both Johnson and Eric pulled out their newly returned phones; neither had thought to check the news. Michelle waited while they caught up.

'I knew the murders were twisted, but this is a whole new level,' Johnson said.

'I think the news coverage caused this,' Michelle said. 'Previously, the suspects tried to hide their kills. They were hard to find, hard to link. But once we announced we knew where the next murders would take place, why hide it?'

'This is awful,' Johnson said. 'Murdering her in the graveyard was done to cause fear and disgust, but it's also hit the headlines in a way none of the others did.'

'Are you suggesting we take advantage of this?' Eric asked, horrified.

'I believe the culprits hope to cause more unrest' Michelle said, 'but we could turn this to our advantage.'

'How does it help us?' Johnson asked. 'I can see more information being phoned through, but nothing that would greatly impact on this investigation.'

'I think that has yet to be seen,' Michelle replied. 'For now, Matt is at the scene of Andi's murder with his team. Her body has been removed to the morgue. Agent Knep is talking to her friends. She had no known family. Agent Fellows is observing the autopsy and a team is doing community enquires. We should get their reports soon.'

'I wish they had waited for us,' Johnson said.

'Do not be foolish. Agents were needed at the scene as quickly as possible, and we did not know when you would be released. Even if the bosses were willing, do you think anyone would have sent you to a murder scene when you nearly were a victim?'

'Then why didn't they take me off the case or send me home?'

'Because you still know more than anyone else,' Michelle said. 'If you can cope with it, your knowledge of the case is invaluable.'

'There seem to be a lot more resources than we had before. Do we get to keep them?' Eric asked.

'I doubt it, but I sure as hell want to know what they're doing with our investigation,' Johnson said.

Chapter 25

MICHELLE HAD SENT them files about the most recent murder and they went to the other end of the office to read them. As the end of the day approached, they saw Michelle get up and start to collect her things. 'You're leaving?' Johnson asked.

'My shift has finished. I have spoken to Agents Knep and Fellows and fed their data into my searches. Do you have anything further to add that cannot wait until morning?'

'No,' Johnson said, 'but...' She didn't like to say that she'd never seen Michelle go home before because it would sound absurd.

'Good. If you want to talk about anything, you are more than welcome to see me out,' Michelle said. 'Anything at all.'

'Of course,' Johnson replied. As Michelle walked past them to the door, she grabbed Eric's arm and pulled him after her.

They left the building in silence. Johnson and Eric followed Michelle as she caught a train; they had no idea where she was going, but they knew they needed to be somewhere private for the questions they wanted to ask.

Michelle got off the train and, after a short walk, they arrived at a small apartment. Entering it, Johnson looked around; it was small and basic with very few personal effects.

'Please sit,' Michelle said. 'Can I get you anything to

eat or drink?'

'No, thanks. Where are we?' Eric asked.

'My home. We can talk privately here. I am sure you have questions.'

'That's for sure,' Johnson said. 'I think it best that you explain who you really are and what is going on. I'm sure there is more than you've told us or we even know to ask about. Once you've finished, we'll ask our questions to fill in the gaps.'

'Alright. However, as I said before, you will have to keep an open mind.' Michelle paused and rubbed her hands against her legs nervously. 'I do not know what year I was born or my original name, but I know I am a few thousand years old. I am the daughter of a human female and an angel.'

'What?' Eric and Johnson said together.

'If you want to know everything, please let me talk. I was not the only one of my kind but I was the only female born from such a union and was often called the "runt". My brothers were known as Nephilim and were much stronger than me. For generations, they helped men that were deemed worthy of conquering lands; they overthrew cruel leaders and brought in better ways.

'After a few centuries, my brothers got bored and decided they wanted power for themselves. They rose up against the rulers they had created and took over their lands. When our father realised what they were doing, he came back to earth to stop them. My brothers tried to fight him because they liked their new way of life, but they were quickly slain. I was allowed to survive because I had divorced myself from my family years before and was considered weak.'

'Are you always as strong and quick as you were last night?' Eric asked.

'How did you go from being shot and bleeding out to

being okay? Is it always like that for you?' Johnson asked.

Michelle was surprised that they focused not on what she had just told them about being half angel, but on her physical powers. The truth would take time to sink in.

'My father stripped me of my powers after my siblings' revolt. Although I was weak compared to my brothers, I was still stronger than any human and he did not want me to take advantage of it. Normally I am as vulnerable as you, though I do know most forms of martial arts and some other forms of combat. That bullet to the chest would have killed this body but not me – but you would never have known that. However, my father wanted me to be able to defend myself against non-human threats. My powers return when a demon is present, and any injury quickly heals. The one those men called "master" was a demon.'

Johnson was looking very confused. 'Do you seriously expect us to believe that?' Eric asked.

Michelle took off her top and he looked away, embarrassed. 'How do you explain my lack of injuries?' she demanded.

Johnson's hand reached out to touch where she had seen the wound. 'I saw it,' she said.

'Yes. And if the master had not arrived, this body would have died.'

'This body? Not you?' Johnson asked.

'Did you kill the master?' Eric said at the same time.

'My soul would not have died and I would have moved into a new body. When that happens, I retain memories of my past life and take on all the memories of the body I have taken over. And no, I did not kill the master because I am not allowed to do so – but I can send him back to his own dimension.'

'So he could come back?' Eric asked.

'Yes, but not in your lifetime. I can put – I suppose a

lock is the best way to explain it – on his path in and it will take him generations to get through it. Though the suspects called him "master", he was not "the master". The ritual that is being performed is to bring over a high-level demon called Egraxan. Enchantments were placed long ago to prevent him from crossing back into this earth, but with society becoming more violent and immoral, I believe a crack has been created that allows lower-level demons that serve him to come through and corrupt those who are susceptible to committing murder. Once the ritual is complete, the crack will open wide enough for Egraxan to come through. I might have sent one demon back, but I expect there is at least one more overseeing the second murder team.'

'I'm sure this is an obvious question, but what is the situation now? They failed to kill me last night, so what is next?' Johnson asked.

'It is only a temporary delay. Only one pentagram needs to be completed. They have one more chance next month before having to start again.'

'What will happen if they succeed?'

'There will be hell on earth,' Michelle replied honestly.

'If we manage to stop them next month, can they start a new pentagram?'

'Yes, I would expect them to start a new one on the next new moon.'

'But if it's so important, why haven't they started a new pentagram each month?'

'I do not know for certain. Those who commit the killings really want to do it, otherwise, they would not be swayed. Maybe there are not enough people who are willing and available. Or perhaps Egraxan does not want to draw attention to what is happening so the pentagram can be completed before a connection is made.'

'So now we know about it, the number of killings could

increase,' Johnson said.

'They've been ahead of us the entire time. Is there nothing we can do to stop them?' Eric asked.

'The final victim of the pentagram will be a female law enforcement officer in Sector 11. We can use that knowledge to try and stop them and buy us more time. To finally end it, though, will be difficult. I had hoped that the suspects would have boasted on occult dark net sites, but there has not been anything I could use,' Michelle admitted. 'The murderers may not be communicating with each other at all. After James and Jonny were arrested, I started to suspect that each murder was committed by someone different.'

'You said before that each murder was separate. I just couldn't understand how you had got there,' Eric commented.

'We can release the information into the press...' Michelle started to explain.

'No way. People are scared enough thinking there are two murderers out there without us telling them that there are eight,' Eric objected.

'Nine, if you included the attack last night,' Michelle corrected.

'Why do you think releasing this information would be helpful?' Johnson asked.

'Egraxan can influence others, and lower-level demons can cross over due to our society's disintegration. Egraxan can wield his power through them. So far his control has been over those disposed to violence so there are limitations on who he can use. I think we can restrict that even further.'

'How do you mean?'

'We build a sense of community, of goodwill. We turn fear into support for each other.'

'Seriously? How would that help?' Johnson demanded.

Her experience had not taught her to have faith.

'I read the transcripts of all the suspects you interviewed. Many were horrified about the allegations that they were the killers. Even though they had committed serious crimes, they were still revolted by the ritual murders.'

'So?'

'That suggests that although things have become bad, we are not beyond redemption. We need to get people to unite, get communities working together. If we can drive people together, we could close the crack that Egraxan is exploiting and stop further pentagrams from starting.'

'But we can't stop the current one?' Johnson asked.

'No, it is too late for that. The demon is already here. Goodwill and community are not built overnight and they are unlikely to stop another killing next month. But if we do not do this, it will not stop until Egraxan succeeds.'

'So even if this plan works, we could be looking at months of murders?'

'Unfortunately yes. But now we know who we are dealing with, it will help us locate possible suspects.'

'I honestly don't know if I can get my head around what you've told me,' Johnson admitted. 'If you had said all this before, I would have thought you mad – but I saw you shot, heal and fight. I can't make sense of it.'

'I know...' Michelle started to say.

'No, I don't think you do. Thank you for trusting us, but it will take me time to process this.' Johnson stood up and left.

Growing up where Johnson had, demons and hell had been an important part of her childhood, with threats of going to hell if she was naughty. She had never believed in any of it; she believed in what she could see and touch. But what she had seen undermined those beliefs.

Getting into her flat, she logged onto her laptop and searched for information about demons. Were the articles accurate? Or was the real thing worse?

⚭

The next day neither Eric nor Johnson wanted to discuss Michelle's revelations but they agreed there would be nothing lost in trying to build a stronger community as Michelle had suggested. They decided to start with Danny, since he had been working hard to unite people after Reverend Adamson's death.

Arriving at his church, they were surprised by how many people were present. There was a definite sense of togetherness and support. Maybe Michelle was onto something, Johnson thought.

'Can I help you?' a young man approached them and asked.

'We're looking for Danny Jones. Is he here?' Eric asked, showing his badge.

'Of course. Follow me.' He led them through the church towards the office at the back. Danny was surrounded by a lot of people; he looked up and acknowledged them but didn't leave. Eric and Johnson knew he would join them shortly.

They were shown into the same office as before and it was not long before Danny joined them, eager for information. 'Do you have any more news about Jenny's murder? I've seen the news about the other victims – I know about Andi Wallace. Knowing what happened here, her congregation contacted me for support.'

'We have information, but we've not been asked not to release it yet,' Johnson said.

Danny was silent for a moment before he understood the double negative. 'Meaning you don't think your supervisors would approve of you telling me, but you haven't specifically been told not to? I'll be discreet, I promise.'

'I was targeted as one of the victims the other night,' Johnson said, 'I was lucky. Unfortunately my attackers were not, so we can't interrogate them.'

'I'm so sorry,' Danny started.

Johnson held up her hand to stop him. 'We think we've identified a pattern to the murders.' She explained the pentagram theory, who the last victim would be and her concerns over another pentagram starting.

'I didn't expect that much information,' Danny said. 'Why are you telling me all of this? And the pentagrams – what can I tell people about those?'

'If you plot the murders on a map, you can see the pattern. I've checked social media and the news and the information is already out there, so you could have pieced it together yourself. We want you to release some of these details and get people looking out for each other. Though Jenny was much loved and your congregation has come together stronger than ever, many of the victims had no one who cared when they went missing. Use the information we give you to try and get people to look after each other. Show them how to do it.'

'Of course, I'm more than happy to try – but won't it get you into trouble?'

'Only if you say where you got the information from,' Johnson replied. 'I've just helped you join the dots on information that's already in the public domain. Here are some websites that you might want to look at.' She handed over a list of URLs that Michelle had collated.

'Why do you think I can help you? Why not approach the media?'

'We thought about it, but the newspapers are more interested in what will sell copies,' Johnson said. The previous attempt to use them to circulate information had increased fear in the community, the opposite of what they wanted. 'We thought, with what you have achieved here, people would listen to you.'

'I can't reach as many people as the media can.'

'Not at first, but in time you will. Many people out there pay more attention to social media than the news and we have an analyst who can show you how to get a wider audience,' Eric said. 'Will you help?'

'Of course, if it will stop these atrocities.'

Chapter 26

MICHELLE PACKED UP her things. Johnson and Eric had finished for the day some time earlier. Since she had explained what she was, their behaviour towards her had changed. Gone was the easy banter and the regular drop-ins at her desk; now they just called in for information. She couldn't blame them – it was a lot for them to accept – but it saddened her because she had started to enjoy their company. Such was her curse, she had to spend too much time alone.

As she left the building and walked down the road, Michelle saw a shadow break away and follow her. It was human, she knew that. She turned down the next road, one that wouldn't lead to the train station, to see if the shadow followed her and cursed as it did. She had expected something to happen after she'd prevented Johnson's murder. There weren't many who could send a demon back to hell and she would have attracted Egraxan's attention.

As the shadow closed in, Michelle guessed this was it. She just hoped whoever took over her work didn't mess it up. She pulled out her phone and called Johnson; there was nothing Johnson could do, but Michelle wanted to be found as quickly as possible so there might still be a chance of her assisting in the investigation.

'Michelle, have you found out something significant?' Johnson asked as she answered the phone.

'I have just left headquarters. I am being followed. I

turned down... Aaghhh.'

Michelle dropped the phone as the knife slid into her back. She fell to her knees, expecting that to be the end of it. Such an injury would probably leave her paralysed from the waist down. She would never walk again.

Then the knife was pulled out and drawn across her throat. Idiots – they were killing her. She had not expected that! As she felt her blood run down her body, and knowing there was no hope of survival, she smiled.

∞

Johnson had almost ignored Michelle's call; she'd been trying to avoid her since Michelle had explained what she was.

When she was growing up in a church orphanage, Johnson had been taught about angels and demons. She had believed in them until the religious riots, then later she had lost her faith. She didn't know what to think now. Had she been wrong to turn her back on the church?

She felt guilty that she couldn't talk to Michelle because that would mean she accepted what Michelle had told her, then again, she had seen the evidence when Michelle saved her. Johnson had never witnessed anything like it...

Hating her jumbled thoughts, she answered the phone; Michelle wouldn't be calling at the end of the day if it wasn't important. Her heart sank when she heard what Michelle had to say, then it sounded like the phone was dropped. There was a gurgling noise and the line went quiet.

She had to hang up to ring the control room and get a unit sent to where she thought Michelle might be. At that time of night there would be no agents in CLEA headquarters – they would all be deployed on operations or at home like her – so she called the sector police.

Logging onto her laptop while she waited for the call

to be answered, she sent messages to Eric and Inspector Kerten, then pulled up a map of the area. She knew the route Michelle took home, and the train station was only a short walk from headquarters. There were only three side roads she could have taken.

Eric responded to her message, saying he was heading back to headquarters; she gave him the road names where she thought Michelle might be.

'Sector control, how can I direct your call?' Finally!

'I am Agent Johnson with CLEA. My analyst, Michelle, has been attacked between our headquarters in Sector 1 and the train station. I believe she tried to lose her attacker by going down a side road. I've lost contact with her.'

'We will send the next available unit. Do you have any information that can assist?'

'No. I was on the phone with her when she said she was being followed. I heard her shout then I lost contact.'

'Thank you. Should you have any further information, please call us back and quote reference 200156.' Control terminated the call.

Frustrated, Johnson headed out to where Michelle might be.

∞

When she arrived at the crime scene, Eric and Inspector Kerten were already there. 'Is it Michelle?' she asked as she approached them.

'Yes. She was stabbed in the back and then her throat was cut. You said you were on the phone with her when she was attacked,' Inspector Kerten said.

'She said she was being followed then stopped talking to me. I had to hang up to call control for help.'

'I wasn't asking to criticise you, Johnson. I'm asking because no phone was found on her. The sector police are saying it was a robbery gone wrong.'

'You don't believe that?' she asked, horrified.

'I don't. It was a clean kill. Michelle could easily have been targeted and then her property stolen to make it look like a robbery – although we can't rule out that it was just a very efficient robber.' As Johnson started to protest, Kerten stopped her. 'I've said I don't think it was, but this is Michelle, and we have to explore all avenues to be sure. She was working exclusively on the serial killing case. Do you think she took any material home with her?'

'No. She worked long hours in the office and sometimes slept there. I can't believe she'd take work home,' Johnson defended her.

'Eric said the same thing. We need to assume she was targeted because of her work – but how did anyone know what she was working on? Go through her computers, call in another analyst if you need to, and let me know if any of her enquiries could have led to this. But be aware that IIB will have to be informed.'

'Michelle didn't talk to members of the public – she gave us details of those we needed to approach,' Johnson said, trying to think of who Michelle might have communicated with.

'Even online? I gave her the authority to interact on social media and the dark net where she needed to identify who owned profiles.'

'Of course.' Johnson had forgotten about that. 'I wouldn't know how to get access to her computer,' she admitted.

'All analysts have to register their online profiles and passwords and I can tell you where they are recorded. Be careful. IIB will track everything you do, so make sure you can justify everything. If you find anything Michelle did that was inappropriate, you must report it.'

'Yes, sir,' Johnson said.

'Michelle was our best analyst, and I know you both got close to her during this case. I'll make sure CLEA do their best to find out who did this,' Inspector Kerten said before walking over to a senior sector officer who had just arrived.

'I can't believe this,' Johnson whispered to Eric. 'How can she be dead when she can do what she can do?'

'We need to discuss it elsewhere,' Eric replied. 'Officer,' he called to one of the sector police, 'do you need us for anything else or are we free to leave?' When they were waved off, Eric took Johnson's arm and pulled her towards headquarters.

'My car!' Johnson protested.

'Don't worry about it now.'

Johnson allowed herself to be dragged into head-quarters. She expected Eric to take her to Michelle's desk, but he led her to the canteen and sat her at a table in the corner. 'I can't believe she's dead; I thought...' Johnson started.

'Only when a...' Eric looked around, checking to see if anyone was near enough to hear '...demon is near.'

'I know.' Johnson took his hand. 'I don't think she died because of what she found as an analyst. I think it was payback for saving me.'

'Possibly. She said her soul moved into another body but she didn't say how. For all we know, she's a newborn baby.'

'Yeah. I wish we had clarity on that one,' Johnson agreed.

'We have to assume she isn't coming back into our lives and go through everything she was working on to see if there's anything she didn't tell us about.'

'She saved my life and I was rude to her. I blanked her.'

'So did I, but we can't think about that now. If they went

after Michelle, we could be next – and unlike her, we won't be coming back. We need to find out who did this.'

Chapter 27

Michelle hurt. She was lying on a hard cold surface and the first thought that went through her mind was, 'Please do not let me be in a morgue.'

As she became more aware of her surroundings, she felt rain on her face and heard people shouting. She didn't know where she was or what had happened, but she definitely wasn't in a morgue. She tried to sit up and wondered how many bones were broken as she felt them grind together.

'Sweety, please don't try to move,' said a lady she'd never seen before who tried to push her back down. She looked scared.

Michelle allowed the woman to ease her back down and looked around. She was lying on the road next to a car. A man was arguing with the crowd. Whoever's body she had taken over had just been killed in a road traffic accident. From what she could see of the car, she guessed she had been hit front on. The driver couldn't leave without driving over her and it sounded as if the crowd were stopping him from running off. Good for them.

Michelle lay back and closed her eyes. No, not Michelle anymore; she must stop thinking about that identity. She always felt disorientated when one life ended and another started. Her death had been quick, which had surprised her. She had known that she would be targeted because of her actions, but she'd expected to be kidnapped, tortured and left in a coma. She wondered what the people who attacked her had been told, or what the demon knew about her. It had been a very long time –a few hundred years – since she'd been involved with demons.

'Aisha, we have called for help. You'll be alright,' the woman said.

Aisha: so that was her name now. She opened her eyes. The woman was starting to look familiar and was obviously her mother. The memories from this new body would filter through during the next few hours. For any lapses now, she could easily blame the shock of the accident. 'I am alright, Mother, just sore.'

'I'm sure you will be.'

The old Aisha would have died instantly when she was hit by the car. As Michelle took over her body, most of the injuries had healed though she still had a few. She just hoped they wouldn't stop her getting back to Eric and Johnson.

∞

Johnson and Eric wanted to go to Michelle's home to see if there was anything that could help find her, or anything personal they could keep safe for her. They hoped they would see her again. When they approached Kerten to ask permission, he tried to dissuade them. The sector police would go there soon enough.

'Whoever did this has her house keys and possibly her address,' Johnson said. 'Don't you think they might be tempted to see if there's anything to steal? And she may have made notes at home that are relevant to the case.'

'You know where she lived?' Kerten asked. Johnson nodded. 'Fine, go – but tell the sector police and let them know about anything you find.'

They took Eric's car. 'Do you think there'll be anything

there?' he asked.

'I don't know, but I can't stand the thought that the murderers might go there,' Johnson said. 'And there may be something that will give us some answers.'

'I think she's too clever to have left anything at home, though she must have some place somewhere so she doesn't lose everything every time she dies.'

'God, what an awful thing to always have to think of.'

⊕

Arriving at Michelle's flat, they were reassured that it was in darkness and the front door and windows were secure. 'That's a good sign. Now we're here, have you any idea how to get in?' Eric asked.

'Her security is very lax – no security bars – so I am thinking about going old school.' Johnson pulled out her baton and patted his arm with it. 'I just hope Michelle doesn't have any crazy security we don't know about. I didn't recall seeing anything the other day, so I'm hoping she hasn't any nasty surprises for us.' Going up to the door, Johnson tried the handle to make sure it was locked then smashed the window next to it and reached in to unlock it.

'I confess I didn't look,' Eric said as Johnson opened the door.

'It was a habit I got into when I was in the sector police, from the time I went to take witness statements and realised that I had to get out quickly or be killed.'

'I didn't know you were sector?'

'I did five years in Sector 16 before joining CLEA,' Johnson said.

The living room appeared more barren than before. The computer on the small table by a wall was the only indication that Michelle had ever lived there.

'I'll see if I can log on. Do you want to check the rest of

the flat?' Eric asked.

Johnson investigated the other rooms. The kitchen was spotless, the cupboards and fridge practically empty. The bathroom was the same – nothing personal, only the absolute necessities. She left the bedroom, a person's most intimate space, until last. She paused as she went to open the door, wondering if here she would find out something more about her friend.

The room was as stark as the others and it looked unused. Johnson opened the wardrobe door and saw a number of similar-looking outfits. Did Michelle not care what she wore, or did she wear the same clothes to disguise how rarely she went home?

Searching the rooms depressed Johnson. Michelle seemed to have no life other than her work, and she had deliberately avoided connecting with anyone. Is that what happened when you lived for such a long time? Did you divorce yourself from everything but work?

Johnson went to see how Eric was doing. To her surprise, he had gained access to Michelle's computer. 'You were able to get past her encryption?'

'She didn't even have a password,' Eric said. 'I've been looking through her files and there's very little here. It's an old computer – I think she had it just to manage bills and place orders.'

'Even so, I'd have expected some security to keep her shopping and banking accounts safe.'

'Those are secure. I guess she didn't bother because there was nothing to hide. What about you?'

'Nothing. I've never seen someone live so basically,' Johnson said.

'We only just learnt what she was; we have no idea how that impacts her existence. I imagine she wouldn't leave behind anything that would give her away.'

'I get leaving behind old lives, old memories, but she

has nothing for this life. It's as if she rented this flat for the weekend and nothing more.'

'Maybe she does have somewhere else, somewhere she knows won't be found,' Eric said.

'If she does, there is no evidence of it here. But I think you're right; she pulled that weapon out of somewhere.'

'Weapon?' Eric asked, confused.

'In the fight, when she became something else, her hand disappeared and came back with the blade that she used to kill the master and my attacker.'

'I thought I imagined that,' Eric said.

'So did I, at the time, but where else did it come from?'

Eric was saved from having to answer by a knock on the door and a tentative 'hello?'. Someone poked their head around the door. 'Hi, can we help you?' Johnson asked.

'I live next door. You aren't Michelle and you don't look like burglars – I was just checking that everything was okay.'

'I'm Agent Johnson from CLEA and this is my colleague, Agent Badu.' She showed her badge.

'Pat Me,' the neighbour said.

'What did you say? Where did you hear that from?' Johnson snapped.

'Michelle said if an Agent Johnson came around I should say "Pat Me" and she'd get really angry. Anyone else would think what I said was weird.'

'Why would she tell you to say that?'

'She said ID can be faked and that was a really personal detail. And she showed me a picture of you to make sure I said it to the right person. She said that soon there would be a day when she didn't come back and the CLEA and sector police would come around. She would be okay but wouldn't be contactable. She had a package for you – she said you'd come here and I should look out for you.'

'What package?' Johnson asked.

'Give me a minute.' The neighbour disappeared. Johnson and Eric glanced at each other, confused. She returned a moment later with a large case. Johnson took it and saw a pad with a small red light over the flap that fastened it.

'Michelle said it needs a right thumbprint or the contents will be lost,' the neighbour said.

Johnson placed her right thumb on the pad and the red light turned green. She opened the case and saw a laptop and notebooks. 'Thank you. We'll go once we've secured Michelle's flat.'

'Don't worry about that small window, I can fix it for you.' She disappeared for a moment and came back with a piece of wood, screws and a drill. 'Around here, it's always easiest if you can fix breaks yourself.'

Chapter 28

Once Michelle's flat was secured, Johnson and Eric called in what they had discovered in the property to the sector police but didn't mention anything about the case.

'You going to tell Inspector Kerten about it?' Eric asked as they climbed into the car.

'Not until I've looked at it. It's 2am, and we've already been told that we haven't got Michelle's murder to investigate. I just want to go home, have a lot of coffee and takeout, and look at what Michelle has left me. You can either drop me back at headquarters so I can pick up my car, or you can come back to my place and join me. Though there is only a sofa for you to crash on,' Johnson warned.

'Coffee and takeout are good.'

'Great. I'll start looking at the food options while you drive.'

Back at Johnson's flat they listened out for the pizza they had ordered, then sat down together and opened the case. Pulling out the laptop, they saw it was much newer than the one in Michelle's flat – and it was password protected.

'Any ideas?' Eric asked.

'Maybe.' Johnson took it and typed in a password. Access was granted.

'How did you know what it was?' Eric asked, surprised.

'I don't know how she knew I used to be mocked with "Pat Me" because I never told her that. She could have given the neighbour other information to identify me with, so I thought it must be important. The password was the person who first taunted me with that name.'

They were glad they weren't in the office as they looked through the information; they could understand why Michelle didn't want anyone else to see it. It documented how she knew about the pentagrams, the relevance of the chosen victims and what would happen if a pentagram was completed. It was clear how Michelle had tried to feed the information into the investigation as best she could. The only thing that was not documented, and would raise questions, was how she'd know to look for this pattern.

'She knew more than she let on,' Johnson said.

'I know. I'm surprised at how much she worked into the investigation. She really relied on us not knowing her identity. How can we explain the rest of this?'

'We can't, without explaining that she's a Nephilim.'

'Okay, but no one is going to accept that.'

'We need to keep this between ourselves.' Johnson watched as Eric navigated the files, 'I'm surprised that she has it all on here.'

'I guess she wanted a record somewhere, just in case,' Eric said. 'But this isn't a secure laptop. It doesn't have the encryption our CLEA ones have.'

'I wouldn't be so sure. I've tried to link it to my internet and it won't. I think Michelle has disabled it somehow, so I guess it can't be hacked. Also, Michelle knows her way around IT. I bet she had her own security measures if someone tried something.'

'Let me see.' Eric took the laptop and tried to connect it to the internet.

'Seriously?' Johnson said.

'Sorry, I've never seen that before,' he apologised and handed it back.

'There was the failsafe with the thumbprint. If I got the password wrong, I bet the laptop would have corrupted. Michelle wanted to pass information to me and nobody else.'

'What can we do with this intelligence? We can explain some of it, as she did, but the demon aspect has to stay between us,' Eric said.

'I agree. But Michelle knew where to search for information. It won't be so easy for us – we don't have her skills to complete the research and we can't give this to her replacement.'

'What about this bit where she was looking at various demonic groups? It looks like she visited a few clubs, though nothing came of it. Do you think we can get some more undercovers to follow it up?'

Johnson read the information, which included locations and passwords to get into the clubs. 'I can't see it hurting, but she seemed to think that generally the clubs were against the murders because they brought unwanted attention.'

'Maybe we can be more forward and ask them outright,' Eric said. 'She made the connections with the pentagrams and the professions of the victims. Now we need to use this for the questions we ask and find information to support what Michelle already knew.'

�co

Eric and Johnson travelled in together the next day. The crime scene barriers had been removed and there was no visible evidence of what had occurred last night. It was as if it had never happened.

Neither of them had had much sleep. Eric had been glad of the overnight bag he kept in the back of his car so he was presentable after having a few hours' sleep on Johnson's sofa.

They went into the CLEA headquarters to Michelle's desk. A different analyst was already there, going through the information she had left behind. It felt as if they had been punched in the gut that she had been replaced so quickly.

'Hi, who are you?' Eric asked.

'I'm Philip. I've been asked to take over Michelle's work on the serial killers. You must be Agents Badu and Johnson.'

'Yes. Did you know Michelle?' Johnson challenged.

'I knew who she was, but she kept very much to herself. I understand she worked closely with you over the last few months. I'm sorry for your loss.'

'Thank you. Is there anything we can do to get you up to speed?' Eric asked.

'No, she left an excellent handover and has categorised everything efficiently. It shouldn't take me long to go through it all. Inspector Kerten wanted to talk to you when you got in. He asked me to tell you to find him in his office.'

'Thanks. We'll come back later.' Johnson turned around and walked off.

'Sorry, she's not taking Michelle's death well,' Eric apologised before following her.

'Is it me, or is it strange to see Michelle replaced so quickly?' Johnson fumed as Eric caught up with her.

'They need someone to finish her work – the murders aren't going to just stop,' Eric reasoned.

Kerten's door was propped open. As they entered, they saw he was wearing the same clothes as the previous night when they'd met him at the crime scene; it looked like he had not been home. 'How are you both doing?' he asked.

'We want to find out what happened to Michelle,' Eric said.

'I've claimed jurisdiction on the investigation, but I've handed it to Agents Knep and Fellows to progress. No, don't start,' he said as Johnson went to argue. 'I know she was your friend, but you have the serial killer case. The only reason I didn't take you off that after you were attacked is because it would take too long for other agents to get up to speed.'

'You aren't going down the robbery gone wrong route, are you?' Johnson asked.

'As I said last night, I don't believe it – though it's the motive the sector police are working to. That's why I was so keen to take it on as a CLEA case.'

'Thank you, sir. I worry that this case made Michelle a target. She was able to give defined locations for the attacks,' Johnson said.

'I appreciate your concerns, but unless there was a leak in the department, how would the killer have known she was the lead analyst on the case? You and Eric have been out there asking a lot of questions and your names are known, but Michelle's activities were more discreet. Unless something comes up on the internet or dark net, it will be hard to make that connection – though I'm not ruling it out.'

'Sir,' Johnson started.

'Don't. I know what she fed into this investigation but I'm not prepared to assume that it was the only reason she was targeted.' When Johnson remained silent, he continued, 'A new analyst has been assigned to the case.'

'We've met,' Johnson said.

'Good. Philip has a very good track record in linked series of deaths. Please work with him. He has a difficult job taking over so don't make it harder.' Kerten looked pointedly at Johnson.

'No, sir.'

Chapter 29

It was two nights before the new moon. No matter who Johnson, Eric or anyone else in CLEA brought in for questioning, the people they interviewed all denied knowledge of the murders. The agents were struggling to get ahead of the case –there were too many criminals out there.

They invited the organisers of the demonic clubs to come in. Michelle had not found any links by going to them, so Johnson and Eric agreed that undercover would have even less success. They hoped that an upfront approach might lead to a different result. The club bosses gave details of men who were 'too into it' and had been barred, but that led nowhere. One was the guy that had attacked Michelle, but she had already ruled him out weeks earlier.

The investigation into the murder of Andi Wallace had given them no DNA, no fingerprints and no leads.

They targeted any criminals they had grounds to arrest in the hope of preventing further killings. A bonus was that the residents were reassured by the increased number of arrests that law enforcement was doing its best to protect the female population.

'I can't believe we are in the same position as last month,' Eric complained to Johnson.

'I know. The intelligence that's come in has been amazing, but it's not leading to the right people. Part of me hoped that Michelle would show up. I wish I'd asked more about what happened... She said the body would die, but I didn't believe it for some reason,' Johnson said.

'She could be anywhere, in a body of any age. If she could have found a way to return or reach out, she'd have done so.'

'I think she would have come to us by now if she could. We need to follow what she left us and assume we won't see or hear from her again.'

⋒

Johnson and Eric kept in regular contact with Danny. He had reached out to Andi Wallace's congregation to offer spiritual support and guidance.

People were quick to follow him. Having supporters in both Sectors 15 and 12 Danny started there first, then linked with other churches in surrounding sectors. The speed at which he worked was surprising. People were looking for someone to follow, to give them purpose and hope, and Danny had a message they could get behind.

Other religious leaders took heart from his success and started to build on the sense of community. Churches, synagogues and mosques recorded increased numbers of people attending and reached out to vulnerable or isolated people. Many were not interested in joining a religious community but were happy to stay in contact so they had somewhere to go if they were in need.

Danny started separate support networks for those who didn't want anything to do with the church; some were location-based, but others were for people in similar circumstances so they could help each other without outside interference.

At the start, Danny's work supported what CLEA was trying to achieve as people came forward to report illegal behaviour; soon, that spread to other organisations. Johnson hoped it would help seal the crack Michelle had talked about. Even if it didn't, it was bringing in the biggest conviction rate ever.

∞

Johnson and Eric left headquarters and went back to her apartment. It had become a regular habit after Michelle died; they wanted to review new developments against the information Michelle had left, and they didn't want to do it where others could overhear.

As they got out of the car, there was the sound of a shot and the window next to Eric shattered. He ducked down behind the car door. 'You okay?' Johnson shouted, taking cover and pulling out her gun.

'Yeah. Do you have eyes on the shooter?'

'No, I can't see anything. You?'

'No. I'm going to move to the front of the car behind the engine block.' As Eric started to move, another shot rang out; this one went through the car door and hit his arm. He bit down on shouting out in pain and moved to the front of the car.

Johnson met him there. 'Are you alright?' she asked.

'I think so. It clipped me in the same bloody area as before.'

'Come out. You can't hide,' a voice shouted.

They didn't respond to the taunt. Being off duty, neither of them had their radios. Johnson pulled out her phone and cursed under her breath when she saw there was no signal.

She inched forward until she was next to Eric then put down her gun. She ripped a sleeve off her suit jacket and tied it around his wound to stop the bleeding. Picking up her gun again, she looked over the car roof to see if she could spot the suspect. There was nothing. 'I don't like it. Where is the shooter?' she asked.

'I'm here.' They turned to see a man dressed in black,

his face covered, pointing a gun at them. They expected him to fire, but suddenly his head twisted to the side and he fell to the floor, dead.

'Are you alright?' A young girl was standing in front of them.

'Who are you?' Johnson demanded.

'You would have known me as Michelle, Pat Me,' the girl said. 'There is no threat now. Do you want to go into your apartment and I can explain?'

If the term 'Pat Me' had not reassured them that this was Michelle in another body, the girl's incredibly precise language would have done.

⊙

Johnson wasn't sure how they got inside her flat, where the girl started patching up Eric's arm. All she knew was that this person had saved them and knew something about Michelle – or was *she* Michelle?

As the shock wore off, Johnson wondered why she let this stranger into her home. 'Who are you?' she asked as the girl neatly tied the bandage on Eric's arm.

'Do you remember a month ago, when I was Michelle, I told you my soul would go into another body when I died and then I would live that life? When Michelle was murdered, my soul went into *this* body.'

'I don't understand. Are you saying you are Michelle?' Johnson asked. 'And if you are, how do I know that?'

'Really, Pat Me? I left you my laptop. Do you not trust me?'

'Explain how this works. You said you came back but not *how*. Are you still Michelle, or someone else?' Johnson demanded.

'When I die, my soul goes into a body that has just died. It is always female and a pre-teen. I think my father thought he was doing me a favour when he set that as a rule. I appreciated it at first, but now it is a nuisance.'

'Why?' Johnson asked at the random disclosure.

'Would you want to go through puberty every fifty years? It gets frustrating. I do not know what men go through, but at least that would be a bit of variety. Even better would be going into a slightly older body. However, it is how it is. Anyway, I digress; where my soul moves to can wait. When I stopped you from being murdered, Johnson, I knew that they would come after me.'

'Why didn't you tell us?'

'I did not know how much more information you could accept. I put precautions in place so you would get what you needed. I did not expect to be killed, though, which is their error.'

'Why?' Eric asked.

'Because I came back. If they had kidnapped me or placed me in a coma, they could have ensured I was no longer involved.'

'Maybe they'll think you're not a threat because of your age? No offence, but you look about ten,' Eric pointed out.

'I was twelve yesterday, thank you very much. But this body does not matter. It is frail, as yours are frail and as Michelle's was frail. It is what happens when I become Nephilim that is important. Then my body becomes irrelevant.'

'How were you able to kill that guy so efficiently?' Johnson asked.

'I retain all the memories from my different lives. I spent hundreds of years learning to fight and putting it into practice.'

'Does that mean you remember what we were working on?'

'Of course. Why else do you think I am here? I take it you got my laptop?' When they nodded, she continued,

'Was it helpful?'

'Yes,' Johnson replied. 'But first, why did it take you so long to come back? Was it a coincidence that you arrived when we needed you most?'

'The body I moved into was killed in a traffic accident, though to onlookers it only looked as if I had been injured. It took time for the wounds to heal. My mother is very protective of me at the moment, so trying to sneak out proved interesting. Also, my memories of the old life are competing with the new, which is difficult to manage,' she admitted. 'Now, tell me what has been happening.'

'Danny has been doing a great job in the community, and we've brought in a lot of criminals, but nothing has led us to who is behind this. We need you,' Johnson admitted.

'No, you do not. You will not find the demon behind it and neither could I. All we can do is to identify and disrupt those that the demon uses in order to stop the next murder.'

'I can't say I understand all of this, but it is good to have you back,' Johnson said. 'What should we call you now? I'm guessing you're not Michelle anymore.'

'Call me Aisha.'

Chapter 30

'WE NEED TO protect those who are most likely to be victims,' Johnson argued.

'So all law-enforcement females,' Inspector Kerten stated.

'We appreciate it's a huge ask. If the murders had all happened in public parks then it could be managed, but they've also taken place in private gardens. How can we protect all potential victims?' Eric asked.

'We post the females with male officers to ensure their safety,' Kerten offered.

'That might not be enough to protect them,' Johnson argued.

'It was enough for you,' Inspector Kerten retorted.

Johnson had to hold her tongue; she couldn't explain how close she had come to dying because she couldn't explain what Michelle had done. 'I got lucky, really lucky. I'm just worried that someone else might not be.'

'I understand your concerns, but even if I could convince the sector police chief, how can we guarantee that the murderer won't find their victim?'

Johnson had to admit Kerten had a fair point. 'I don't know.'

'I don't want another death any more than you do,' Kerten said. 'Believe me, CLEA and the sector will be working together to do our best to prevent it.'

But Johnson wasn't convinced. They had spent a month arresting everyone they could for any reason; it was the only tactic they had left but it wasn't enough.

Aisha hadn't been able to pinpoint any potential suspects for the next murder. 'The demon uses different murderers each time,' she had said 'The way Egraxan works means that he can exploit anyone who has violent leanings. I can help you with the possible location and to identify who might be a victim, but not who the killers will be.'

'Can't you do *anything*? Haven't you other ways to find out information?' Eric asked.

'No. Unless a demon is near me, I am just as human as you are. On the upside, I will know about it if one approaches me.'

'Do you have any way to find Egraxan or the people he is using?'

'Not unless they use a platform that I can monitor. I check what I can for information, but no one is commenting.'

'Can your father help?'

Aisha laughed. 'I have not spoken to him since he killed my brothers. He would not get involved with this.'

'Why not? Isn't it worth asking?'

'No. There is a balance between heaven and hell. If I contacted him and he got involved, the other side would escalate its attacks. Trust me, you do not want that.'

They tried to understand, but it was clear that this was a very different level of diplomacy and one they didn't want to get involved in. Aisha gave them her mobile number and said she would respond when she could, but she reminded them that she was a schoolgirl now and phones weren't allowed in class.

'We could talk to the school...' Johnson started to say before she realised it was a stupid suggestion. What could they say that could make any sense? Aisha laughed and promised to meet them at the next new moon.

⚭

Johnson sat with Eric at sunset on the night of the new moon. All female law enforcement officers had been paired with two male officers, and none had been given the day off. Many of the women complained that they could defend themselves, but they were told patrols of three people were being recommended because of the level of violence that was involved in the murders.

'Want to go out on patrol?' Johnson asked.

'God, yes. Let's head to the area Aisha marked out first.' Aisha had highlighted a park within Sector 11 where a murder was most likely to happen.

⚭

They went to the park. En route, they saw more patrols than ever before; Johnson wondered if the police were taking the murders more seriously now that one of their own was at risk. Both CLEA and the sector police were aware of the attack she had experienced.

As they started to walk, Johnson said, 'There's something about this that I just don't like. There's been nothing since that last attack on us.'

'Which would have succeeded if Aisha hadn't arrived.'

'But she isn't with us all the time, so why not try again?'

Eric didn't have an answer.

They stopped when they saw a group of people, dressed like the ones who had attacked Johnson last month. This time there were more than two. She realised why there had not been another attack – she was still the intended victim.

Johnson and Eric pulled their guns, but more men came up behind them, surprising and disarming them. Eric was forced to his knees while Johnson was dragged forward. Gags were forced into their mouths, preventing them from shouting out.

The leader of the group spoke. 'We didn't plan to try

and kill you again, but when the master realised how important you were to that runt Nephilim, we couldn't resist.'

They forced Johnson onto the ground. Multiple hands grabbed her and tied down her wrists and ankles.

'Don't worry,' the leader said. 'We'll take our time. We want your Nephilim friend to show up again.'

It was still early – the other killings had happened much later – but Johnson had no idea where Aisha was. The girl had slipped out once or twice to see her, which had led to her being grounded by her parents who were now watching her very closely. But Aisha had promised to be at the park tonight, though she hadn't given a time.

The man with the knife ripped open Johnson's shirt and she tensed, waiting for pain. Then he paused as he towered over her. Slowly, blood started to seep out of his mouth and he collapsed. Johnson saw Aisha standing behind him with what looked like kitchen knives strapped to her hips.

'We're so pleased you made it,' another man said. 'Though this time, the master isn't here. Let's see how a child does against all of us.'

'You are foolish to underestimate me, regardless of how I appear.' Aisha pulled the blade out of the dead man's body. 'If I was just a little girl, I could not have sneaked up behind him and killed him with a carving knife, could I?'

'You're so small that we didn't see you. Now we do,' the male taunted. It was the last thing he said before Aisha's blade went through his throat.

The other men rushed forward but she pulled out the blade, turned and slashed at the nearest one, stabbed the man behind him and then a third. Someone grabbed her from behind, forcing the blade down. Aisha pulled a knife from her hip with her free hand and stabbed his throat.

Another attacker was right in front of her, inches away from driving a blade into her, when a gunshot rang out. In their rush to get to Aisha, the attackers had let Eric go.

One more man was standing in front of her. She smiled. 'Want to try?' she asked and held up her knife. He ran off.

Eric grabbed his radio and called in the fleeing suspect as Aisha bent down next to Johnson, pulled the gag from her mouth and cut her bonds. 'Thank you,' Johnson murmured. 'I honestly didn't think they'd come after me a second time.'

'I do not think that was the original plan, but because I came to your aid the last time they thought they could use you to draw me out. They wanted to incapacitate or kill me again so they could complete their ritual. I am not sure if you are the target or just a way to distract me from the intended victim.'

'If Johnson isn't the intended victim, who else could it be? This is the only park around here,' Eric said.

'There are other places closer to the points of the pentagram, though they are not open to the public.'

'Someone's private garden,' Eric realised. 'How would we know where to look?'

'All female CLEA and sector police were ordered to work, though there might be one or two who are off sick. But I can guarantee no CLEA agent or sector police officer could afford a property with a garden in *any* sector,' Johnson pointed out.

'Then we need to look for any calls for assistance in the area,' Aisha said. 'Can you see if there have been any deployments to an address nearby?'

His hands shaking slightly, Eric asked for an update on any calls in the vicinity but the only one had been his. It was a surprisingly quiet night.

'Either they have not made their move yet, or the attacker stopped a call being made,' Aisha said.

'Is there any way you can tell?' Eric asked hopefully.

'If a demon was present, yes, but not otherwise. Our best chance would be old-fashioned door-to-door enquiries.'

'But wouldn't a demon be present like last time?'

'No, the demons do not have to be there to complete the ritual. They would like to be there to see their master freed, but if there is a risk their presence might hinder the release they would not appear.'

'Damn,' Eric cursed.

'I hate this,' Johnson said.

'We need to look for anything, no matter how small, how irrelevant,' Aisha said. 'Do you have a laptop I can use?'

'In the car,' Eric said. They made their way to the vehicle. 'Should we have left the bodies there before the sector police show up?'

'I think we can justify it. One suspect got away so we're at risk of further attack if we stay here – and we have another potential victim to find quickly. I wouldn't want someone else to die because we stayed here,' Johnson said.

Aisha started typing. 'We need to check 3 Altern Road. The owner is the director of intelligence.'

'How the hell did that not come up in any briefings?' Eric demanded.

'I guess it was considered sensitive information,' Aisha said sarcastically.

'Then how did you get it?'

'You really do not want to know,' Aisha said.

'We're going to have to be creative as to why we've gone there,' Johnson said.

'Say that you are checking nearby addresses after what happened in the park. Number 3 is directly opposite the park entrance,' Aisha said.

'It unnerves me how well you do this,' Johnson retorted.

'I've had a few centuries of experience.' Aisha smiled at them.

Chapter 31

WHEN THEY GOT to the address, the door was slightly ajar. Raising their weapons, Johnson and Eric went inside. There were signs of a struggle similar to those at the Edwards' property, and a body was lying on the floor. Johnson checked for a pulse and felt nothing.

'I know him – it's Agent Toms. He does security assignments. We're going to have to call this in.' Eric reached for his radio but Aisha placed her hand over his to stop him.

'Not yet. Give me a chance to see what is happening outside.' She nodded towards the garden.

'We have a dead body,' Eric pointed out.

'Five minutes will not alter that, but calling it in means more people will be in my way. Check the rest of the property and see if anyone was injured.' With that, Aisha headed outside.

She didn't have to go far. Immediately in front of her was a large group of men restraining a young child and a man. Both had been gagged, their hands were tied behind them and tears were rolling down their faces. Two men were holding the director of intelligence, Maria Garcia, trying to push her down, but she wasn't making it easy for them. Director Garcia hadn't always been behind a desk; she had been a field agent of some repute.

'Get down on the ground, and we won't kill your husband or daughter,' Aisha heard one of the men shout. The man holding Garcia's husband tightened his grip, and Mr Garcia screamed through his gag.

Aisha watched as the director fell to her knees. 'Please don't kill them,' she begged.

'That all depends on you,' the man said.

'No, that depends on me,' Aisha stated, walking forward.

'What do you think you can do, little girl?' The man didn't pay her any attention. Was he so arrogant as to believe that he could beat her, or didn't he realise who she was?

'You would be surprised.' Aisha pulled out one of her knives and threw it at the man who was holding a blade to the child's throat. He collapsed to the floor. The child froze for a moment, then she was on her feet and running into the house.

'Leave her; it's not as if there is anything she can do,' the man holding the director said as one of the others made to go after her. 'I thought you'd been disposed of,' he continued, finally turning his attention to Aisha.

'I am not dealt with easily. This is your last chance to let them go.'

He responded by grabbing the director by her hair and pulling her head back.

'You will not cut her throat,' Aisha said. 'You need her for the ritual. Kill her like that, and the pentagram will not be completed.'

'You're right – but we don't need him,' he said, indicating Mr Garcia.

Aisha was already ahead of him. She threw a second knife that went through the throat of the man who was holding the director's husband. Then she pulled out a large carving knife and ran at the one holding Director Garcia.

∞

The girl ran through the house straight into Johnson and Eric as they came down the stairs after checking the house for more bodies. They were shocked to see her and stopped her headlong flight. Absolutely terrified, she struggled at first but Eric held her while Johnson showed her badge. They took out the child's gag and cut her restraints.

'You're safe with us,' Johnson said. 'Tell us what happened.'

'They're outside! They're going to kill my mummy and daddy,' the child cried.

They led her to the car and told her to lie down so no one could see her, then Eric called in the attack. The child clung to Eric, begging them not to leave her. 'We need to go back in,' Johnson said, pulling her gun.

'No,' the girl whispered, tightening her grip on Eric.

'We can't leave her here alone,' he said.

'I know – and I don't think she'll let you go. Stay here with her. I'll go in.'

'No, it's you they were trying to kill.'

'If they still want to do that, then it's best if I'm not near her.'

Reluctantly Eric agreed and watched as Johnson went back into the house.

Johnson saw a group of men in the garden. No one paid her any attention as she inched closer. They were focusing on Director Garcia. Aisha was standing next to her, carving knife in hand, a body at her feet.

One of the men pulled out a gun and pointed it at Aisha. 'I bet you can't survive a gunshot.'

Aisha lunged forward quickly and drove the knife up into his armpit, severing a major artery. 'Don't talk, do,' she told him as he screamed in pain. Death was only minutes away.

'You can't get us all before we shoot you,' one of them said.

'She isn't alone,' Johnson said, walking up behind them, gun raised.

The director of intelligence had started inching her way towards the house and an escape when another man grabbed her.

'I can't risk that you will prevent the ritual', a different voice said. It was deep and sent fear through everyone there.

Turning towards the sound of the voice, Aisha saw another servant of Egraxan had appeared behind the director; he leaned down and ran a finger down her cheek. Director Garcia had gone white in fear. 'Thank you for joining us,' Aisha said.

'Don't confuse me with the demon you returned to hell, I am Olroth, one of Egraxan's most trusted.' Darkness emanated from him, curling around him; one of the tendrils touched the man holding Director Garcia and he screamed in pain and collapsed to the floor. Burn marks appeared on his face.

'Get behind me,' Aisha called out to Johnson.

Johnson wasn't sure what was happening but she did as Aisha said, even as the darkness approached her.

Aisha called her wings; where there should have been feathers, there were blades. She spread them out to protect Johnson, and as the darkness hit them it dispersed. Shocked, Johnson stared at her. She knew Aisha was half-angel but these wings surprised her.

'You will have to do better than that,' Aisha said to Olroth.

The darkness receded, swirled and formed wings that replicated Aisha's behind the demon.

'Leave. Get Garcia and her husband out of here now,' Aisha ordered Johnson. Then the strange portal appeared again and Aisha reached in and pulled out her sword. She ran forward to meet the demon.

As one of the men tried to stand between her and the demon, Aisha swept her wing and the hundred blades that had replaced the feathers cut him in half. Then she attacked Olroth with her sword and used her wings to defend herself. He tried to fight back but she countered every blow he made.

'You fool! You think my weapons and wings are only effective against humans but I was bred to fight *you*, not mankind.' Aisha continued to slash and stab at him. Demons were not good at combatting knife wings in battle; they relied on the fear that they caused. Aisha had centuries of experience using her wings as weapons and had been trained by angels.

She slashed at him until he was forced onto the ground. She had expected more of a challenge, and she was angry at being underestimated yet again, but she also knew she could use it in her favour.

'When you go back to hell, tell your master to stop this. If you continue, I might have to change my stance on anonymity. If I reveal what I am, it will add credence to my saying that demons exist and my explanation of what you are doing with the pentagrams. How well do you think that will do down with your master?'

'As well as it will go down with your father, I would imagine,' the demon hissed.

'My father has not cared about what I do for centuries. What I do know is that "daughter of an angel" never sounds bad. Even if people do not believe me, many will be tempted by religion. I understand that is already happening.'

'Why would anyone believe you?' the demon asked.

'Three people have seen what I am. But do not think it is the only evidence I have. I have lived in this world for a very long time.' Aisha didn't wait for him to say anything else before she started to chant and sent him back to hell. 'Pass on the message,' she said as she finished chanting. She drove her blade through him and the demon disappeared.

Chapter 32

Those of the demon's followers who remained alive watched in horror as their master was vanquished by what they had thought was a young girl but later realised was an angel.

For a moment, there was absolute stillness then, seeing the demon beaten, they panicked and fled towards the house. None of them heard the approaching sirens.

Johnson radioed Eric to let him know the suspects were heading his way. She had been able to get the director and her husband away from the fight but had not made it further than the edge of the garden.

'Do you know where my daughter is?' Mr Garcia asked as Johnson removed his gag.

'She is safe with my colleague.'

'Thank God.'

Aisha helped her cut the ties around the director's wrists. 'You are safe now,' she said. With the demon gone, she had returned to being a young girl and the wings had disappeared. 'Are you hurt?' She held out her hand to help Director Garcia stand.

'No, I don't think so. What did I just witness?'

'More than I can explain just now. Let us see how your family are,' Aisha said. The director allowed herself to be pulled up then turned to her husband and they embraced.

'I'm going to check on Eric,' Johnson said. She was worried that he hadn't come out with the child. As she got to the front door, she saw teams of CLEA and sector police arresting the suspects as they tried to flee. Eric was trying to direct them as best he could with the child still clinging to his leg. She smiled.

'Is everything okay?' he asked.

'Yes, but her parents are worried about her.' Johnson crouched down to the girl. 'It's safe now. The bad guys are gone and your parents really want to see you. I can take you to them.' She opened her arms and the girl let go of Eric's leg and stepped into them.

Johnson picked her up. 'You okay out here?' she asked. Eric nodded and she returned to the garden. As soon as the Garcias saw their daughter, they ran to her, Johnson handed her over before going to Aisha.

'So what now?' she asked as they looked at the agents who were arriving. Questions were going to be asked, a lot of them.

'I honestly do not know. The last time a high-level demon tried to come through was a few hundred years ago and it was dealt with. There was no printing press in those days, let alone social media, and those that survived learned to keep quiet because no one believed them. I just hope Director Garcia and her husband can be convinced to keep quiet about what happened.'

'I imagine they will, if only because they'll fear that it's a ridiculous story. But we need to explain the dead bodies.'

'Let us hope you are right that they remain silent. As for the dead bodies, how are your knife skills?'

'Not funny.'

'Just a suggestion. I have other ideas. Let us say that they turned on each other, each wanting the honour of the kill. I can help you to make the forensics work' Aisha promised. 'I need to go, I cannot be seen here.'

'We'll need to catch up soon.'

'Of course. I will reach out to you.' And with that, Aisha was gone.

The attackers were taken into custody and kept under constant watch; the authorities worried they would kill themselves like the one who had attacked Johnson the previous month. Fingerprints and DNA were taken; and they were all well-known to CLEA for violent crimes.

Knowing who had been arrested, Philip researched them on the CLEA systems, online and dark net. Johnson went up to see him but he told her to leave because she was a distraction – he would contact her when he had any information. Then he ignored her and Johnson remembered why she had never bothered coming to this floor before working with Michelle.

She joined Eric at his desk. 'The morgue has sent through a preliminary report on the bodies,' he said. 'They've all been identified.'

'Let me guess – they are all well known to us?'

'You bet.' He handed over the file. 'I've sent the details up to the analysts.'

Some of the men knew each other, others didn't. The analysts found one thing they all had in common: they communicated on the dark net. They thought this might be a major breakthrough, but the dark net website the men had used led nowhere. There was a reference to the user @ourlordeggracon, and references to what would happen to those that displeased the master. The only bonus was the other names on the site; work was being done to identify them and arrange search warrants.

The suspects were interviewed but they said 'no comment' and created no new leads.

Though the authorities could charge those arrested at the director's home for the assault on her family, there was nothing to tie them to the other murders. None of the missing property from the other victims was found at their addresses, and their movements didn't place them at any of the other scenes.

Johnson couldn't believe the leads were still so slim. She had no idea where to go with the information she had. Michelle – no, *Aisha* – would have seen a connection if one existed. She was about to call her when her phone rang. Seeing the caller ID, she answered.

'Are you still at headquarters?' Kerten asked.

'Yes, sir...'

'Good. Come to my office immediately.' He hung up.

Johnson put her phone in her pocket; she would call Aisha later. Kerten didn't often summon her like that and she assumed he wanted to talk about the lack of progress in the case.

Arriving at his office, she knocked, walked in and paused; Kerten was not there. 'Ma'am,' Johnson said as she saw Maria Garcia.

'Close the door, Agent Johnson. We need to talk.' Garcia was sitting in Kerten's chair. 'I want to know what happened last night at my house. Before you repeat the lies in your statement, I want to show you something.'

The director turned Kerten's monitor towards Johnson and started to play some CCTV footage. Johnson's heart sank; it came from the director's garden. Johnson watched as Maria, her husband, and her daughter appeared with the men who had attacked them. Then Aisha arrived, a seemingly harmless young girl – until she started to fight and kill the men. Her movements were efficient; she was definitely not an ordinary girl.

Then it got worse. The daughter ran off, and a short while later Johnson saw herself arriving at the scene. She squirmed; it was clear she was not surprised by what she was seeing. But that was nothing compared to the demon materialising and the wings that appeared on Aisha...

'Stop!' Johnson said. She didn't need to see the rest.

'I admit that I doubted what I saw when it happened, so I said nothing. I didn't tell the CLEA that there was CCTV because I wanted to look through it first,' Director Garcia said. 'Now I have even more questions. Other than you, who seemed very calm when everything was going on, I don't know who to ask.'

'Does Inspector Kerten know about this?'

'Not yet. I want the truth. When I get it – or not, if you refuse to answer – then I'll decide what to do.'

'I wasn't calm,' Johnson admitted. 'But I had seen something similar before, when I was attacked. It wasn't in my report because I didn't think anyone would believe me.'

'You talked to this girl – or whatever she is – as if you knew her.'

'No, I...'

'Don't lie to me. Tell me what is going on or I'll release her image to the media as a person of interest.'

'You can't do that!'

'I don't want to, but I have to know what's going on. If you don't give me the information I need, I'll get it another way.'

'I can't speak for her. Give me time to talk to her.'

'You have one hour then I want you back in this office.'

Johnson left, pulled out her phone and called Aisha. It went to voicemail; she left a message asking the girl to call her urgently. Looking at the time, she cursed. Aisha wouldn't pick up the message if she were in class. Johnson followed up with a text message. Now she just had to keep her fingers crossed and hope she saw the message.

⬭

Aisha had her phone on silent. After the events of the previous night, she was concerned that Johnson or Eric might need her so she checked for messages when she could. She bent to pull a book out of her bag, quickly looked at her phone and saw a missed call and text message from Johnson saying they needed to talk within the next hour. She sat up and put her hand up.

'Aisha?'

'Please, teacher, I need to go to the toilet.' She rubbed her stomach and looking pained. It was one of the few advantages of being this age again.

'Fine, but don't be long.'

Aisha grabbed her bag and left. In the toilets, she made sure no one else was there and called Johnson. 'What is so urgent?' she whispered.

'The director of intelligence has CCTV of you transforming and killing a demon – or whatever you did to it. She wants to know who you are or she'll release the footage to the media. I have an hour to give her the information.'

'What is your take on her?'

'You're not worried by this?'

'Not particularly. She releases the video, I kill myself, I skip to another body, and her footage looks like a cruel prank.'

'You have got to be kidding me. You can't do that!' Johnson said.

'Why not?'

'You can't kill yourself. And what about the soul of the person whose body you took over?'

'Aisha was dead when I entered her body. I cannot enter a body where a soul still exists, and my soul cannot die. But if you trust Garcia and think she will accept what I have to say, then why not tell her? If these murders continue, having her on our side would be a benefit.'

'She has kept the footage to herself so far. She wants answers, but I don't know if I trust her. I don't know her.'

'Do you know anything about her? What is her reputation?'

'Respected.'

'I finish at school at 3pm so I can be at headquarters at four. If Garcia cannot wait that long, she will have to find an excuse to pull me out of school, with a positive reason.' Aisha passed over the details of her school, hung up, hid her phone in her bag and returned to class.

∞

Director Garcia was still Kerten's office. 'Well?' she asked.

'She is happy to talk and she can be here at 4pm. She can come sooner if you can find a reason – preferably a good one – to pull her out of school.' Johnson handed over the details.

'I can get her out of school, though the 'good' reason amuses me.'

'She is always clear about her preferences.'

'She's *twelve*?' Maria asked, looking at the year group Aisha was in.

'No. It's hard to explain *what* she is.'

'Having seen the CCTV, I can believe it. I'll get an analyst to check her details.'

'They won't tell you anything.'

'Why?

'I think Aisha needs to explain that to you. It took me some time to get my head around it, and I'm not sure I fully understand everything.'

'I'll have a unit collect her as a witness to a crime. You'd better not be lying to me.'

'I'm not.'

When Johnson left the office, she went to find Eric. She pulled him aside so they could talk in private and told him about the conversation with the director. 'Damn,' he said.

'You weren't in the garden, so you're not on the CCTV. She doesn't have any evidence to tie you to Aisha.'

'If she knows that you saw the Nephilim and demon when you were attacked, how do you explain that I didn't?'

'You'd been shot. You can be excused not recalling it,' Johnson said weakly.

'Do you want me to come with you when Aisha arrives?'

'No. I'd like you to be there, but I think it best you keep away in case Garcia doesn't accept Aisha and I go down. Then at least there will still be someone who understands what is going on.'

'I don't like this.'

'Neither do I. We have to be careful from now on.'

∞

Director Garcia had sent a car to collect Aisha from school, so it wasn't long before Johnson was called back to Kerten's office. Aisha was sitting opposite the director and it was clear they had been talking. Johnson was annoyed; she felt protective towards Aisha but had to remember that, regardless of her appearance, she was very old. She must have had a lot of experience in explaining who she was.

'Thank you for joining us. Aisha is happy to explain everything that happened,' Director Garcia said.

Aisha started by saying that she was Nephilim and what that meant, before explaining that her previous body had been Michelle. She had worked for CLEA and lead the intelligence for the investigation, which explained how she knew Johnson. Finally, Aisha explained how demons were driving the murders. When she finished talking, the room fell silent for a moment.

'You're not surprised by this?' Director Garcia asked Johnson.

'No. I knew Michelle well. When I was attacked, I saw her turn into Nephilim, and she saved me from a demon. Later she was murdered and returned as Aisha. I am very open to the unusual by now,' Johnson said.

'If I hadn't seen what I did, I doubt I'd have believed you. But I did see it and I have this.' She indicated the CCTV. 'What I need to know now is how to stop more murders.'

'We've been working to close the gap the demons have been coming through.' Johnson explained what they were doing with Danny and other religious organisations. 'We don't know yet if it's enough. If another murder has occurred, we'll know we haven't succeeded. We need to wait for any reports – and hope the new analyst is as good at making connections as Michelle was.'

'He should be. I left my search parameters in my files,' Aisha said.

Johnson tried hard to keep a straight face.

'Then I guess we must wait to see if another murder has happened,' Director Garcia said. 'From what you've said, can I assume Agent Eric Badu is aware of all this?'

'Yes, ma'am,' Johnson admitted.

'And Inspector Kerten?'

'No.'

'Do you think we should include him? He was in military intelligence, wasn't he? That's why he is an inspector, not an agent? Or don't you trust him?'

'I trust him, but with no proof of the existence of Nephilim and demons, how could I have explained it to him?'

'We have the CCTV now.' Garcia pulled out her phone and asked Kerten to come to the office.

Chapter 33

A WEEK WENT by and there were no murders reported. The seventy-two-hour missing person threshold had been temporarily lifted, so if someone was unaccounted for CLEA should have got the news quickly. But that would only account for victims who would be missed by their family and friends.

'It does not mean that there has not been a killing. If a new pentagram has been started, a murder could have taken place in any sector,' Aisha pointed out. She had come over after school to talk to Johnson and Eric. Director Garcia and Kerten had joined them. As far as Aisha's parents were aware, she was at a friend's house.

'I'll get an all-sector police briefing out to make sure all park areas are checked as a matter of priority,' Director Garcia said.

'What happens if someone was killed in a garden?' Johnson asked.

'I'll ask the media to advise friends or family of any missing women to report them to the police immediately. That way, we will at least have addresses to search.'

'It's a good sign that no one has been found yet, isn't it?' Eric asked.

'I would like to say yes, but our society is not renowned for looking out for each other,' Johnson responded. 'And I don't think Danny has made enough of an impact yet. The suspects could have picked out someone they knew wouldn't be missed for a while.'

'I agree,' Director Garcia said. 'We must be cautious and assume that there is a victim out there that we haven't found yet. While we wait, we continue to bring in as many people as possible for outstanding offences.'

'There are organisations we can link into other than religious ones,' Kerten added. 'More than one victim was interested in fitness, and a lot of sports and exercise clubs are small and local. If we start to bring them together, it will build a different type of community. I know some ex-military who run them – I can ask them to start to work on this.'

'That's a good idea. There are a lot of organisations of all descriptions out there that could help – but we're law enforcement, not a community organisation.' Garcia said.

'You do not need to be,' Aisha said. 'People look for connections with each other, but our society makes it difficult. Do a call to arms – tell people to get out there and join together to stay safe. Show what the religious community is doing as an example. If Kerten can get the fitness clubs to link up, it will give others the idea. You will find that other organisations and charities follow naturally.'

'You can't know that for sure,' Garcia said.

'Not for sure, but I have been alive for a very long time. I know human nature; people want to belong.'

∞

The director of intelligence ordered that all green areas were to be searched. There was a lot of grumbling by the sector police but they obeyed, and the body was found quickly: a teacher in Sector 13.

When Johnson and Eric heard the news, their hearts sank. They had been so hopeful that the killings had ended. When they attended the scene and saw the body, they knew it was linked to the other murders.

Johnson witnessed the autopsy while Eric stayed behind. Once Matt arrived for forensics, he went to talk to people living nearby. Deep down, Johnson and Eric knew that they would find nothing to assist with the investigation. As Johnson watched the autopsy, she felt depressed at how they had fallen into a routine with these cases.

☾

'Having read the previous reports, I can't say I'm surprised another body was found,' Director Garcia said when they met with her the following day. 'You were both very thorough, and I can't see that you've missed anything, but I don't want to wait until the next new moon to try and catch the murderer. Pulling in suspects or anyone with outstanding warrants against them has built confidence, but it hasn't stopped the killings.'

'We don't know what else to try,' Kerten said. 'The demon behind this is clever. We've appealed to members of the public but it hasn't led to anything useful. And we can't mount surveillance across all the sectors – the area is too wide.'

'I didn't mean it as a criticism. I'm just wondering if you have any other ideas?' Garcia asked. Johnson and Eric shook their heads.

'Aisha, you are being very quiet!' The director turned to her.

'I have an idea, but it is not a good one.'

'I'm open to anything at this point.'

'I would not be so sure about that. The demons and humans under Egraxan's control have gone after Johnson three times. If we make her a bigger target we could draw out a demon, I can summon Egraxan through him. I can fight him in this world,' Aisha explained. She was met with silence. 'I did say it was a bad idea,' she qualified.

'Is there anything special about me that makes me a target?' Johnson questioned.

'The failed murder attempt must have upset their plans and they might be keen to even the score with you.' She paused and considered her next words. 'But there is something else about you, a mark on your soul. I did not see it until the demon arrived and I became Nephilim again, but the mark would be offensive to a demon.'

'What sort of mark?' Johnson questioned.

'A sacrifice mark. You were willing to die for another at some point in your life and that leaves a mark on the soul. Over time, it can be eroded by selfish acts, but it is still powerful on you.'

'Am I the only one with this mark?'

'I do not know,' Aisha said. 'I can only see a soul when a demon is present.'

'Did I have it?' Director Garcia asked.

'No.'

'So it won't be something all the victims had in common,' Garcia stated, and Aisha nodded.

'How would my mark make a difference?' Johnson asked.

'It is what it represents to the demons. The immorality of society has given them a crack to exploit, but people like you threaten that.'

'Did they come after me because of it?'

'I do not think they did at first – I expect you were targeted because you were law enforcement, working in the right sector and were leading the investigation. You were just convenient. But when the demon arrived he will have seen the mark, which is why they have kept coming after you.'

'So, as I am already a target, you just want to make me a bigger one?' Johnson guessed.

'If we push you as a survivor and get groups like Danny's to unite behind you, the risk that the gap could close would increase. You will be a focus for the demons.'

'I don't like it,' Director Garcia said.

'Would you be there?' Johnson asked Aisha.

'I cannot be there the whole time,' Aisha admitted. 'If a human attacks you, there is not much I can do if you have a CLEA team following you and you will have to rely on your own defences. A demon is a different matter. I know when one is near and I can materialise at the location.'

'Materialise?'

'Similar to how I get my weapons that I store elsewhere.'

Johnson thought of the times a portal had appeared and Aisha had grabbed a sword. 'If it ends this, I'll do it,' she said.

'No, the risk is too high,' Garcia and Kerten said together.

'This is why Johnson's mark is still pronounced,' Aisha pointed out.

'Still...' Kerten started to say.

'This will not end soon. Trust me – summoning Egraxan before the ritual is complete will make him easier for me to defeat. I can also choose where to fight him and take him out of a populated area. It is not a good plan, but it is all we have.'

'I say we go for it. I really don't want to go to another murder scene or autopsy for another victim,' Johnson said.

'We will get you protection at all times from armed units. Aisha, do you promise me that if a demon comes through to attack Johnson, you'll come running – or whatever it is you do?' Kerten demanded.

'Of course, I will.'

'You sure you want to do this, Johnson?' Garcia asked.

'Yes, ma'am.'

The application for a 24/7 protection detail was submitted and approved quickly. The team was briefed that Johnson would put herself out there on both the news and social media as someone who had survived one of these murders to encourage the communities to support each other.

They decided not to go through the news agencies but to wait for them to pick up the story. Instead, Johnson went to Danny's church to talk to him. His following had grown massively over the last few weeks, but she was still surprised to see how many people were at the church compared to the previous times she'd been. As soon as Danny realised Johnson was there, he started towards his office. She followed him. 'I didn't expect to see you again so soon,' he admitted as they sat down.

'You've done an amazing job with the social media campaign.'

'I couldn't have done it without Michelle's help. I heard about her murder. I'm sorry.'

'Thank you – she will be missed. I'm afraid I have another favour to ask you. I want you to post that I survived an attempted murder.'

'Why do you want me to put that information out now when you didn't before?' Danny asked. 'Don't get me wrong. The news that someone survived an attack will bring hope – but why do it through me rather than the media? Why release it at all?'

'Considering how your network has grown, I feel you can reach more people.'

'You're hoping that whoever is behind this will be angry and come after you again,' he guessed. 'No, Johnson, I can't do that. What if it goes wrong and you're killed? It will be my fault.'

'It won't be your fault, Danny. I believe they'll come

after me again anyway – the truth is that they tried a second time when the first attempt failed. Hopefully, we'll be better prepared for them if they try again. I also want women to get behind this, to give them the strength and courage to fight back.'

'By getting yourself attacked for a *third* time?'

'There were other reasons for the second attack that don't apply to anyone else.' Johnson couldn't explain about the demon trying to get to Michelle through her. 'I know the risks, Danny, and I'll have a security team with me the whole time. If this works, we can end this series of murders. I think the risk is worth it. I've written down information you can use.'

Danny finally agreed to post Johnson's survival on social media and announce it in the church; he would ask his contacts in other faiths to do the same. The information would be released in two hours, which gave Johnson time to get back to headquarters.

∞

Kerten had gone to some ex-military friends who were starting to unite the fitness community; they shared information and used it to encourage people to join self-defence classes.

Johnson left work with a team of specialist CLEA officers. Agent McKay was assigned as the lead and travelled home in her car, and the others followed behind. They didn't want to make it obvious that Johnson had an armed guard.

In her flat, she checked Danny's website and saw he had been true to his word.

CLEA Agent Johnson, a survivor of a demonic attack.

The headline was followed by the pictures she had given him and the details she wanted to be released.

Hundreds of people quickly shared it and the information that she'd survived one of the ritual murders was already all over social media. She had made sure that it said that she'd been disarmed but had fought off her attackers. That was not true, but she could hardly say a Nephilim had saved the day.

She smiled as she read some of the comments. Several times it was pointed out that she was trained in self-defence because she was a CLEA agent, but others said that would only have got her so far. Some links were posted to Kerten's friends' classes. Women seemed to be rallying and no longer willing to live in fear.

Agent McKay came into her flat with her while the others stayed outside keeping watch.

'I can't believe how much attention I'm getting,' Johnson said.

'That's the plan, isn't it?'

She knew it was but reading Danny's social media accounts and the supportive comments made her want to reach out to engage with these people. Unsure if that was a good idea or not, she asked Inspector Kerten and Director Garcia if it would be possible. Kerten said it would probably increase interest and that might help draw out the next killer.

Johnson decided that tomorrow she would ask Danny to help her engage with his followers. With that thought, and Agent McKay asleep on the couch, she went to bed.

Chapter 34

Johnson woke when something crashed to the floor next door. As she jumped out of bed, she heard gunfire. Someone had come for her. She had not expected it to happen so quickly.

She grabbed her gun from the nightstand and edged her way to the bedroom door. She was about to enter the living room to help Agent McKay when she heard Aisha's voice saying, 'Your gun is worthless here. Put it away before someone ends up as collateral damage, then get out of my way.'

Johnson realised that it was a demon that had come rather than a human who working for them. She knew it was best to keep out of Aisha's way.

At that moment her bedroom door burst open as Agent McKay was thrown through it. He groaned but didn't get up. Johnson saw the demon looking straight at her and for a moment she panicked because she had nowhere to run to. Then she saw Aisha come up behind him and grab him around the throat. He tried to break free but her grip was strong as she started to chant.

'You can send me back to hell, but another will follow,' the demon gasped.

'I do not plan to send you to hell. I plan to use you to call Egraxan.'

'No!' the demon started to fight harder, but he wasn't strong enough to break her grip.

'Aisha!' Johnson called out, concerned.

Aisha looked up and cursed. Egraxan couldn't come into this small apartment. She spread her wings and flew both herself and the demon out of the door.

Johnson ran to the entrance and watched as they disappeared mid air; she had no idea where Aisha had taken the demon and hoped she knew what she was doing. Knowing there was nothing she could do to help, Johnson turned to Agent McKay. She called in the attack and hoped the other agents in the car outside were alright.

∞

Aisha arrived in a waste dump several miles away from the sectors' borders. Three cities used the area to dump waste they couldn't otherwise get rid of. There were planned transits once a month; other than that, no one came here and no one would want to. Nothing grew here and any attempt at building had failed. It was the only area Aisha knew where she wouldn't have to worry about other people being in the way. After what happened when the first demon had come through, she knew she couldn't be near anyone for this fight.

The demon tried to break free but failed. Aisha's chanting increased and then, with a scream of fear, the demon disappeared beneath her hands.

She felt the cold creep around her and quickly cast the portal so she could grab her blades. 'Egraxan, so glad to finally meet you,' she said as she turned around.

'Thank you for summoning me. You have saved me so much trouble with all the murders I had to orchestrate.'

In front of her was a demon straight out of horror stories. His skin was black and layered in scales; smoke emanated from his mouth and nostrils, horns curled from his head and he had huge bat-like wings.

'If you think your appearance will scare me, think

again. I know your tricks. I have only brought you here to end this so no one else will be killed.'

'Once I've killed you, the runt of a Nephilim, there will be hell on earth.'

'I am not that easy to kill.' Aisha spread her wings, each feather a blade. They clicked together lethally. In each hand she held a sword.

As she ran at Egraxan, he aimed a blast of fire at her and forced her to stop and pull her wings in front of herself. The power of the blast pushed her back and flames started to lick at her feet.

Aisha launched herself into the sky, bringing her wings back to gain altitude. Momentarily she was hit by fire, but it was nothing she couldn't heal from in this form. Egraxan shouted in anger as his prey escaped him and tried to redirect the flames, but Aisha easily avoided him. She dived, came up behind him and plunged one of her blades into him. He shouted in pain. Nothing forged on this earth would hurt him – but Aisha's blades were a gift from her father.

She turned and dived for a second attack but, as her blade went in, it slowed her. Egraxan was prepared; he grabbed her arm and pulled her to him, forcing her to drop one of her swords. His hand moved, ready to break her neck, confident that they were too close for her to use the second sword. She felt the heat from his hand, and she knew that she didn't have much time before either the burns killed her or he broke her neck.

They were too close for her to use her sword, so she dropped it. With her arm free, she pulled out a knife and drove it through Egraxan's wrist. He screamed in pain as he released her.

Aisha landed next to him and, regardless of her pain, she smiled. She had never hoped to get this close. She reached down and picked up her sword. Before he could stop her, she drove it through his chest. He shouted and lashed out at her, but Aisha ducked and pulled the blade out before plunging it in again.

This time, Egraxan was able to hit her and sent her tumbling away. He grabbed the blade, pulled it out and dropped it on the floor before moving towards her. He grabbed her, pulling her close. 'Where are your blades now?' he sneered.

'Where they have always been.' Aisha twisted sharply, bringing one of her wings up and slicing through Egraxan's wrist. He dropped her, damning her to hell as smoke filled the void she had created. She didn't wait for him to come at her again; she charged, bringing her wings up and relentlessly slashing at him, ripping his body apart and chanting as she did so.

Egraxan realised he had erred. He called the fire again, hoping the heat would destroy her. She continued her assault as the scrap heap went up in flames.

∞

CLEA arrived at Johnson's address. The agents outside were unharmed and hadn't realised anything was wrong until the call came in. McKay had started to regain consciousness, but he was concussed and couldn't say what had happened. Johnson hoped it remained that way as she praised him for seeing off her attacker, whom she claimed had run off.

There was a slight rattle through the apartment block and the lights flickered. A minor quake, someone said, but Johnson wasn't so sure.

She turned and looked out of the window to where she had last seen Aisha and hoped she was alright. If Aisha lost to Egraxan, they would know sooner rather than later. Could the demon actually kill her permanently?

Because of the information that Johnson had twice

been a victim before, the area was soon swarming with reporters telling the world that another attempt had been made on her life and praising her for being a true heroine.

Inspector Kerten arrived and wanted to remove her from the scene. 'Are you alright?' he asked.

'Yes. Aisha arrived and took the demon away. Have you heard from her?'

'Not yet – but it's not as if she's linked into our communication network.'

'We shouldn't have let her fight Egraxan. What if she loses?'

'He would have come through anyway,' Kerten pointed out. 'This way, Aisha has an advantage. We need to trust her.'

Kerten wanted Johnson to return to headquarters where she would be away from the reporters and there was better security, but she refused. She was worried that Aisha wouldn't go there, and she needed to know that her friend was alright.

'We can't do anything with the press if you stay here,' Kerten pointed out.

'If I stay here, they won't get a story. In the morning, I'll go directly to work. The reporters will get bored once a press release has been made and their attention will be drawn elsewhere.'

Reluctantly, Kerten agreed she could stay in her apartment. The armed unit would remain outside and drive her to work next day.

As Johnson lay in bed, she worried about Aisha. She drifted off to sleep in the early hours of the morning and woke when her alarm went off, half expecting Aisha to be in her room telling her everything was alright.

Sighing, she got up and showered before heading for the door. She didn't get that far; Aisha was in her sitting room, drinking hot chocolate. There was a cup of coffee on the side table with a box of pastries next to it. 'I understand the need for security, but it does make it difficult to sneak in. Pastry?' she said.

Johnson sat down opposite her. It brought back memories of when Aisha was Michelle and she felt a moment of grief.

'It is alright to mourn Michelle,' Aisha said. 'She is gone, and I will never be her.'

'But you are both the same person.'

'Yes and no, I remember everything I did when I was Michelle, but Aisha's life and the memories she had mean that now I am someone different.'

'It's so confusing.'

'I know.'

'I think it's funny that you still talk so precisely. Will that stop?'

'No, that is me. How I talk is the one thing I can control, no matter whose life I live.'

'Don't people think it is strange?'

'Yes, but over time it becomes irrelevant. For me, it is the only part of my existence, my personality, that I feel is really mine.'

'That's so sad.' Johnson suddenly understood what it meant to always take over another life and 'fit in'.

'It is my existence. It has been for over a thousand years and it will probably be for many more.'

'Are you going to tell me how it went last night?' Johnson asked, not knowing what else to say.

'I sent Egraxan back to hell. Any lower demon serving him will have been pulled back as well. There should be no more murders.'

'That's it?'

'You need to keep up the work with Danny. Just because Egraxan is gone does not mean another demon will not exploit the gap. Now it is down to society to build a better community.'

'So what happens next?'

'You may find that the demonic influence that drove people to murder will go. Some of the killers might come forward.'

'It would be good to get some arrests,' Johnson admitted. 'But what about us?'

'You get on with your life. I think you should go out with Matt,' Aisha advised.

'That's it? What about you?' Johnson asked.

'I will live this new life and see where it takes me. Call me if you come across anything else demonic – and not just here.'

'What does that mean?'

'Other cities have their own issues, Danny and others could close the gap in this area, but the demons may find somewhere else to exploit.'

'Is that possible?'

'Anything is. Just be vigilant.'

'This feels very anticlimactic.'

'That is a good thing,' Aisha promised.

Chapter 35

Johnson walked into the office the next day. Eric had beaten her to it. 'I heard it was an interesting night for you,' he said.

She smiled. 'You could say that.'

'Kerten filled me in last night but told me not to go to your flat. How are you doing?'

'I'm alright. Aisha came to see me after everyone left.' She recounted their conversation.

'Do you think we'll see her again?'

'Only if we need her. It felt very much like a goodbye,' Johnson admitted.

'Sorry, agents,' one of the support staff interrupted them. 'There is a man here saying he wants to talk to you.'

'Why us? We're still working on the linked murder cases.'

'That's just it – he says he wants to confess to the murder of Amy Hood and will only talk to you. He's in one of our interview rooms.'

Johnson recognised the man immediately as the security guard at the hospital she had spoken to about CCTV. She would never have guessed he had killed Amy. He refused legal advice, so they went straight into an interview.

'I'm sorry, I did it,' were the first words out of his mouth.

'I'll remind you again, you have the right to legal advice. You are here under suspicion of committing a murder.

Do you understand that?' Johnson said.

He nodded. 'I don't need no solicitor. Other than telling me not to talk, they can't help. I want to admit what I did.'

'So tell us what happened,' Johnson said.

He explained that he had a criminal history but had lied about his identity to get the job. 'They wouldn't have given it to me otherwise and I needed the work. I get short-tempered, like a bit of a fight, so security seemed like a good idea.'

He admitted he had fantasised about killing someone. He had caused serious injury in his time and been sent down for it but had never gone 'that far'. Then he met Amy, but she ignored him. 'I don't even think she knew I existed.' It angered him, and he had thought about ways to make her pay.

'Then it went from thinking about it to really wanting to kill her. I felt it was the right thing to do, that someone *wanted* me to do it. Now it feels insane!' He hit the desk angrily before he continued. 'I watched her and got to know her routine, then one day I made sure my shift ended at the same time as hers. I followed her home. A week later, I was in a shop buying a knife, rope, fucking chloroform. I thought I was doing right. How is that right?'

He didn't expect a reply. 'I waited for her on the route she took home and I grabbed her. For the rest of what I did to her – something came over me. I knew I really wanted to do it.'

'Do what?' Johnson asked.

'How I killed her.' He hung his head in shame as he recounted how he had tied her down and cut the symbol into her before cutting her throat. 'At the time, I loved it – I got off on it. It was like all my dreams come true. Then this morning I woke up and couldn't believe what I'd done, couldn't believe I'd killed Amy. I didn't want her to die – I wanted her to notice me.' He burst into tears.

He answered all their questions. He had blindfolded Amy because he knew she would recognise him from the hospital and he couldn't bear to see her disapproval. He didn't know what had happened to her phone; it had fallen when he'd grabbed her, but he hadn't wasted time picking it up and he didn't go back afterwards to look for it.

Eric had him taken back to his cell. Johnson couldn't look at him anymore. When he came back, she said, 'When I went to the hospital the investigate, I spoke to him. He gave me the CCTV.'

'There was nothing to tie him to the murder. You know that.'

'I know. It just makes me feel guilty for not seeing it.'

'Stop it!' Eric demanded. 'There is no blame here. He wasn't involved in the other murders. Even if you'd realised he was the suspect, it wouldn't have helped the other victims. But what he told us *could* help. He was on the periphery of her life, someone we would never have looked at. Are the other murderers the same?'

'If that's the case, the number of suspects could be huge.'

'Yes, but you said that the demon's influence will start to fade. I guess that's why Amy's killer came in today. Others might come in or start to show different behaviour that we can ask people to look out for.'

Checks on the security guard's real name showed that he had an extensive history of serious assaults. Would he have killed anyone if Egraxan had not persuaded him? Seeing the guilt that seemed to be affecting him now, Johnson doubted it – though she didn't feel sorry for him. The crimes he had previously committed showed that he was a risk to the public.

ꙮ

He was not the last to come in. Over the following weeks, more men turned themselves in. Johnson longed to reach out to Aisha to talk to her about it, but she didn't. She hoped that maybe one day she would be able to.

As Michelle had stated during the investigation, a different person had committed every murder.

Katy Jones was killed by one of her clients through BB's app. He'd been infatuated with her and enraged when she rejected him. He had followed her after she'd cleaned his house and stalked her for some time before killing her.

Carol Jenkins was murdered by a man from her running club. She had not been aware of his interest but other members of the club had, and they reported it to the hotline.

Jenny Adamson was killed by the abusive ex-partner of one of the women she was helping on the Utofia estate.

Rose Yu's killer was one of the nurses at the hospital who resented her superior attitude and her relationship with her house mate.

Olna Farmer's murderer was one of the homeless who camped in the park where she walked Alfie. He had fantasised about being part of her life. He had abandoned Alife when he couldn't stop the baby crying.

Tami Rankin was killed by a man from her fitness class. One of the instructors saw some photos on his phone that caused concern, and when they searched his home the police found a lot of sado-masochist material.

Andi Wallace was killed by a member of her congregation who felt they deserved more of her time and a bigger share of the charitable donations.

Crime rates were down. People were sharing information and that made criminals wary because society was no longer turning a blind eye to their misdemeanours. Attendance at religious institutions and community groups was continuing to increase.

Society was better now than at any time Johnson could remember; even so, she waited for something to go wrong. But as the next new moon came and went and no new murders were reported, she started to relax.

The officer who had shared the photograph was dismissed, but there were still unanswered questions. They had not found out how the original call for assistance was cancelled, or how the suspect had killed himself in his cell, or who had leaked information to the press. IIB was still investigating, but Johnson didn't know if they would ever find the answers.

She'd hoped to hear from Aisha at the new moon but there was nothing. Worried, Johnson decided to visit the school and catch her as she left. Before she could get out of her car, she saw Aisha come through the gates, smiling and flirting with a boy like any normal teenage girl.

Johnson remembered what Aisha had said about getting on with her life. She picked up her phone and dialled a number.

'Hi Johnson, where's the scene,' Matt said when he answered.

'No scene.' She paused, worried about the response she would get. 'I was wondering if you wanted to go out for dinner some time?'

'Yeah, I would love to.'

www.ingramcontent.com/pod-product-compliance
Lightning Source LLC
Chambersburg PA
CBHW070440170726
48291CB00002B/593